Rocking the
BOAT
Christopher Koehler

Dreamspinner Press

Published by
Dreamspinner Press
4760 Preston Road
Suite 244-149
Frisco, TX 75034
http://www.dreamspinnerpress.com/

Rocking the Boat
Copyright © 2011 by Christopher Koehler

Cover Art by Paul Richmond   http://www.paulrichmondstudio.com

ISBN: 978-1-61581-843-3

Printed in the United States of America
First Edition
February 2011

eBook edition available
eBook ISBN: 978-1-61581-844-0

For Burch Bryant, Jr.,
the best husband, partner,
and friend a boy could ask for.

To our dearest
Princess Lala-
a thousand
smootchies xx

love
Hydraaph

Acknowledgments

WHILE writing is among life's great solitary pleasures, not even writers do it alone, and I'd like very much to thank certain people for their assistance: Jeff Weaver, for answering questions about rowing shells I should've been able to figure out myself; John Gamber, for answering questions about comparative literature in lavish detail; coach extraordinaire Tricia Blocher, for her input on simultaneously coaching and going to grad school and for working me like the dog that I am; and Julie "Come for the Coffee, Stay for the Abuse" Taylor, who runs my favorite coffee shop.

I also gratefully acknowledge the help of Dahlia Adler Fisch, whose close editorial scrutiny made Rocking the Boat a better book. Matthew Carlton is a true friend, and his unflagging support and enthusiasm for this project and virtually everything else I write keeps me going. Finally, my husband Burch Bryant, Jr., who reads everything I write whether he wants to or not and gladly supports my writing.

Lastly, I'd like to thank Elizabeth, Lynn, Mara, Paul, Ariel, and everyone else at Dreamspinner Press for making the publication of my first novel the joyous process it was.

Author's Note

ROWING is a full-body, no- to low-impact aerobic endurance sport suitable for far more people than just the college hard-bodies depicted here, from adolescents to octogenarians and everyone in between. Many rowing clubs now offer adult learn-to-row camps each spring, and masters rowing (age 27 and over) is one of the fastest growing segments of this wonderful and enriching sport. Google "rowing + [name of your city]" or check out Boathouse Finder at http://www.bhfinder.com and look for a club near you (last accessed 1/14/11).

Chapter
ONE

COACH NICK BEDFORD watched the eight men—his athletes, sweaty and pushed to the edge, their sides heaving like thoroughbreds—do their best to beat each other on the boathouse ergometers. The ergs, specialized rowing machines that duplicated the rowing stroke almost exactly, were his rowers' best friends and worst enemies, building their conditioning and strength but also devouring everything they had to give and demanding more. He often shared their workouts, but not today. Today he walked around each athlete's erg, looking for flaws in his technique. The crew's coxswain helped him, but he was still the coach. It was his job to get them in shape.

They were a small crew, and California Pacific College was a small school. A former college rower himself, Nick was a graduate student working on his master's degree in exercise physiology at a not-too-distant state university, and around the boathouse, he did it all. He was the resident expert on bodies in motion, guiding each athlete through workouts on land and water, each designed to make the boat go faster. He was the dietician, trying to keep a group whose natural prey was pizza and beer on the nutritional straight and narrow to build muscle and fuel recovery. He was their sport psychologist, helping them through losses and guiding the young men through the shoals of school, rowing, and life. He spent his free time immersed in exercise science literature, reading, reading, reading, anything to give his men that extra edge.

He even rigged the boats, adjusting the hardware and making minor repairs.

Eight varsity athletes, eight seats in the varsity boat. Nick was lucky they were so competitive, even with each other. Posting their erg scores meant someone would be pulling harder next time. He also had a standing offer to the junior varsity rowers: any JV athlete who beat a varsity rower on the ergs could challenge him for a seat in the boat. He'd only had to make good once. Each of his eight rowers put the "I" in team, each determined to beat the others. For a small program, it was ideal. For eye candy, it was unbeatable.

"What'd you think, Coach?" his coxswain asked, coming to stand next to him.

Nick was lucky. Stuart Cochrane had coxed in high school, and the junior pre-med major was as skilled as they came. "There's room to improve," Nick said, never taking his eyes off his athletes. "Look at Sundstrom. He's hunching his shoulders. On the ergs, it'll hurt, but on the water, it'll strain his muscles and make it hard for him to stay in synch."

"He's never going to catch Morgan without fixing his technique, either. I'm on it," Stuart said. He walked over and knelt down next to the large rower, watching intently for a few strokes before correcting him. Stuart returned, his coxswain's strut even more pronounced.

Nick had to smile. The best coxswains were small and light so they didn't slow the boat with weight that wasn't pulling an oar, and they had Napoleon complexes. Stuart fitted the bill, short and cocky and determined to win. "That worked."

"Of course it did," Stuart smirked. "Keep your eye on Estrada. Have you noticed how he speeds up just a bit during the last 2k? That's part of how he keeps beating Brad."

"I like a nice, friendly rivalry," Nick said, grinning. "It keeps the erg times fast."

"I'm not sure how friendly it is. Brad was the fastest until Morgan joined the team and hasn't taken kindly to being beaten," Stuart added quietly, his voice just loud enough to reach Nick's ears over the sounds of the ergs. "And some of the other guys are beating him too."

"Then Brad needs to up his game," Nick said. He didn't want to know about rivalries like that. He'd seen crews torn apart by such distractions. So long as his rowers left their differences on the dock when they rowed, he didn't care. As he'd told Stuart, a rivalry on the ergs would move the boat faster.

Nick returned his focus to the ergs. He'd kept an eye on Morgan Estrada, all right. It was hard not to. Collegiate rowers were in fantastic shape, but there was something about Morgan that drew his eye. He was tall, taller than Nick (who, at six feet, wasn't short), but then, rowing selected for tall men and turned them into muscular ones. Sweat dripped from one wavy brown lock, running down his cheek, but Morgan ignored it.

Nick noticed it, however. It defined Morgan's cheek, flushed red with effort, but normally very fair. There was more conquistador than conquered in Morgan Estrada's background. All Nick's men were good looking in one way or another, but there was something about Morgan that pulled him in, something that threatened to swallow him.

Eye candy was a perk of his job, but Nick tried not to stare too much. They were his boys; he was their coach. There was a trust there, and he took that trust very seriously.

Still, watching Morgan strain, sweaty and grunting and red, made Nick think of crossing that line.

OVER on the erg, Morgan concentrated intently. He liked the ergs. They demanded strength and concentration to move his body in sequence: drive with the legs, pivot from the hips to swing his torso back, pull the arms into his chest to bounce the handle off his sternum, and then arms back out, torso forward as the legs slowly brought him back to the start. His kinesthetic sense told him where his body was, leaving his mind free to think of anything or nothing but the strain of his muscles and the desperate need for air. He held his chin high, breathing deeply, oxygen to fuel the burn in his legs. He felt his skin prickle, like someone was watching.

Morgan glanced around. On the ergs, looking around wasn't a big deal. In the racing shells, where even a subtle shift destabilized the boat, it could cost them crucial fractions of a second.

He didn't see anything. Then Morgan looked in the mirrors that lined the wall ahead of them. They let rowers check their form, but Morgan wasn't the only one looking. Coach Bedford stared at him, his light brown eyes intense. Now hyper-aware, Morgan made sure his technique was the best it could be, sitting up straight from his lower back, chin high, self-conscious and nervous. When Coach Bedford saw him looking, he jerked his eyes away. Morgan couldn't overanalyze it right then, but there was something about his coach's eyes that made him sweat in a way that had nothing to do with heart rate or aerobic capacity.

Morgan gritted his teeth. He was coming to the last five hundred meters of the piece. He couldn't afford to get distracted, not with the others dogging his heels, not when one of them might be closer to the end.

But Morgan's eyes kept straying to Coach Bedford, now studiously looking elsewhere. Almost as tall as he was, the coach had floated Morgan's boat from the moment he'd first seen him. There had been something about Coach Bedford's passion for the sport that had drawn Morgan in when he had given a recruiting pitch to the incoming freshmen, and in that moment, the former high-school oarsman Morgan knew that despite wanting a break, he'd row, if only to see to Nick Bedford's brown eyes and muscular build up close all the time. The day he'd made the varsity team as a sophomore by challenging a varsity rower for his seat had been a dream come true.

A screaming grunt from the next erg jerked Morgan's attention back to the workout. One down. He pulled hard, pouring everything he had into the last few seconds as his vision tunneled. Then Morgan near-collapsed as he slumped on the seat, done and spent.

"Get some water, walk it off when you can," Coach Bedford told him, one hand on his shoulder. The touch tingled, but it could've just been oxygen deprivation.

NICK and Stuart wrote down the numbers on the monitors from each erg's display. With this test, a set distance, the goal was to finish as fast as possible, and to gauge each athlete's progress, they checked each athlete's speed at five-hundred-meter intervals. "Once you catch your breath, get some water and go for a short run to work the lactic acid out of your muscles. Be back in fifteen minutes."

"Keep it slow, this is a recovery run!" Stuart yelled.

Eight drained men hauled themselves up and filed slowly out of the boathouse.

"Recover by exhausting ourselves again," Brad Sundstrom muttered.

"That's Coach Bedford. The last workout is history, it's the next one that's important," Morgan said.

Brad gave him a sour look. "Yeah, but we can't do the next one until we recover from this one."

"Then it's part of the same piece, isn't it?" Morgan said, taking off at a slow jog.

A quarter-hour later, they came back to the boathouse and headed right for the water cooler.

"Stretch it out, guys," Nick ordered, watching them. Watching him.

Stuart motioned, and the rowers sat down on the ground. "So how'd that feel, guys?" Nick asked.

"Like shit, Coach," Brad snorted.

"It was six minutes in hell," Morgan said. He leaned over one leg, lengthening the Achilles tendon. The reach stretched the muscles of his back tight under his T-shirt.

Nick smiled slightly. He'd been there himself. His eyes traced the strong lats under Morgan's shirt. He was just checking for form and to see that he'd developed no asymmetries, or at least that's what he told himself. "Obviously I haven't cooked the numbers to compensate for weight or age, but based on this, some of the JV rowers are nipping at your heels. If you want to keep your seats in the boat, you need to apply yourselves." Nick looked at Brad meaningfully.

"Ergs don't float," Brad said as his teammates looked everywhere but at him.

"Granted. We all know speed on the erg doesn't translate to speed on the water, but if you want to go fast on the water, you've got to pull hard on the ergs. It's not all of it, but it's part of it," Nick said. "The Pacific Coast Rowing Championships are in ten weeks. We had a good fall season, but you're going to have to work hard between now and then if you don't want powerhouses like the University of Washington and Cal Berkeley to hand you your asses. This was just the first test. There'll be tests just about every week from now until then."

Nick's announcement was met with loud groans. "For the JV too," Stuart said, glaring at the rowers, because he had a stake in this too. Coxswains competed amongst themselves, and it was a matter of pride to cox a winning crew. To coxswains, rowers were meat that moved boats, and Stuart wanted his boat to move the fastest.

"Yeah, it's going to suck, but you guys are strong. You'll get stronger. It's going to take work. There's a reason I keep telling you guys to take a lighter course load in the spring," Nick reminded them. He met each athlete's eyes for moment. "Since today was the first day of spring break, I'll let you take the morning off, but you know what comes next. Double days. We'll be on the water in the morning, in the boathouse or the gym in the afternoons. Dig up those diet handouts from wherever you're composting them and follow them. Take naps after lunch. Do some yoga. No more booze or anything else for the duration, not until after the PCRCs. I know college students party, but you're here in this boathouse because you want to be, so dig in and commit. Before this is done, you'll go so far into the pain cave you'll forget what daylight looks like. In return, I'll give you nothing less than the best I have to give."

Nick saw some heads nodding. They'd done this before. They knew, just like they knew he shared as much of the burden as he could. "C'mon, circle up," Nick said.

They hauled themselves to their feet, some weary, some stretching their spines. Nick put one hand in the middle, and the athletes—his athletes, as dedicated to him as he to them—put their hands on top. "Remember the Five Cs. They make the CalPac Crew great. Coach, coxswain, crew, communication, commitment."

It was corny, but by the time Nick was on the second C, they all said it with him. They knew he meant it. It was the basis of the close relationship between coach and athletes. They were a small band, united by shared misery in pursuit of a common goal. He loved them for it. He hoped they returned his devotion.

"See you tomorrow morning. I want you ready to put your hands on the boat at six a.m., so be here early to warm up and get the equipment ready," Nick said, the old familiar spiel.

The rowers left the erg room, heading for the showers. Morgan held back.

Nick looked up. "Good piece. Did you need something?"

Morgan hesitated. "See you in the morning, Coach," he said before jogging to catch up with his ride.

THE week passed for all of them in a blur of morning rows and afternoon strength training. After the last row of double days on a Saturday morning, the men of the CalPac Crew were ready to cut loose. Nick knew it. He expected it. He was used to conversations that cut off the moment he was noticed. His rowers were barely over twenty, so it went with the territory.

But there was something off-key about it this time that he didn't recognize and didn't like. Something that made his coach's Spidey sense tingle. Usually, the varsity crew alone managed to produce a cacophony like a flock of chickens, squawking and pecking and cackling about the minutiae of collegiate life. Bringing the JV rowers into the mix jacked the noise level so much it often drove Nick into the coaches' office with the door closed.

Before practice that Saturday morning, he hadn't thought much about their tight-lipped unanimity. It was early; they were tired. The only sounds in the boathouse were the whirl of the ergs as athletes warmed up and the quiet conversations between coaches and coxswains about the upcoming row.

After practice, however, the rowers had been tight-lipped and smug. Sure, Brad and Stuart always looked smug, but this time it had been all of them. When Nick could hear himself think with both squads present and accounted for, something was definitely up. A little judicious eavesdropping gave him an idea of what was astir.

So Nick had bided his time throughout the day and made some calls to a few of his fellow coaches with CPC's other athletics programs. They confirmed his suspicions, but since their sports weren't approaching end-of-season finales, they were more philosophical about it. He couldn't afford to be.

After dinner, Nick headed for the scene of the future crime, a house in the student ghetto just off campus. He borrowed his best friend Drew St. Charles's almost-new BMW, since his rowers might recognize his battered Honda. Given the dizzying cost of CalPac's tuition, the 3 Series BMW wouldn't even stick out. It was the perfect blind from which to lie in wait for his flock.

From behind the cover of a newspaper, Nick counted as his rowers went into the party. Since it was hosted by some players on the men's lacrosse team, he didn't recognize most of the people heading inside. But that just made it easier to count off his athletes as they entered.

Morgan and Stuart walked by, the last two. Nick sank further in the seat. For all that Morgan had been on the varsity squad the previous year, Nick had only started noticing him as more than just an athlete a few months before, and now suddenly he couldn't keep his eyes off the junior. Morgan. He sighed. What was it about that kid that got under his skin? For starters, he realized ruefully, Morgan was no kid. From what he'd seen in practice, he was all man. Tall and muscular and just hairy enough to turn Nick's crank. Dark hair that curled across sculpted pecs and swirled around dark nipples just begging to be played with before plunging down the ridges and contours of Morgan's abs and on down to what Nick could only imagine. Not that he'd looked. Because that would be wrong.

Nick knew he'd have to do something about that, maybe join Drew on one of his trips to Aspects, the more civilized of the local gay watering holes. It been way too long since he'd gotten laid, and terminal sperm poisoning was clearly setting in. It was prime time on a Saturday night and he was slumped down in the front seat of a borrowed sports car to stalk his rowers, mentally macking on a guy who hadn't even graduated from college yet. He should've been out with a boyfriend, or better yet, cuddled up at home with one, reading together or watching a movie before keeping each other up all night.

Instead, Nick was spying on his crew, waiting to spring a trap. Suddenly he just felt pathetic and far older than twenty-eight.

He looked at the dashboard clock. Nine thirty p.m. Time enough for them to get into trouble.

MORGAN surveyed the scene when he and Stuart entered. The party was at a typical college-student rental. Sagging, disreputable couches that had clearly seen better, beer-free days had been plunked down in the middle of the living room across from a large television. Scuffed IKEA tables and lopsided bookcases loitered against walls that no one had painted with anything but primer. It was borderline nasty when he thought about it, but they weren't there to pick up design tips. They were there to par-tay.

Stuart knew some people on the lacrosse team, which was how the men's crew had landed an invitation. Truth be told, parties were about body count, not faces, and another team meant more beer.

Morgan might not have gone without Stuart there. Having a gay wingman rocked; being a gay wingman was a sacred obligation. He didn't spot any non-rowers he knew right away, but Stuart hailed some guys across the room, and he tagged along.

There were beer bongs and the real deal, as well as the inevitable game of beer pong and a table with bottles of hard liquor. Morgan grabbed a beer, making sure it was unopened. He didn't plan on drinking much, not like some of the guys on the team or many others at the party. Stomach pumps weren't on the short list of things that went down his throat. That was pretty much limited to food and beverages, plus the occasional cock. Lately, he'd been thinking about Coach Bedford's. A lot. But it was getting out of hand. Certainly not in hand, at least not his.

Maybe he'd find someone to distract him. There were bound to be a few hot guys. Out athletes were relatively rare even at liberal California Pacific. He himself wasn't officially out to his team, but he'd never hidden it and just assumed they all knew. Based on the glances thrown his way at that party, however, there were plenty of closeted jocks. He knew the signs; he'd played the game. He was just tired of it and ready for something more.

Morgan wanted a boyfriend. He'd been out to his family since he was sixteen. He'd done the casual dating and even more casual fucking. It had been fun, but it wasn't for him, not over the long term. He didn't want the little house with the white picket fence, at least not yet, but he wanted someone special, someone he could give himself to, someone who'd do the same for him. Someone who wanted the same things he did. He wanted Mr. Right.

But Morgan also knew that Mr. Right Now would do. He wasn't dressed to attract attention, but he drew it anyway. His loose shirt was tight enough to hint at the cobbled abs that roaming hands would find underneath, the jeans cut low and his briefs lower, with just a hint of skin and treasure trail between shirt and pants.

Morgan made conversation, but his attention was on the men around him. Stuart caught his eye and winked. He was doing the same thing. Morgan smiled to himself. Having a gay teammate who was also a friend and roommate was even better than having a gay wingman.

Nearby, in a knot of guys he didn't know but who had the built look of athletes, someone met his eyes. He was shorter than Morgan, but broader, more muscular, his dark eyes beckoning, promising. Morgan had seen him around. He was a lacrosse player, but not one of the ones he knew. So much the better.

Morgan didn't move yet. Timing was everything. He kept talking to Stuart and his friends, glancing back every so often to make sure the other man still smoldered.

The lacrosse player moved from his position, and they began their slow, steady dance around the room. Morgan shifted his position again, always keeping the other guy in sight. There was a rhythm to these furtive seductions, and it was important to make sure they followed the same beat.

Morgan made eye contact again, mouthing pleasantries that didn't matter to people who weren't important at this point in time. He casually rubbed his chest, his hand straying to his pecs. He gave one nip a brief flick. The other man's eyes flared.

Then it was his turn to move, to draw the other man to him. Another cluster of people, another conversation he wasn't hooked into, another can of beer he hardly touched.

Morgan rubbed his crotch to tell the guy it was now or never. That was another reason to find a boyfriend, he thought. It'd be nice to have sex without having to make sure the guy was drunk enough to be willing but not too drunk to perform. Timing was everything.

"I'll see you guys later. There's someone I gotta talk to," Morgan said.

He wandered purposefully towards the back of the house. He couldn't just make a beeline for it. That would be too obvious. He had an itch to scratch, not an urge to cause talk.

One stop along the way was enough, a stop with a final burning look over his shoulder. Then he was in the shadows of a long hallway, separated from the rest of the house by a ninety-degree turn.

Morgan didn't wait long. A minute more, and the object of that night's affections was on him. He craned his neck as the man moved in hungrily and a hand pawed its way under his shirt.

"Gonna gimme that boy pussy?" he said, slurring slightly.

"You sure know how to charm a boy," Morgan said. He pushed the other man back into the wall and made for his neck. He'd learned the hard way not to kiss guys like this on the lips. Six-pack gays, men just drunk enough to admit they kinda sorta liked guys, got angry when you kissed them on the lips because it made them gay. Or something. So Morgan sucked and nipped behind one ear while he tugged the other guy's shirt open. His thumbs circled the hardening nipples; then he flicked them, gauging the reaction. A sharp hiss, and he flicked them again. The other man's breath grew ragged as Morgan licked a trail down his neck.

Morgan had him gasping in short order. Morgan knew what he wanted that night and how to get it, and they were standing right there in the hall. They could be discovered at any moment, but the man made no move for a bedroom. That was fine with Morgan. It was part of the sizzle.

Even as his short-term lover grappled with the button fly on Morgan's jeans, Morgan freed a hand for the other man's shorts. They were loose, so he plunged his hand down, fingers probing for underwear, then over the elastic and into the boxers.

His own pants were undone and his cock freed. He was rock hard, and it felt so good. For just a moment, he reveled, sensation blotting out thought.

Then he grabbed the guy's cock, enjoying the heft of the shaft. His fingers danced over the soft skin, teasing and caressing.

"Ohhh, baby," the other man whimpered.

Morgan tightened his grip. The cock in his hands further stiffened, fueling Morgan's own fire. Another's rod in his hands aroused him like nothing else. The pulsing, vital measure of another man filled him with power. In that way, in that moment, that other man was entirely his.

Even as his own shirt was lifted up and one nipple sucked into the other's mouth, Morgan ran his thumb across the head of the man's cock, savoring the feeling of the head under his fingers. The current ran between his hand, the mouth on his nipple, and the hand on his own shaft. He breathed deeply, eyes rolling up, as the fire rose around him. He burned, and it felt so good.

The cock in Morgan's hand dripped precum, and he smoothed it around, slicking the head and shaft. Spitting into his hand, he started jacking. It felt like a steel piston in his palm. He caressed the head, then slammed his hand down the shaft, loving the rush. The other man writhed in his grip, but Morgan was relentless.

Light coiled around Morgan's spine. It wouldn't be long, not for him, not for the man moaning on the other end of the cock in his hand. He let it build, soaring on the feeling racing out from his groin.

Morgan held out as long as he could and then let go. "Unnh!" Three seismic spurts and an aftershock or two and he was done.

His partner for the moment followed quickly. "Ooohaaah!"

The other man sagged against the wall for a moment. "Duuude. That was so hot. Do you ever go to the third-floor library bathroom? We should totally do that again sometime."

Morgan, carefully wiping the guy's load into one pocket, shook his head. He didn't say anything. The emptiness, as insidious as fog, had already whispered around him, cutting him off from even the ersatz connection he'd felt moments before.

It was the flip side of the rush Morgan felt moments before when the other man had been his because of the cock in Morgan's hand. Jacking him off, Morgan had felt, for a moment, connected to the other man, but that connection ended when they came. They shared nothing; they had nothing; they were nothing together. It was why Morgan had more or less stopped tricking. It hurt too much when it ended, and it always ended too soon.

Feeling more alone than he had in a long time, Morgan walked out, not even bothering to find the bathroom. He grabbed a beer, wishing for something stronger. Then he looked up.

Standing there as cold and remote as a statue was Coach Bedford. He met Morgan's eyes, and Morgan swore he saw into his soul. There was no way his coach knew he'd just jacked off a stranger in the back of the house, but it felt that way to Morgan.

His coach walked into the room, drawing looks, but most people ignored him. They didn't know him, so it didn't matter. But to his athletes, to Morgan, it felt like everything had stopped. The music, the fun, the party all withered and died at the touch his coach's icy demeanor.

Coach Bedford stalked up to Stuart. "Everyone will be at the boathouse tomorrow at six a.m., or there will be hell to pay."

Chapter
TWO

NICK stood on the dock looking out to the river. The river, as familiar to him as the street he lived on, always calmed him. When he was on the water, conflicts and problems and dilemmas receded like the tide. The water's Zen was what he missed most about coaching, not the rowing, not the camaraderie. He had his own boat, a single-man shell. It had a few miles on it and was a little battered, but it was still almost as stiff as when it had first come off the line, just like him. That was all that mattered.

He'd gotten up early and taken it out, letting the water claim his anxious mind in the predawn stillness. But he was off the water now, and the tide came back in. He glanced at his watch. It was a few minutes past six a.m. Time for him to find out if he still had a crew.

Oars over his shoulders, Nick opened the boathouse's small side door, and there they were. Some looked a bit worse for wear, some at least had the decency to appear ashamed, and at least one looked downright belligerent, but he could deal with Brad.

He didn't say anything right away. He took his oars back to the rack, making sure they were stowed. He was stalling, and he knew it. He paused for a moment, gathering himself. "All right," he said, turning around. "Who wants to tell me what that was about last night?"

The nine men facing him didn't say anything. One or two shifted uncomfortably. He noticed that Morgan stared at the floor, refusing to meet his eyes.

"Really? Nine of the gossipiest men I know, and no one's got anything to say? All right, I'll go," Nick said. He'd achieved a certain detachment out there on the water, but his growing anger punched through it like it was wet tissue paper. "This is how you show me your commitment?"

"Hey, you work us hard, we need to relax," Brad barked. He looked at the others for support. "Am I right, guys?"

Nick raked his eyes across the larger man, always the voice of impulsiveness on the crew. "Not like that, you don't. Not on my crew, and not during the season. Aside from the fact that alcohol isn't really a part of the training diet, there was pot and God knows what else there. After that scandal three years ago, the athletic department instituted random mandatory drug testing for all athletes. You know that. Any jock who tests positive is off his team, and five of you are on scholarships. Can you make up the difference? Have you told your parents that?" Nick expanded the swath of destruction to include the other eight. "Nine weeks, gentlemen, and I use the term loosely. I own your sorry asses for nine more weeks. After the season's over, your time is your own."

"You can't tell us what to do during our time off!" Brad yelled. Then he winced at the noise.

"Sure I can," Nick said. "You've got your athletics contract with the school, and we've got a contract here too. In return for the very best coaching I can give you, you give me your utmost effort and dedication."

"I didn't sign anything, and neither did these other guys," Brad said sullenly.

"Leaving aside the fact that yes, five of you indeed signed something when you accepted your rowing scholarships, there's still an implied contract," Nick said. He accepted a certain amount of give and take, but when it came to coaching, the boathouse was not a democracy. "Tell me what happens if you lose the PCRCs."

"We don't win," said Robert Allen, who rowed seven seat in the boat.

Nick let his contempt show through for a split second. "That logic must dazzle your professors. If we don't win, the alumni oversight committee doesn't hire me back and good luck finding a replacement on short notice. So I give you everything I've got. In return, I expect the same. You have a problem with the coaching, you talk to me. You have a problem with the discipline, get off the team."

Morgan nodded slowly, lifting his gaze from the floor for the first time since Nick had started in on them. "The Five Cs...."

"That's right," Nick said, "and three of them are standing right here—the coach, the coxswain, and the crew. The other two are communication and commitment. I'm communicating to you *right now* that you need to step up your commitment or get out of this boathouse *right now*. I'll find JV rowers to fill your seats. I'm taking a shower. You've got until I'm done to figure out what you want."

Nick stalked off to his office to grab his duffle bag and then headed for the locker room, sick with the dread of impending failure. He knew he might not have a crew by the time he was dressed. He hated to gamble, and this was an epic roll of the dice.

MORGAN watched Coach Bedford retreat to the locker room. That's what it was too—a retreat. First he tossed a bomb in their midst; then he ran off to avoid the fallout.

Where the hell did Bedford get off making those accusations? He'd only had a few beers. He knew his limits and was nowhere near them. At six-three and over 190 pounds, he could have three beers in an hour without being drunk according to the DMV, and that was all he'd had all night. He'd have been fine to drive with the addition of some water and another hour. If those three beers lost them the PCRCs, they had bigger trouble than a party, Morgan thought.

Morgan was committed. The accusation that he wasn't pissed him off. He was plenty committed to the sport and to the team. His hands alone showed that, his palms full of calluses and blisters. He'd learned to stop letting people see his hands when he rowed in high school. He now had firm opinions about brands of bandages and sports tape. That was commitment.

Commitment was being in his seventh year of a sport that took a great deal of his energy and exacted a high price physically, mentally, emotionally, and socially. Hell, even academically, since it was looking like he was on the five-year plan for his bachelor's degree, all thanks to the time commitment (there was that word again) crew required.

No, crew exacted a high price, and Morgan paid it willingly because it fulfilled him in a way nothing else ever had or would.

But that didn't mean he was an indentured servant. They were scholar-athletes in CalPac's rhetoric, and without the schooling, he and his teammates couldn't have been athletes. Coach Bedford didn't own his life and sure as hell didn't own him, Morgan thought angrily.

The thought made him shiver. A little voice whispered that Coach Bedford could own him if he wanted to, could own Morgan lock, stock, and barrel….

He shoved it down.

But Morgan's anger was broken. He sighed to himself. Coach Bedford was right. He gave the team everything. The guy couldn't have much of a life, and he knew Coach Bedford didn't have a girlfriend, at least one he'd ever mentioned.

Given that, the crew needed to match coach's commitment. "Well?" Morgan said to the others.

"Aww, shit," Brad said. "Coach is right. Go talk to him, will you, Cockring?"

Stuart held his hands up. "Not me, asshole. I've never seen him this mad. And stop calling me that."

They all stared at each other, no one eager to face what they now realized was their coach's righteous anger.

"I'll go, bitches," Morgan said.

As he walked to the locker room, Morgan wondered why Coach Bedford's good opinion mattered so much to him. Coach Bedford's accusation cut him to the quick. He knew he hadn't done anything wrong, but it still bothered him. A lot. Yeah, the unfairness just infuriated him, but it was more than that. Morgan felt like Coach Bedford had accused him personally of letting him down. Coach Bedford's good opinion wasn't lightly earned and wouldn't be lightly earned back.

It wasn't like he'd caught Morgan in the act, but he might as well have, with a load of another man's spunk wiped into a pocket. Morgan knew in that instant that letting down his coach—this coach—would slay him. He never wanted to see the cold, hard look in the other man's eyes again and would do anything to avoid a repeat.

Morgan walked into the locker room, now steamy from the shower. His throat went dry. Coach Bedford stood with his back to him, a towel wrapped around his narrow waist. Conscious thought deserted Morgan as he drank in the sight of those impossibly wide shoulders and the built lats that plunged down to a perfect ass, unfairly hidden beneath the towel. Calves, righteously defined and hairy, reappeared from the bottom of the towel.

Morgan wanted to reach out and rip the towel away, letting it flutter to the floor. He could do it. Just a few strides of his own long legs and he could be so close to his coach, close enough to feel him, close enough to taste him. Of their own volition, he felt his quads bunch to start him moving, felt his bicep twitch to rip the towel away.

Morgan coughed. "Coach?"

MEANWHILE, the tension left Nick as the locker room door shut behind him. Tired from his row, deflated after confronting his athletes, he wanted nothing more than a hot shower and an afternoon of not thinking about things. At least he could have the shower. That the situation out in the boathouse was unresolved took the shine off the rest of it.

Nick didn't know what to do. He'd never had a crew that had a real chance of winning the PCRCs before. CalPac was rarely DFL, or

Dead Fucking Last, a technical rowing term, but rarely out in front. Not this year. This year, they had a shot.

But Nick also had never had a crew so apparently bent on sabotaging that shot. There was nothing wrong with letting off steam, and he had nothing against parties per se. But not during the buildup to the biggest race of the spring season. For the seniors, it'd be the last race of their collegiate careers. The casual attitude baffled him.

As the hot water hit his shoulders, Nick craned his neck, stretching the kinks out. The hot water stung the blisters on his hands. Blisters. Their very presence hinted at deeper issues, since he only got them when he had a death grip on the oar handles, and he only had a death grip when he was tense and angry.

He couldn't get the image of Morgan walking out of the back of the house out of his mind. It could've been completely innocent. The bathroom had to be somewhere, after all. But he'd been a semi-closeted college athlete once and had a pretty good idea of what kinds of things went on in darkened rooms at parties. He didn't know for sure that Morgan was gay, but he'd heard rumors. Normally he ignored boathouse scuttlebutt, but this time….

The thought of Morgan sullying himself like that made Nick ill. He told himself it wasn't jealousy. Morgan deserved better. He hadn't lifted his eyes off the ground during his entire tirade.

Guilty conscience or just angry? Nick would never know. *Project much, Nick?* he thought.

He took some soap from the dispenser mounted on the wall. Rubbing his hands to form lather, he started in to clean himself. With no washcloth, it might not be as thorough, but then, sweat was water-soluble, and he hadn't been all that dirty to begin with. Right, soap where it stank. Armpits, ass, groin.

He lifted his cock to wash under it and felt the old familiar zing. He couldn't, not there, not in the locker room.

Could he? His rapidly filling cock sure thought he could and should. Right there in the locker room, his oarsmen on the other side of the door? Yeah, right there in the showers.

Groaning softly, he slicked up. Holding the base of his cock steady with one hand, he slowly moved the other up and down the rest of its length. He shuddered as waves of pleasure raced up his spine.

It'd been a long time since he'd had someone to touch him. Practiced ease combined with the thrill of danger took him right to the edge.

And he stayed there.

Nick reached one soapy hand up to a nipple. He rolled it back and forth. His nips had always been wired, and the pleasure bloomed behind his eyes. He dropped his head back, moaning softly.

It felt good. Damned good. Up and down. Slippery friction.

He was almost… there. Right at the edge.

But not over it. Something was missing. The overpowering lust began to recede as the rubbing on his cock degraded from pleasure to irritation.

He just wanted to cum, damn it. It had felt so good just a moment before. He tweaked the other nipple hard. If he could just….

Morgan. An image of the rower straining in the boat popped into his mind, and just like that, he was harder than granite. The defined muscles of the rower's back visible through his tank top had Nick shaking with need.

"Morgan," he gasped, and he blew his load onto the tile wall of the shower in three sharp blasts that left him seeing stars.

His knees shook as his vision cleared and he came to his senses. Had he just… jeez. The evidence was right there on the wall. He angrily washed his spunk off the wall with his hand.

He'd just jacked off to one of his athletes. There was a line between coach and athlete that no decent coach dared cross, and even with those twisted fantasies, Nick felt like he was dangerously close. This had to stop.

He finished in the shower and dried himself off roughly, pissed at his lack of control. He was a man and a coach, damn it, not some horny teenage hormone case. He should be able to control himself better than that.

He wrapped the towel around his waist and walked into the locker room. Someone had written "hurt" on his locker's door, the hurt locker. He smiled despite himself as he rummaged for his toiletries.

"Coach?"

Nick jumped. He hadn't heard the door open. He turned around, and there was Morgan. In the flesh. The last person Nick wanted to see at that moment. How long had he been standing there? How much had he seen? How much had he heard?

"Yeah?" Nick said gruffly, pathetically grateful the towel was plush enough to hide his dwindling hard-on. He hoped.

"We… um," Morgan said. "We're sorry. We'll do what we need to do."

Relief washed over Nick. He still had a crew. "Will you tell them to get oars down to the dock and my launch set up? We'll go out for a steady row to work on conditioning, nothing too cruel this morning."

Nick turned to his locker. He had to dress fast. He had a practice to run. All his attention was on business now, his erection thankfully gone, and just as he was about to drop the towel, he realized Morgan still stood there. "Yes?"

Morgan looked up, his face red, from the steam or uncertainty, Nick couldn't tell. "Thanks for not giving up on us, Coach."

Nick nodded. "Go warm up. I'll be out soon."

IT WAS a beautiful spring afternoon, but not out on the river. The wind was up, and it was perfect sailing weather. Too bad they were a rowing team. Nick managed well enough. He was in a safety launch. The crew might object to the increased challenge the chop provided, but it'd be good for them. They couldn't always row on flat water, after all, and he wasn't working them that hard, not after the week he'd already inflicted on them.

They had earned a second week of double days, the men of the CalPac Crew, and this was the last row before they resumed the regular training schedule. He'd pulled their class schedules too, so he knew when everyone was available. There'd been some creative time management, but everyone had made it. Just to be on the safe side, he'd notified their professors, as well, but that early in the semester, there was no worry about midterms or projects.

Nick was going easy on them today, partly because of the more challenging water, partly because of what he had planned for the next day on the ergs, but partly because of physiology. The whole point to training was to provoke an adaptation that would result in greater strength. But that strength only came through recovery. He knew just how close to the edge to push them that week before he backed way off. For a little while, at least.

For a time he just watched without shouting through the megaphone. They were the varsity crew; he'd given them instructions. It was time to let them figure it out, time for Stuart to work the bugs out, time for him to observe without comment. It took literally thousands of strokes to lay down new muscle memory, so he got out of the way to let his men work.

Watching was critical. He'd learned a lot about rowing through coaching. It gave him a perspective he'd never had before, a series of "Aha! So *that's* what that looks like" moments that allowed him to connect his own experiences in a boat to the training of others. He had a keen eye for the subtle movements his crew made as they rowed, the same sequence of movements endlessly repeated. The minute lift of a shoulder at the wrong moment or a hunched back jumped out when he was quiet and watching. That eye made a difference and separated the good coaches from the babysitters in motorboats.

Nick also watched for the pure pleasure of watching. Boats rowed by novices resembled nothing so much as epileptic spiders, eight limbs flailing without rhyme or reason. But the men of his varsity crew, some of whom had been at it for six or seven years, knew how to row. Good rowing looked effortless, and today, his crew looked like they'd found their rhythm, bodies swinging together, the blades of the oars at the same height off the water as they moved back into position to take another stroke. Eight blades knifing into the water together, eight athletes using their oars as levers to pry the boat past them, eight bodies moving as one.

Nick glanced at his five-seat. Morgan. He found himself watching Morgan a lot. He told himself he was watching because Morgan was such a good rower. Graceful, yet powerful, all the parts moving in sequence to harness all the power a human body could muster in just the right order. It was beautiful to see. He was gorgeous, muscled without being overbuilt, handsome without being pretty, a male body in poetic motion.

But it was more than that. Morgan wasn't just handsome, he was hot. He could see Morgan's ass encased in Spandex shorts, enticing him. It made Nick long to come behind him and grab hold, running his hands down the slick fabric of the shorts as he kissed him roughly from behind before yanking those shorts down, rubbing his painfully hard erection between those perfect cheeks, and fucking him senseless. Watching that amazing body work made him yearn to see it work in other ways, to see that effort and sweat put into riding his cock.

Nick groaned as his pants grew too tight, even painful. He shifted, trying to ease his sudden discomfort. He was just glad the crew couldn't see him pitch a trouser tent like that. He'd never hear the end of the razzing. Shifting did nothing to relieve Nick's growing problem. Making sure his boat's course was set, he leaned back to reach down his pants and adjust, pushing an epic hard-on to one side. He was just glad no one could see.

He watched Morgan a little longer. He told himself it was just to check his technique, but still he lingered. Then Morgan glanced over, catching his eye. Nick flushed. Caught looking. What a freshman move. But still he held Morgan's eye just a little longer. His mouth twitched into a one-sided smile at the other man. He couldn't help it. There was just something about him that made Nick smile.

Then Nick tore his gaze away, suddenly guilty and shamefaced, his face burning. Crushing on a rower like this. It just wasn't healthy. He had a job to do, and it didn't involve leering.

IT WAS the last day of the second week of double days, made all the more hellish because classes were gearing up for the term. Morgan never understood why all professors, and in this he included his coach, assumed that their course was the only demand on his time. He may not have had midterms yet, but as an upper-division literature student, he had plenty to think about, and that was before crew twice a day. Lately crew had brought its own distractions above and beyond the usual— and something else to think about.

Coach Bedford.

Morgan never knew what to make of him. Early in that second week of double days, he'd stalked around the boathouse like a demon. He watched their every move and pounced on any technical flaw, no matter how inconsequential. "Big flaws are made of little flaws!" Coach Bedford had said, practically screaming.

Morgan felt picked on and said as much to Stuart one evening.

"He's after all of us," Stuart pointed out. "In case you haven't noticed, there's not a whole lot I can do right on the water this week. Hell, he's even got me on the ergs with you guys. Like that'll make the boat go faster."

"Maybe not, but it'll skinny your ass down," Morgan smirked.

"My ass is just fine the way it is, thank you. It's you dumb brutes who move the boat, not me, so why should I suffer?" Stuart said. Then he considered the matter. "You may be right about him picking on you, though. I'll start paying more attention."

But the crew had a party to pay for, and Coach Bedford had ridden them hard that week. He made no bones about it.

Then Morgan thought about what he had seen under that towel the day in the locker room, about Coach Bedford adjusting himself in the launch. That had to be what he was doing. Morgan thought about the bulge in Coach Bedford's pants. Even through those dire Dockers he had on he could tell it'd be big. So yeah, there was a bone he'd like to ride hard.

By the end of the week, it seemed like Coach Bedford had relaxed, as if Morgan and the others had atoned for their sins, as if they'd proven themselves worthy once again. Morgan knew he'd been determined to make it up to his coach. While there was the desire to please and the need to prove to himself that he could take what his coach dished out, Morgan knew there was more to it than that. He wanted to impress Coach Bedford. He wanted to be back in his coach's good graces for reasons that had nothing to do with rowing. He just didn't want to dig too deeply into the reasons why just yet.

When Morgan had caught his coach watching him on the water, it had been magical. He shouldn't have turned his head like that, but when he did, Coach Bedford didn't yell. He just kept looking. He even smiled, and not an evil "ah-ha!" smile. It had been tentative, almost shy. For some reason, that warmed Morgan like a hot cup of coffee on a cold day. He wanted to see that smile again.

And now it was time for the last land workout of the second double-days week.

"All right, listen up," Coach Bedford said. "It's been a long, hard week, but you've done well. Starting with tomorrow's row, we resume our normal practice schedule. Yesterday afternoon's row was an easy one, so you know what that means." Coach Bedford grinned as his rowers groaned.

"You're in such a good mood that you're going to let us go without tormenting us today?" Brad said hopefully.

"Would someone please pinch Sundstrom awake? He's dreaming," Coach Bedford said. "In fact, on the dry-erase board is today's erg workout. While you lot are setting up nine ergs, perhaps Brad will unveil today's practice?"

As the others set up the ergometers, Brad turned the dry-erase board around. He glanced at it, then whistled. "Wow. You must really hate us."

"No more so than usual, Brad," Coach Bedford said.

The rest of the crew read the workout with varying degrees of amazement and horror.

"Even me?" Stuart said, green around the gills.

Coach Bedford pulled his sweatshirt off to reveal a skin-tight technical-fiber top. "As a matter of fact, no. You're the coxswain, and as inspiring as it is to the crew for you to share their suffering, there's no real need for you to spend so much time doing horrible things around your anaerobic threshold."

"But there's nine ergs," Stuart protested.

"Yes," Coach Bedford said, "there are." He toed his shoes off and dropped trou. The skin-tight top proved to be the top half of a unisuit, the single piece tank and shorts many crews favored. They were made of Lycra and left nothing to the imagination. He sat on an erg's seat and put his shoes back on. "Stuart, you're the coach for this workout. You know what to look for. Show no mercy."

"Does that include you?" Stuart said, a glint forming in his eye.

"Yes."

Morgan's eyes popped out of his head. The uni looked like it had been sprayed onto his coach's body. His coach in Spandex was even better in real life than he'd imagined. He wondered how he'd made it so far under Bedford's coaching without seeing the man in Spandex, but he wasn't arguing. There he was in his old uniform, large as life and twice as hot.

Coach Bedford wore the blue and gold of the University of California, and Morgan knew that he'd rowed for UC San Diego as an undergrad. Some former collegiate athletes got soft the moment their athletic careers ended, but not Coach Bedford. The uni fit him just as well as it had when he'd been Morgan's age.

Morgan snapped his jaws shut but continued to admire the view even as he sat on an erg next to him. It always made him hyper-aware to erg next to his coach, like every little flaw or problem would be instantly spotted and corrected, even if rationally he knew that his coach would be too distracted by the grueling workout before them.

But really, how unfair was the world that he couldn't see his coach's chest without the uni, a front view to match the view of his back that still made Morgan salivate.

"So what do we get if we beat you?" Brad said.

"Bragging rights?" Coach Bedford suggested.

Brad shook his head. "We throw you off the dock."

"But what if you beat them?" Stuart asked.

Coach Bedford grinned like a cat in front of a cage full of fat, flightless birds. "If I beat *any* of you, shall we say another week of double days? I'll even make it raw scores, not adjusted for age and weight. Because I'm such a nice guy."

"Oh hell no," Brad said. "You pussies better pull hard, because I am so not doing another one of those."

"Ready all!" Stuart called.

The nine of them, athletes and coach, took erg handles in hand and sat at the ready.

"Row!"

And then the hum of the ergs and the burning in his legs drove all other thoughts from Morgan's head.

Chapter
THREE

NICK lost the erg challenge he'd used as the culmination of the second week of double days by a few seconds. When he cooked the numbers for age and weight, he'd actually beaten three of them, but that wasn't part of the bargain. As promised, Brad had thrown him off the dock. He didn't mind, not if it cemented the crew's loyalty and determination.

After that, he and his crew settled into a routine, he with his graduate work and they with their undergraduate studies, and everyone worked to make them the best athletes they could be in time for that final, all-important race of the season.

Nick spent his days after practice at his own school, taking graduate seminars, teaching undergraduate courses, and doing his own research. He devoted his evenings to studying or grading or working on materials for coaching—practice plans, reading the latest research in human sports physiology and deciding whether it applied to rowing and, if so, how to apply it to his crew, or, like that Saturday afternoon, tabulating the results of the latest round of erg testing.

Every other week Nick put them through a 2k erg test, and every fourth week they spent a day on more comprehensive testing. He was both pleased and impressed with the results. The latest 2k time told him seven of his athletes were getting faster, and the eighth had a cold. Nick wasn't worried. Even a fraction of a second made a difference at that level of competition; winning by a tenth of a second was still a win. Not only that, the more comprehensive testing showed that overall fitness had increased, as well. Sure, any dumb jock could pull hard for six minutes and change, but his boys… well, with their recent fitness gains on top of what they brought with them, they could pull harder and recover faster. Since some regattas had heats, which meant same-day or even back-to-back races, the CalPac Crew would be well situated to win.

Nick carefully entered the information into the spreadsheet that held previous results and studied the data. All of his rowers were improving, but one stood out. Morgan. Morgan had always been competitive. Nick had known that since he'd started gunning for a seat in the varsity boat early in his sophomore year. By the end of it, Morgan had displaced one of his varsity rowers.

But now, judging by the data, Morgan was gunning for someone again. He'd pulled out in front of his teammates and continued to pull away. He had someone in his sights, no question. Nick just couldn't figure out who. He'd already surpassed Brad. Maybe Morgan just wanted to see how far he could go.

Nick leaned back in his chair, stretching the kinks out of his neck. Morgan. What was he going to do about Morgan? What could he do? He knew what he wanted to do. He wanted to nail Morgan's ass to the mattress. Or the wall. Either one. Better yet, both. Just the thought made his cock begin to fill.

Morgan was one of the nine men Nick shouldn't be looking at because he was one of his rowers. He was also the only person to interest Nick in a long time.

Sighing, he logged onto one of his favorite pay-per-view sites. It featured hot young men doing the kinds of things horny guys did to and with each other. It rarely failed to soothe, but for some reason it just wasn't doing the trick tonight. He was distracted and not all that revved up to begin with.

Nick found himself lingering over the ending, the part after the moaning ended and the two men showed what great and good friends they were, tenderly cleaning each other up in the shower before settling in for a nap. The shortest part of the movie, it occupied the greater part of his attention.

Nick pictured him and Morgan doing that, gently washing each other, holding each other before drifting off to sleep. He smiled without realizing it, his expression softening to wistful yearning as he wondered what Morgan liked for breakfast. Maybe an omelet and toast with juice. He'd serve it on a tray with a flower in a little vase. Or maybe pancakes that they'd feed each other before licking the syrup from each other's fingers.

He almost fell out of his chair when he caught up to where his mind was headed. He wasn't fantasizing about sex. He was picturing a relationship. Was that it? Was his subconscious telling him he wanted a relationship with Morgan? The idea blew him away. He'd never gone in for relationships much, not as an undergrad devoted to rowing and avoiding the flack from other athletes, not as a coach and grad student. He sought companionship when he needed it but otherwise steered clear of more substantial entanglements. Relationships took time, and he had none, not between coaching and grad school. The few boyfriends he'd had inevitably came to resent the time and discipline the sport required. Even as a coach, there were few late nights and many early mornings and a lot of attention paid to other men—hot men—in between.

A little voice whispered that if he dated a rower....

Nick squelched the thought. He didn't know many out men who rowed with the local clubs for the post-college set, and those few were happily partnered. He'd never interfere with that, ever. And dating his own athletes? What a cliché, an ugly and immoral stereotype, a coach poaching his own athletes. You don't shit where you eat, or in this case, fuck where you coach.

But damn, Nick wanted to know what it felt like to hold Morgan. He could imagine what his cock would feel like balls deep in Morgan's ass, because he'd fucked guys before. But he'd never held someone, not like that, not someone he wanted to hold that way for a long time to come. The longing to hold, to be held, made him shake. Damn. He wanted to see himself with Morgan for the long term, someone he could maybe share a life with, just as they shared a passion for crew.

Then his shoulders slumped, and Nick leaned forward to pillow his head on his arms. Morgan. He'd be disgusted if he knew where his coach's mind headed every time he walked into the boathouse. As far as Nick knew, Morgan was straight. At least, Morgan had never indicated he wasn't. Of course, that meant nothing, and then there was that party…. What *had* Morgan been doing back there?

Nick laughed helplessly. He was making himself crazy. He'd finally found someone he both wanted and who would understand the demands on his time, and Nick couldn't touch him, even assuming he was gay, and beyond that, assuming he was interested.

Nick shook his head, banishing the thought to the back of his mind. He hated wanting what he couldn't have. But out of idle curiosity, or so he told himself, Nick pulled his books of rules and regulations from USRowing and the International Rowing Federation. He made a note to check NCAA regulations too. All were sure to take a lively interest in relationships between coaches and their athletes.

Three very unhappy hours later, he called his best friend, Drew. "Can we talk?"

"Aren't we talking right now?" Drew said. "Wait… you sound dreadful. What's wrong?"

"It's complicated," Nick said.

"Let's go get some dinner and work it through," Drew said.

"No, this has to be behind closed doors."

"That bad?" Drew murmured.

"It's not good," Nick said.

On the other end of the line, Drew thought for a moment. "Okay, here's what you're going to do. First, you're going to put some decent clothes on, because I want to go dancing later and it sounds like you need to be distracted. Then you're going to pick something up and come over here and we'll talk it to death."

"Drew, I don't—"

"You're wasting time!" Drew said. Then he hung up.

Nick shook his head. He knew better than to argue with Drew when he wanted to dance.

AN HOUR later, dressed and with take-out on the seat next to him, Nick pulled up in front of Drew's house. The neighborhood always made him self-conscious because it reminded him that he could've lived there too, if he'd stayed in the business world after graduating from college like Drew had. But where Nick went into coaching, Drew moved into real estate. Lately, he'd taken to buying and flipping foreclosed-on and abandoned houses, catching the rebounding housing market. Drew did quite well for himself too, despite the economy.

For the love of rowing, Nick gave that possibility up and went into coaching and back to school, since virtually all collegiate coaches had master's degrees in some form of exercise science. Most days, he didn't regret it, even as he rushed from the boathouse to the lab to the classroom. It was the nights that had turned problematic, he thought dryly.

Nick rang the bell, and immediately Drew opened the door. "Hey there, babydoll," Drew said, diving in for a hug, plastering himself to Nick's side like a lover. Drew had been calling him "babydoll" since their first week in the dorms as freshmen at UC San Diego. The very much out Drew had sized up the still-closeted Nick and latched onto him. He'd held on tight until Nick got over himself and came out, to his friends if not his team, and they'd been best friends ever since.

"Hey yourself," Nick said indulgently. He looked Drew up and down. "I swear, you keep getting better looking every week. How is it that I'm the working athletic professional, but you're in better shape?"

Drew was a few inches shorter than Nick, with brown hair and blue eyes that should've made him look like the poster boy for generic American gay, but a steady intelligence and sparkling wit, plus diligent work at the gym, made him the man everyone at the clubs wanted to dance with. For his part, Drew was in no hurry to settle down, but Nick knew he didn't believe in just giving it away, either.

Drew pushed at his hair a la Mae West. "A girl's got her secrets. Are you going to feed me or just bore me to death with whatever's got you gnawing your guts out?"

"Food first, definitely. I know what happens to you when you're not fed regularly," Nick said with a shudder.

"A boy's gotta have one flaw," Drew said, dragging Nick to the dining room, where he'd already set out dishes.

"Dishes, Drew? And flatware?" Nick said, one eyebrow set on "stun."

"It's not food if it's not on a plate," Drew said, shuddering. "It's just not."

Nick, who ate most meals anywhere but his apartment's tiny eat-in kitchen, wisely kept silent.

"So tell me, what has you tied in knots?" Drew said, serving first Nick and then himself.

Nick squirmed. "The usual, only more so."

"Wait, don't tell me," Drew said. He closed his eyes and put his fingers to temples like he was tuning in to Nick's brainwaves. "It's the crew."

"It's always the crew," Nick sighed.

"I know, that's what makes you so easy to figure out." Drew smirked. It made his dimples pop, which he knew.

"Remember a few weeks ago when I borrowed your car? It goes back to that, maybe even before," Nick said, explaining his stakeout operation at the end of spring break.

"You did what?" Drew said, pausing with a fork halfway to his mouth.

"Hey now, you told me I could borrow your car," Nick said.

Drew sat back in his chair and shook his head. "Obviously I should've asked why. For some odd reason, I thought you had a date you wanted to impress or something, but now that I think about it"—Drew sighed—"you'd actually have to date someone, or even be interested in a man for a reason other than how fast he can move a boat. I should've known that was too much to ask for."

Nick didn't say anything. He pushed uneaten food around on his plate, refusing to meet Drew's eyes.

Drew noticed. He stared at him through narrowed eyes. "Or have you? Is Nicky holding out on me? Because that would be bad, very bad. Very, very bad. That would make me angry, and you wouldn't like me when I'm angry."

"Will you turn green? Because you've already grown like four sizes since a year ago. You juicing?"

"Don't deflect," Drew said as he dabbed his lips with a napkin. "Soft tissue. Vulnerable. Kill! Kill!"

"I suppose if I don't confess, you'll wrestle it out of me?" Nick said with a sly smile.

"I thought we'd given up friends with benefits years ago," Drew joked.

"Yeah, we did, since the 'benefits' part didn't work very well and threatened the 'friends' part. This isn't easy for me, okay? I'm going to have to circle around to it. Yes, I've got it bad for someone, and he doesn't know I exist. I mean, he does, he just doesn't know I like him."

"'Like'? You 'like' like him? What is this, grade school? You're attracted to someone. You want to fuck someone. You want to marry someone. You don't 'like' someone," Drew said.

"Drew, please. This is hard enough without you parsing everything. Yes, I'm interested in someone, but it violates every canon of professional ethics there is," Nick said, throwing his napkin down.

Drew's jaw dropped. "You've fallen for one of your rowers. O my God, you horndog! You, Mr. Scrupulous himself. After all these years, the sight of all that male flesh has finally gotten to you, stud."

"I'm so glad my problems amuse you," Nick snapped.

Drew reached out and put his hand on Nick's. "You know I love you, and I'm sorry. I was just teasing. Talk me through it."

"There's not a lot to talk through," Nick said. "Coaches don't date their athletes. The NCAA, USRowing, even the US Olympic Committee... they all come down very hard on it, and all for the same reason: the power dynamic. Because of the authority coaches have—I have—it's far too easy for the element of consent to be removed."

"Nick, you're not like that."

"I hope I'm not, but how could I be sure? What if he's gay, and I approach him? What if he acts flattered, goes along with it, all that stuff, just because he's afraid of making me angry or afraid I'll drop him from the team? That's not consensual, not really."

"No, it's not," Drew said, "but we both know it happens all the time. We both saw it when we were student athletes ourselves. Granted, it was between male coaches and female athletes. They were called 'honeybuns', I believe."

"And when it blew up—and it always did—it was ugly," Nick said.

"You're not like that," Drew repeated, "and consider this: there are all those rules against it because it's a lot more common than anyone wants to admit. What would happen if you told him?"

"Drew, I'm not even out at the boathouse. Sex is a distraction, and straight men can be so paranoid if they think you're looking at their asses," Nick sighed.

"Which you are."

"Which I am. The best coach I ever had was epically lesbotronic. Sex never even entered into the equation. I've tried to model myself after her."

"Then you should've coached women's crew," Drew laughed.

Nick didn't say anything. He slumped in his chair, dejected and depressed. He'd tried to be so careful, and now he had a huge mess on his hands, or could very easily. "If I speak up, I could lose everything… a job I love, Morgan's respect. If I keep quiet, at least I keep my job and my self-respect and can still be his coach, even if nothing more."

"If you keep quiet, you lose a chance at love," Drew said softly, all traces of joking gone.

"I don't know what to do," Nick whispered.

Drew left him alone with his thoughts while he cleared the remnants of dinner. When he was done and Nick had not so much as moved to the sofa in the den, he sat down next to him, one hand on his shoulder. "Perhaps there is no answer, not right now."

Nick looked at him and smiled a sad, one-sided smile. "Sorry to be such a downer."

"You're not a downer. But this isn't healthy. You need to go out, get laid."

"We decided we were better friends than lovers, remember," Nick said with a laugh. "It didn't work very well."

"Weird, that. We're compatible in every way, even top and bottom, but the chemistry just wasn't there." Drew shrugged. "Besides, I didn't mean me. We're going dancing, remember? You can let off some steam. You can also drive. I want a drink with an umbrella in it. But my car, if you please. I don't wish to be seen in yours."

Nick rolled his eyes, smiling in spite of himself. "Any place in particular?"

"Aspects, I think. The bartender there is a known expert in the making of sticky little drinks."

"Then your chariot awaits, just as soon as you hand over the keys."

"DUDE, you're going to bed at eight forty-five on a Saturday night?" Stuart said.

Morgan glared at his roommate. "Don't start. Just don't start. It's been a hellish day, all downhill after practice. I've done what I need to do. I'm going to sleep, hitting restart, whatever."

"You're getting old," Stuart said.

"Fuck you," Morgan muttered on his way by.

"Bend over," Stuart called. He watched Morgan's fine ass sashay down the hallway to the bedrooms. He sighed and went back to his books, an enigmatic look on his face in the blue light of the muted television.

Once in his room, Morgan shuffled through his evening routine, doing the bare minimum. It was just time to be done. He climbed under the covers and was mercifully out in moments.

Rough day? Nick said, kneading his shoulders. Morgan just sighed, his head limp on his neck. He didn't reply. *Lie down. I'll take care of it, but first you have to get undressed.*

As Nick watched him, Morgan stripped down, slowly pulling his shirt over his head, then, with his eyes fixed on Nick, dropping his shorts to the floor. He lay down on his belly, face turned to one side. Then Nick sat beside him, clad only in his racing uni, the tank pulled down. Moran floated in the sensation of Nick's hands, his large, strong hands, working the knots out of his neck and shoulders, then moving down his back.

Then Nick stopped and climbed over him. Morgan looked over his shoulder, and there was Nick, straddling him, sitting just below his ass. *I can do your back more easily this way.*

Morgan just nodded, and hands returned, stroking up and down his back, making him feel good, easing the day away.

Then the hands strayed lower, caressing his ass as Nick leaned forward. Morgan felt the weight of Nick's body, felt the hard rod pressing into him. He tingled all over. *Roll over*, Nick breathed into his ear.

The pressure eased from his back as Nick stood, and Morgan rolled over. He looked up and Nick loomed over him, a god. His chest was broad and muscled without an ounce of fat. Soft brown hair covered each pec and traced a path between his abs down his chest, disappearing into his uni. Nick's cock tented the already-tight Spandex, precum staining its dark blue to black.

Then Nick lowered himself again, straddling Morgan's quads. Morgan could see right to Nick's package, could see what he most wanted, just feet away. It was huge, and Nick's cock strained against the pliant fabric. All he need to was reach out....

Then Nick caught his hands. *No. You've been bad. You don't get to touch.*

Morgan groaned but didn't struggle. Nick released his hands and continued the massage. First it was just the front of the deltoids and biceps, but he quickly moved on to the pecs. He put his hands over them, thumbs over the sternum before smoothing outwards.

Morgan gasped when Nick's thumbs brushed his nips. *You like that?* Nick said, brushing each one again, harder, longer. Morgan's breathing deepened, and his own cock, already semi-hard, filled so fast it hurt.

Morgan turned his face to one side, blushing furiously, but Nick look down and smiled. *Don't worry. It happens all the time with massage therapy.*

Nick moved his hands down Morgan's abs. His own chest was much hairier than Nick's, but Nick didn't seem to mind. He took care with each part of the abs, the stroke of the massage giving way to a caress.

No, you were a very bad boy a few weeks ago. Why would you settle for a handjob in the dark when you could have this whenever you wanted it? You could have it so much better.

Morgan groaned again, louder, deeper, thrusting his hips, trying to increase the rush as Nick moved his hands away. Nick leaned over Morgan, looking deep into his eyes. Morgan stared back until he thought he would drown, and then he closed his eyes.

He felt Nick kiss each closed lid, felt Nick's mouth brushing a trail down one cheek. His lips parted slightly as Nick kissed him. Morgan sighed into the kiss, electricity zinging through his body. He floated in a sea of sensation, anchored only by Nick.

Then Morgan felt a hand on one nipple and gasped. His hips rocked harder as his coach, the man for whom he'd longed, rubbed it, rolling it back and forth between his fingers.

Morgan protested when Nick's lips left his but then felt them move to his nip, the other one. *So it doesn't feel neglected.* Nick swirled his tongue across it as it hardened. Then he nipped it, kissed it, and swirled his tongue again to ease the pain, and under him, Morgan writhed.

"Please," Morgan breathed.

Please, what? You can have it all, everything you ever wanted, only give yourself to me.

"Yes...."

Nick's lips and tongue continued south as he brushed his hand across Morgan's now painfully hard erection. He ran his fingers through the precum pooling on Morgan's belly. *You're leaking.*

"Yes...."

Morgan bucked as Nick fisted his cock and brought his mouth over it.

Is this what you want?

"Yes...."

Nick lapped at the head lazily, like he had all the time in the world. Then he blew gently across the wet skin, sending shudders through Morgan's body.

"Please...."

Please, what?

"Love me," Morgan said, almost sobbing.

You have no idea how long I've waited to hear you say that. Nick hovered over Morgan's cock, which was jumping in time with his pulse. Then he engulfed it, swallowing it to the root.

Morgan wasn't small, he knew that much, but Nick took him all the way. He could feel the muscles of Nick's throat flutter around his cock, sending seismic shudders through his body.

His hips thrust again and again as Nick sucked, humming with pleasure, humming to give pleasure. Light and heat and pressure grew in his groin as Nick worked, taking him closer and closer.

Then Morgan felt a finger tease at his opening, circle it to stoke the sensitive skin. His head swam, and then all at once he was there. He pumped burst after burst down Nick's throat, but Nick never let up, never stopped, not until Morgan was done....

Morgan's eyes fluttered open, the pleasure lingering but fading with the growing awareness of quickly cooling pleasure in his underwear.

Wow, he thought, still dazed from the imagined encounter, still stunned with pleasure. One hand strayed across his chest as he savored the memory. Some dreams faded, but he knew he'd remember this one for a long time.

Morgan rolled over, hugging his pillow to him. He'd never get back to sleep, not after that. He'd blown one of the most intense loads he could remember, and it hadn't even been real. His partner had been a figment of his imagination generated by his subconscious's fevered desires, and the man that figment was based on didn't even know he existed, not like that.

There in his room, at that moment, he'd never felt more alone. The man of his dreams was just that—a dream. He knew he was being melodramatic. He was young. He'd get over it and meet someone else. He hoped. He didn't want to be that pathetic, lonely person crushing on someone he could never have, left out in the cold by life.

He reached a hand down his underwear. Speaking of cold….

Cold and lonely. What a combo. What had been hot was now just sticky and unpleasant, and Morgan got up, stripping his underwear off and using it to wipe himself clean.

He got dressed again and trudged into the living room where Stuart still studied, his face buried in a physiology text. "You look like crap," Stuart said without looking up.

"Can't sleep," Morgan grumbled.

"And?"

Morgan made a face. Stuart could be insightful, but his hard-charging coxswain's personality often spilled over into other areas of life. Stuart was a busy man and didn't take the time for byplay and chit-chat. Should he tell him? It was one thing when Stuart didn't know the guy involved but quite another when it was their coach. It all came down to how much he trusted his friend.

"Out with it," Stuart prompted. "I know you're upset, and I know it's boy trouble."

"That's spooky," Morgan said.

Stuart shrugged. "It's just this thing I do. Try not to let it overwhelm you. And don't think you can throw me off the scent, because you can't. You're hung up on someone. I can tell."

Morgan slumped on the sofa. He marshaled his thoughts. "Yep, it's boy trouble. Or man trouble, as the case may be."

"Isn't that a John Waters movie?" Stuart said, looking up from his book for the first time since Morgan had interrupted him, a smile playing around his lips.

Morgan smiled back. "That would be *Female Trouble*, I believe."

"So are you going to tell me about it?"

"Yeah, I like a guy and he doesn't know I exist. He's handsome and smart and gorgeous, and it's totally hopeless," Morgan said. He sighed.

Stuart regarded him for a few minutes, an odd look on his face. "Do I know this guy?"

"Yes," Morgan groaned. He buried his face in the sofa cushions. "It's Coach Bedford."

"For a moment there, I thought you said it was Coach Bedford." Stuart wiggled a finger in one ear to clear it, and his eyes grew wide.

"I did, and you can't tell anyone," Morgan said. "I feel stupid enough as it is. Can you imagine what Brad Sundstrom would make of it?"

Stuart shuddered. "No worries on that score. The last thing you need is something for him to lord over you. So the coach makes you throw a boner, huh?"

"That's such a lovely way to put it, but yes. Oldest story in college sports, isn't it?" Morgan sat up. He pulled his knees up to his chest, resting one cheek on them. "Athlete gets the hots for his coach, his straight, straight coach, and really, how pathetic is that?"

Stuart thought for a moment, searching for words. "It's not pathetic. The heart wants what it wants. So long as it's not immoral or damaging," he said, fixing Morgan with a gimlet stare, "there's no harm in it, at least if it doesn't go on too long. But I do think it's hopeless. I mean, Coach Bedford? Dude, he's as straight as an arrow."

"Yeah, but he's so hot," Morgan said with a sloppy grin.

"At least you didn't say 'dreamy'," Stuart sighed, "so I know you haven't turned into a complete girl. Yet."

Morgan cocked an eyebrow. "For Coach Bedford? I totally would."

"Overshare!"

"So what do I do?" Morgan asked.

"What can you do?" Stuart replied with a shrug. "Just keep on keeping on. Try not to let it get out of hand and try to remember there are other guys out there who are available, ones who share your sexual orientation."

"I know, it's just hard," Morgan said quietly.

"Sounds like someone needs to go dancing," Stuart said, slamming his textbook closed. At Morgan's skeptical look, Stuart said, "C'mon, you need a distraction, and it's not that late. Aspects is just getting going."

Morgan made a face. "Ass-Pecs is such a meat market."

"I know," Stuart said, cackling. "That's why we're going."

Groaning, Morgan hauled himself off the sofa. He knew his friend and roommate. Stuart would cajole and badger him until he gave in, a slower and quieter version of what he did on the water. It was part of what made him so effective a coxswain, but it also sometimes made him a pain in the ass. But Stuart was a friend who always had his best interests at heart. "Gimme ten minutes."

NICK didn't know the name of the techno tune he and Drew were dancing to, but he didn't care. It was working. Drew had been right; it felt good to let go and move. Unlike Drew, he might not have worn the latest designer labels, but it didn't matter. Based on the glances thrown his way, he still looked good. He was an athlete and in great shape. A tight T-shirt and some halfway decent jeans, and he was good to go.

Looking good certainly facilitated flirting. Nick and Drew flirted all the time. It was fun, it was safe, and it was a way for the two to express their mutual affection. But flirting with strangers gratified the ego too. Nick had even gotten a few numbers, which he had no intention of using. Drew had gotten a few of his own, some of which he probably would use. The teasing and the suggestive dancing was so completely different from his usual life that it diverted him, and Drew was there to fend off anything too unwelcome. They had a code, kind of like baseball signals, and at the first sign, one or the other would move in with a grope or a kiss to say, "Hands off, he's mine."

After one such rescue, they swayed together, Drew's hands latched behind Nick's neck, Nick's hands around his friend's waist.

"They let hets in here!" Drew hissed in his ear.

Nick started, jarred from his zone. "What?"

"Bunch of fucking college jocks. This is our bar. They can go slumming somewhere else. Jerks. Jock-jerks," Drew giggled. He was sloppy, but he'd had a few wet ones.

"I thought this place was for grown-ups, not…." Nick turned his head to see the group Drew meant and stopped. The bottom dropped out of his stomach as his blood turned to ice. "They let hets in!"

"That's what I said," Drew laughed. "You should listen better."

Nick fought panic rising like the tide. "No, those're some of my rowers. They let hets in. He's here. Morgan's here. I can't be seen."

"Where? Which one? The tall one with the dark hair? He's hot," Drew said.

Nick was too panicked to agree. He just wasn't ready to be out, to be outed, to his crew. He wasn't prepared to find out how men's crew would react to a gay man as a coach. There were gay rowers, there was even a gay rowing federation, but that didn't mean a college crew was ready for a gay man to be in charge of their hot young asses. Once they found out, the alumni oversight committee would know in hours, and his job would have the longevity of a mayfly. "C'mon, we've gotta get out of here."

"But I wanna dance," Drew pouted.

Nick wasn't listening. He couldn't hear anything over his pulse pounding in his ears. He grabbed Drew's hand and dragged him from the dance floor, intent on escape before he was compromised. He couldn't let Morgan see him.

MORGAN shook the tension out of his shoulders as he danced with Stuart and some people they knew from the women's crew. Stuart was right. It felt good to go out with some friends, to let his body distract his mind.

The women liked girls, they liked boys, so they could bump and grind and be totally shameless without anyone thinking anything about it. Morgan looked around as they danced, just force of habit. He didn't flirt. He knew the signs and ignored them. He was there with friends, not for sex, not for romance. He needed to clear his mind, not clutter it further.

"Oh. My. God," Stuart said over the pounding beat. "Is that...?"

Morgan looked up, and time stopped. It was Coach Bedford and some other guy. Some other hot guy being led by the hand. His vision tunneled in on the retreating back of the man who'd starred in his hottest dreams. Coach Bedford. In a gay bar. With another man. He didn't know whether he should laugh or cry.

Chapter
FOUR

NICK almost managed to forget the close call at a gay bar by slumming straight athletes. Almost. But his life was a house of cards, and he knew it. Job, future, life as it was currently arranged—all depended on staying closeted at work. He'd never thought it'd come to that when he finally admitted the truth to himself and Drew at the end of their freshman year. It had been so freeing to stop lying. He hadn't meant to go back in the closet for work, but it had happened nonetheless. He hadn't been dating anyone when CalPac hired him, and he tried to keep his personal life personal because he was the coach and not his athletes' friend.

But it was still a lie, and now it undergirded his life. He liked his life and didn't want it blowing up in his face. Every time he felt himself getting a little panicky, he headed out to run, or jumped on the ergs, or hit the weights. As a result, by Sunday evening he was exhausted and sore and still anxious and scared. He tried a little one-handed soothing, but he inevitably thought of Morgan, and that just made it worse.

Exhausted by it all, he nonetheless slept fitfully Sunday night, waking up for practice almost as tired as he'd been before he'd gone to bed. One good thing about working in an athletic capacity: he didn't have to clean up before work. He'd scull after coaching his crew and then clean up so he didn't reek all day when he taught or attended classes of his own. So he rolled out of bed, ate, grabbed his bag, and was out the door.

The panic didn't punch him in the guts until he parked in his marked spot in front of the boathouse. He'd been caught at a gay bar by two of his rowers. He rested his forehead on the steering wheel. It wasn't so much that crew was homophobic, but the sport was conservative, still a bastion of country-club elitism even as people of color and the disabled were welcomed. But all the worry flooded back, and the coffee felt like a brick in his stomach. Never before had he been frightened to go into the boathouse.

Nick forced himself to calm down, at least on the outside. It was early; no one was there yet. Morgan would face him when he walked in, not the other way around.

He fumbled for his keys, and his hand shook a little as he unlocked the boathouse. *Get it together*, he told himself as he punched the alarm's code.

He let himself into the coaches' shared office and sat down at his desk in the dark. He made himself take several slow, deep breaths to steady his heart. It worked. He felt himself grow still.

Then he heard voices outside the boathouse, and that blew it to hell. His heart slammed in his chest all over again, and he fought to get himself back under control.

He hurried to switch on his light and look like he cared about the plan for the morning's practice. But under his desk, he bounced his foot up and down, terrified that this day would be his last in the coach's launch.

IT WAS Stuart's turn to drive, and that was just fine with Morgan. Nothing would distract him from delicious anticipation. He was riding high with a silly grin.

"What's gotten into you? You look the Cheshire Cat, and it's just too early for that," Stuart muttered.

"Coach Bedford's gay. We spotted him at Ass-Pecs on Saturday night, remember? That's what's gotten into me. That's what I hope will get into me," Morgan smirked.

"Is that what your deal's been? You were grinning and staring off into space all day yesterday," Stuart said.

Morgan slouched in his seat. "You weren't supposed to notice."

"Yeah," Stuart said, drawing it out. "Speaking of noticing... you noticed, no doubt, that he was there with another guy?"

"Paging Dr. Buzzkiller!" Morgan snapped, folding his arms across his chest to ward off the unwelcome injection of reality.

They drove on in silence. Stuart looked over, and Morgan still had a tight grin going. He just shook his head.

Morgan ignored the looks. Stuart's reality-check wasn't loud enough to drown out his internal chant. *Coach Nick likes the dick, Coach Nick likes the dick*, he singsonged to himself. So what if Coach Bedford had been there with a guy? That didn't mean they were boyfriends any more than Stuart was his boyfriend just because they were seen together at the bar, or that he and Stuart were boning the gals from the women's crew just because they all danced together.

So it was with a you-have-a-secret-and-I-know-what-it-is smile that Morgan walked into the boathouse, ready for practice and ready to see his coach in a whole new light, only to run into a wall of ice a mile high.

NICK forced himself not to react when Morgan walked into the boathouse. If he treated Morgan like every other rower, then he wouldn't have to think about where he'd seen him. Or what he'd thought about afterward.

Then Nick got a load of that ivory skin and dark brown hair, with that lock that always seemed to flop over those brown eyes. He itched to brush it aside and then pull the taller man down and kiss him, at least for starters. He saw himself walk up to Morgan, who'd flash that shy smile of his....

No. Nick knew he couldn't be mooning over one of his athletes like that, not even if he saw him in a gay bar, even if they were interested in the same genitalia. He wouldn't—couldn't—let himself go there. Then Nick stopped cold. He'd seen Morgan in a gay bar, all right, dancing with Stuart and some women he recognized from the women's crew. Dancing dirty, from the looks of it, hands in places he didn't want to think about, touching things on Morgan he thought about far too much.

That threw ice water on Nick's little fantasies of kissing Morgan. He had to do this, he had to kill this… this thing in the cradle for both of them. He couldn't and wouldn't be the coach perving on his athletes, swooping in like a raptor on a helpless rabbit.

"Estrada," Nick said curtly. "Go get oars down. I'll talk to you after practice. Cochrane, let's go over today's practice plan."

His heart screamed in protest, but Nick forced his expression into a mask. It killed him to be frosty to Morgan. The younger man had all but skipped into the boathouse, faltering when he saw Nick's flat expression. The moment when the light died in Morgan's eyes just about killed him, like he'd broken the younger man's heart. He'd remember that for a long time.

"Sure thing," Stuart said, glancing at Morgan.

Nick shook himself and got his mind back on business—or tried. He didn't breathe easily until his men were in their boat and on the water. Nick knew he'd done the right thing, so why did he feel like shit?

MORGAN'S giddiness turned to dread at the sight of Coach Bedford. Sure, he was dressed in ratty jeans and a parka that obscured all the delicious details hinted at by his clothing on Saturday night. But it was the look on Coach Bedford's face that scared him. It was positively funereal.

Morgan trudged to the oar locker and started taking oars to the dock as his teammates trickled into the boathouse and put the coach's launch together. Then it was time to warm up, and he did his best to force his growing apprehension from his mind, letting his body take over as he performed the familiar exercises.

Morgan was a good rower. He'd rowed in high school and tried out for the novice crew his first year at CalPac College. He'd made the varsity team as a sophomore. His body knew what to do. His mind? His mind was on Coach Bedford.

Morgan kept his eyes forward, but from his peripheral vision, he saw the coach staring at him. No corrections or comments came his way. Coach Bedford just stared, Morgan could feel it. He refused to let it unnerve him. Instead, it just pissed him off, and he attacked the water with each stroke.

"Five, you're burying your oar," Stuart's voice crackled over the racing shell's speakers. "The extra surface area of the shaft in the water isn't moving the boat any faster, but it's fucking the set. Knock it off."

The words stung, and Morgan pulled his focus back to where it belonged, but he still felt Coach Bedford watching him. Then his stroke went to hell, and Stuart rode him for the rest of practice.

As they put the shell back on the boat rack and dried it off, Coach Bedford walked up to Morgan. "Can you stick around for a few minutes? I need to talk to you."

The weary, wary rower nodded and continued putting gear away, but still he watched his coach out of the corner of one eye. Coach Bedford gave him one last hot, tortured look, practically fucking him with his eyes, before he retreated to his office, leaving the door open for Morgan.

Morgan rushed through his after-row stretch out, hyperaware of the door gaping open, drawing him in. He said to Stuart, "Coach wants to talk to me. Can you wait?"

Stuart rolled his eyes, already tired of the psychodrama. "Yeah, for a few minutes. I've got lab, so don't be all day."

"I don't think I'll have much say," Morgan said, heading for Coach Bedford's office. His stomach felt leaden. Somehow he didn't think his coach was going to profess undying love. He knocked on the door. "You wanted to see me?"

Coach Bedford looked up and swept Morgan with his gaze. Morgan felt very self-conscious. Was he being checked out? Judged? He couldn't tell, but it was almost enough to make him scream. He coughed. "Coach?"

"Have a seat, Estrada," Coach Bedford said, shaking his head, the color high in his cheeks.

Morgan frowned. Coach Bedford usually called them by their first names, sometimes by what seat they rowed, but rarely just a last name.

His coach shifted in his seat. "So… about Saturday night."

"Yes?" Morgan said. He sat down, a smile ghosting across his lips.

Coach Bedford tried to look Morgan in the eye, but couldn't. He kept dropping his gaze. "Not that I need to explain myself, but before this spreads through the crew like a bad cold, you should probably know that I'm not gay. I was at that bar Saturday night because Drew wanted to go dancing and he's my best friend."

"Oh. That's cool," Morgan said. Then Morgan caught and held his coach's skittish gaze. "I'm gay. That's not a problem, is it?"

It might've sounded like a question, but it was really a statement, and it hung there in the air like a challenge. Morgan was out and proud, and there was no way in hell he was going back in the closet for anyone.

"No, of course not. CPC doesn't discriminate, and neither does this crew. If anyone gives you crap, tell me."

Morgan nodded. There was something unspoken on his coach's part, but Morgan couldn't put his finger on it right then. He didn't trust himself to speak at that moment, so the silence grew and grew.

"Hey, Morgan! Get the lead out!" Stuart called. "Some of us have to go to school, you know."

At that moment, Morgan could've kissed his roommate. He'd never been so embarrassed in his life. He was such an idiot. Of course his coach wasn't gay, and any thought he'd had that Coach Bedford might be too was just wishful thinking. What he wanted was once again impossibly far away, back beyond impossible. "Gotta go."

THAT evening, after sleepwalking through a day of glum distraction punctuated by sharp irritation, Morgan slammed the door to their apartment hard enough to rattle the windows. Stuart looked up. "What's gotten into you?"

"Not Coach Bedford, that's for sure," Morgan snapped. He'd been so sure....

"Is that what this morning was about? You stomped out of the boathouse and then clammed up. So Coach Bedford's dating someone?"

"No, he's straight," Morgan hissed.

Stuart closed the book he'd been reading and sat back. "Oh, really?"

"Yes, apparently he was there just being a friend. His best friend's gay, but he's not. How metrosexual. How much does that suck?"

"Not enough, apparently," Stuart said.

Morgan grimaced. "Please, not right now." He dropped to the couch and lay down, one hand over his eyes in an unconsciously theatrical gesture. "It just hurts, you know? What I wanted seemed like it was so close. Maybe not right within my reach, but close enough I might've had a chance. Now? Further away than ever."

"You out to him?" Stuart asked.

"Duh. After that, I wasn't going to pretend to be straight. I am who I am, and if they don't like cocksuckers on the CalPac Crew, then I'd rather not row."

"Your parents'd be pissed if you lost your scholarship."

Morgan rolled over to face Stuart. "They're fine with me being gay. If I told them why I'd lost it, Coach Bedford and California Pacific College would face the wrath of PFLAG."

"I've always liked your parents," Stuart said. "Mine could learn a thing or two."

"I'm sorry, Stuart, I didn't mean to—"

Stuart held up a hand. "Hush, this is about you. You thought you had something, then it was jerked away. But you didn't think you had it for very long, right? You're out to our coach and you're still rowing, right? These are good things. It's not like you've been doodling his name in your notebooks and dotting the I in 'Nick' with little hearts, right?"

Morgan just groaned and buried his face in the upholstery. "I haven't actually turned into a tween girl. It just feels that way." He sighed. "I'm a complete fool. I had my mancrush on our coach. Okay, fine. It's not like it doesn't happen in collegiate athletics, even if the guy-on-guy angle is a little rarer. Then I see him at a gay bar. Awesome! Score one for the oarsman. I spent all day yesterday imagining how it would go, and what happened this morning wasn't it." He laughed, a pain-filled bark. "I walked into the boathouse this morning convinced I was going to get my man. I slinked out with my tail between my legs. I'm such an idiot. He's older, he's sophisticated. I mean, he's seen things and done things. Been places. Even if he were gay, he'd want someone his equal, someone his age. I'm just some college kid with nothing to offer. I can barely get into bars legally. I'm still in school. What would a man like Nick Bedford want with some young punk like me, anyway?"

Morgan stood up. "Thanks for letting me ramble on. For listening. I'm going to bed. See you on the flip side."

STUART pasted a concerned look on his face and didn't say anything. *What would Coach Bedford want with you? The same thing I do*, he thought.

Stuart nodded as Morgan headed to his bedroom. Morgan didn't notice, just like he always didn't notice. Stuart sighed sadly, an indulgence he rarely allowed himself. He knew exactly what Morgan was going through because he'd been through it himself.

It was the overwrought tragedy of his life. He was surrounded by hot guys who'd never look twice at him, even if they were gay, because he was the better part of a foot shorter than they were. Even once he and Morgan were out to each other, Morgan had taken one look down, and Stuart had been permanently relegated to "friend" status. Stuart took the friendship Morgan offered, because Morgan was a great guy and it was better than nothing. But it still hurt.

Even if the guys would give him a shot, he didn't have the time. Pre-med studies took all the time crew didn't. He opened his textbook to resume studying, but his mind was miles way. Something wasn't quite right about the whole situation, now that he thought about it. Coach Bedford was straight? Looking at him at Ass-Pecs, if Stuart hadn't known him, Stuart would've sworn they batted for the same team, the way those two men danced together, Coach Bedford and his "friend."

Coach Bedford was entitled to his own life outside the boathouse, even to his own secrets and lies. But Stuart was very protective of his friend. He loved crew and he loved coxing for his coach, but Morgan was Morgan, and Morgan was crushing on their coach. He didn't buy Coach Bedford's explanation. He'd keep his eyes open for signs that Bedford had lied to Morgan.

THE boathouse and parking lot in front of it hummed like a beehive. All the crews had a regatta the next day, just a local one, but given that it used the same course as the PCRCs, a lot of schools, not just the CalPac crews, used it to gauge the effectiveness of their training in the months before that final race of the season. The regatta may have been small, but the level of competition was cutthroat for everyone, rowers, coxswains, and coaches, all in their own ways.

The process of moving their shells to another venue involved carefully orchestrated chaos overseen by the two varsity coaches. Nick had lost the coin toss, so he and Stuart oversaw the loading of the shells onto the trailers, while Mandy Brown and her coxswains spearheaded the de-rigging of the boats. On the other end, the women's crews would unload the trailer, and the men's crews would re-rig in the boathouse. That way, everyone ended up doing everything at one time or another, and the junior varsity crews for both squads just went where they were told.

The shells themselves cost more than many cars, at least the kinds of cars Nick imagined buying when his venerable Honda gave up the ghost. The teams took fantastic care of them too. That it was a private school with relatively well-heeled alumni mattered not in the least to Nick and his counterparts. They rammed through the heads of their athletes that respect for the equipment came right behind respect for themselves. When he thought about it, Nick realized that the athletes were themselves a kind of equipment, and in this sport, equipment of all kinds was expensive.

So the boats were taken off the racks and put into slings in the bay of the boathouse, where the women's coxswains oversaw their disassembly. Each part, labeled as to boat and seat, was grouped with the others of its kind, seats with seats, riggers with riggers, and then Nick's crew and the junior-varsity men carefully placed the stripped shells on the trailer and strapped them down for the drive to the regatta. The CalPac crews and virtually every other crew Nick had ever been on or heard of operated on the "you row it, you rig it" philosophy, so everyone was busy before, during, and after races. There were no free rides.

Nick, clipboard in hand, stood in the parking lot, directing his men where to put shells on the trailer.

"In two, up and over heads," Stuart called. "That's one, and two, and... *up!*"

At his command, the varsity men lifted a riggerless shell over their heads, the muscles of their arms and trunks straining.

"Top middle," Nick called. He looked up and noted the novices had left one set of stairs on the other side of the trailer. He jogged over and quickly moved them into position, bending over to nudge them as close as possible to the trailer. After he'd put the stairs down by the boat's stern, he looked up and found himself staring squarely at Morgan's groin. He might've been wearing jeans, but they left little to Nick's imagination. His mouth went dry, and he got out of the way.

Stuart nodded his thanks. "Stack the ends, and up the stairs on my call." Stuart waited while the rowers bunched up on the ends of the shell. "First step, and… *up*! Second step… *up*! Third step…."

Nick pretended he was watching to make sure his athletes didn't mishandle the boat and that the junior varsity men were in position on the trailer to grab it and slide it into position. The truth was that he was glad his crew knew what it was doing, because he couldn't form coherent thoughts, let alone direct traffic.

Nick closed his eyes, reliving the view. Damn. That boy packed some serious meat. Nick felt himself stiffen at the recollection. It was getting to be a regular occurrence for him. See Morgan at practice, get hard, do something about it when he got home. Today, watching Morgan lift boat after boat onto the trailer, stripping his shirt off when he got too hot…. It was too much. His own pants grew tight, way too tight. Using his clipboard as a screen, he reached down to shift his hard-on to one side or the other, anything to relieve the chafing from his underwear and fly.

Nick looked up and discovered he'd been caught. As Morgan headed back to the boathouse with the others to pick up another shell, he'd looked right at him. With a raised eyebrow, he turned his eyes forward and continued into the boathouse just as Nick went to lick his lips.

Nick groaned. The humiliation of being caught with his hand down his pants did nothing to kill his boner, and he'd been caught by the cause of that boner to boot. There was no way he'd make it until he got home. If he didn't do something, he'd embarrass himself further by walking around with pants full of wood all afternoon. The rowers would notice too. They were all horny young men, and they knew what a load of hard cock looked like, since they were all semi-hard themselves half of the time. Granted, most of them were straight, but dick was dick when it was doing something you couldn't control, and that united men, gay or straight. They were all slaves to their cocks.

Not feeling as ashamed as he should, Nick hotfooted it to the men's locker room and its bathroom stalls. He rubbed his palm against the aching bulge in his pants, groaning as a frisson of pleasure shot from his groin. He closed his eyes and let it wash over him. He knew he should've felt guilty, but thoughts were still free. So long as he didn't act on them, everything was golden, right?

Nick shut himself in a stall and dropped his clipboard. It clattered to the floor, loud in the tiled locker room. He fumbled with the button and zipper on the chinos he wore, unable to get them open fast enough. Freed from its confinement, his cock tented his boxer briefs out. He palmed himself again, slowly this time, savoring the waves of pleasure so intense they almost hurt. Leaking precum soaked the fabric. *That's for you, Morgan*, he thought.

He yanked his underwear down and sat down on the toilet. With the thumb of his left hand, he smeared the precum across the head of his penis, riding the sensation, itself enough to make him twitch and bring up more precum, the clear fluid rising up and dribbling down his shaft. Damn, he was hard and ready.

He moved his other hand to one nip, flicking the already-hard nub. It added to the pleasure radiating from his cock, meeting and combining somewhere in his gut. He leaned back against the tank and closed his eyes, the better to recall the images of Morgan lifting the boats, his muscles bunching and flexing in the afternoon sun. He spat into his hand and started jacking. The sensation increased exponentially as he pictured not his hand gripping his cock but Morgan's tight, hot ass. Morgan rode him like a cowboy, head thrown back as Nick made him forget his own name. He'd reach out and grab Morgan's cock as Morgan would lean forward to suck his tongue into his mouth, speared by Nick on both ends.

In his mind, Morgan joined him at the climax, shooting a load of hot spunk onto his chest even as he filled Morgan's ass. But when the light cleared from Nick's eyes, he was alone in a bathroom stall, the only cum his own, flowing sluggishly over his hand and down his shaft to make a mess in his pubic hair. On the way in, he'd been hard and energized by his bone for Morgan. Now, it was cold and awkward, the porcelain of the toilet digging into his back, his ejaculate growing colder by the second. He sighed, alone again, just as he'd been before.

With a sigh, Nick cleaned up and got back to work. He had a team to organize and a regatta to prepare for, and his own desires and needs were beside the point.

THE day of the race had been a long, hard one in many ways. The regatta had gone well—at least, Morgan thought it had. They'd come in third in their primary event, varsity men's eights/small school. But Coach Bedford had also thrown a curve at them and entered them in the varsity men's fours/open. The bow four and stern four were put into four-person boats, with Stuart coaching Morgan and the others who rowed in the stern of their eight. It was an open event, which meant any and all four-man teams were eligible. The bow four had come in third again, but his stern four had won.

Every athlete wanted to win, and the victory in the open four sent Morgan, Stuart, and the other three into orbit. Coach Bedford had nodded in approval when they'd come off the water. There'd be analysis of both races in the days to come, but his coach's grin and "Good job, guys" meant the world to him, for some reason. The medal around his neck made a nice bonus.

A perfect day of racing would have ended with that. But Morgan also spent the entire day playing a complicated game with his coach, more of the same from the de-rigging and loading. He'd look up to catch his coach staring, only to look away a little too quickly. Or he'd spy on his coach out of the corner of his eye, fueling fantasies that hadn't died despite their conversation in the boathouse that morning after practice. He'd eye-fuck his coach, since he couldn't have the real deal, only to have Coach Bedford catch him. Gazes held for long moments, breathing that grew ragged and caught in his throat, desire that swamped him. Morgan knew what he wanted. Something told him that Coach Bedford mightn't be as het as he claimed. Morgan could only pray wishful thinking wasn't clouding his judgment.

The day was warm, and after racing, the sweat flowed freely. Morgan pulled the top of his uni down to his waist, leaving his chest bare. The breeze felt wonderful as it rippled across his skin, drying the sweat to salt in his chest hair. He looked up from where he'd loosened the bolts holding his rigger into place, and there was Coach Bedford and his burning eyes again. Part of him wanted to snap, "Take a picture. It'll last longer." But part of him was turned on knowing his coach was looking at him. What did Coach Bedford do at the end of the day? Morgan let himself imagine that he went home and thought of him. He shivered despite his warmth.

The unisuits were great to race in—no loose fabric to catch on oar handles or seats—but they left nothing to the imagination, and since he didn't have a jock on underneath it, the clinging fabric showed his hard-on in stark relief. Staring at his coach from under his eyebrows, he tweaked one nipple. The previous weeks had been torment, and it felt good to give some back. When he rubbed one hand across his belly, Coach Bedford dropped his wrench in a clatter of embarrassment.

Then Morgan smiled and looked away, hiding his growing problem behind the shell. He didn't think he was wrong, but it was going to be a long afternoon of re-rigging the boats back at the boathouse without the promise of a hot and willing man to reward him at the end of it. Sighing, he went back to work.

Stuart sidled up to him. "You're shameless."

"What?" Morgan protested.

"I've been watching you tease Coach Bedford," Stuart said, smirking.

"Have you been watching him? Because he's been watching me," Morgan said, all wide-eyed innocence. "I'm just giving him something to look at. But if he's straight? I'm—"

"Hey, Cockring!" Brad barked. "You got the adjustable wrench?"

Stuart rolled his eyes. "Don't have too much fun. He still has to drive the trailer back to the boathouse, and since I'm riding with him, I'd prefer it if he didn't drive off the road."

Chapter
FIVE

"SO HOW'RE things going?" Drew asked, sucking a smoothie through a straw with the same technique he used on men to turn their skeletons to jelly.

Nick and Drew strolled along on a pleasant spring Saturday afternoon, soaking up the sun and culture both at an outdoor arts festival.

"The crew's doing really well. They had a regatta last week-end—"

"If that's what I'd asked, I'm sure I'd find that really fascinating, but I didn't, so I don't. I asked how things—as in you, as in that rower—were going," Drew said, peering over his sunglasses at his friend.

Nick's shoulders slumped, and he searched for just the right words. "It's complicated."

"Never mind, babydoll. If you have to parse it, that pretty much answers the question," Drew sighed.

"What do you want me to say? You asked how I am. I'm Morganless," Nick said, shrugging.

"You've really got it bad. At least four guys have checked you out since we got here a half-hour ago," Drew said.

"Really?" Nick asked without much interest.

"Really. So tell me, whatever happened after you so rudely dragged me from Ass-Pecs? I've been dying to know," Drew said.

"Just not badly enough to ask?" Nick said, smiling for the first time that afternoon.

Drew gripped his shoulder. "Nick, if you'd wanted me to know, you'd have told me. But truthfully? The curiosity's killing me."

"There's nothing to tell. The next day, I talked to him, told him I was just there with a friend, that—"

"You didn't," Drew said. "You told him you're straight?"

"I might've," Nick mumbled, staring at the ground.

Drew shook his head. "Unless this boy's a total fool, there's no way he's going to believe you're straight, and if he were a total fool, you wouldn't be pitching a trouser tent over him."

"What a thing to say. You should be ashamed," Nick said.

"Oh no you don't, you don't get out of this so easily. I can't believe you told him you were straight—"

"You don't understand," Nick said.

"I understand a lot more than you give me credit for," Drew snapped, "and don't whine. It's unbecoming."

"I wasn't whining," Nick mumbled. Drew was right about one thing. His whole obsession with Morgan really was unbecoming. It was why he'd lied in the first place, and it clearly hadn't worked. The back-and-forth staring? That had to stop. It distracted them both from what was important. It was unprofessional of him, just like Morgan's games were beneath him, and jeez, he wanted Morgan beneath him.

Nick smacked his forehead. That had to stop. Since this couldn't end the way he wanted it to, with Morgan in his life and in his bed, he had to end it another way. He had to make sure Morgan was unavailable, and that meant getting Morgan off the market. If Morgan were dating someone Nick loved and cared about, then it wouldn't matter how badly he wanted him. He looked at Drew speculatively.

"Drew…."

"Whatever it is, no."

"I've got an idea," Nick said, more animated than he'd been all day.

"No."

"You could at least hear me out."

Drew shook his head. "I recognize that tone. The last time you used it...." He shuddered. "Just, no."

"C'mon, hear me out," Nick wheedled. "If you dated Morgan, then I'd have to get over him, wouldn't I?"

"Oh, jeez, it's worse than I thought. Where do you come up with this shit? Do you find it online, or is it something you store in a box under your bed until it's good and rancid?" Drew shot Nick a dirty look.

Nick put his arm around Drew's shoulder and led him to a bench in the shade of an old oak tree. "Seriously, give it a listen. I'm not asking you to marry him, just distract him for a while so I can get my head together. You're a great guy," Nick wheedled. "You'll be kind to him. I've never known you to be cruel to anyone, and you've always let your exes down gently."

Drew nodded despite himself. "Go on."

"All you have to do is date him for a while, show him a good time—without messing up my training plan—and then let him down easy, just like you always do with men when you're done with them. He's a bright guy, and you're not nearly as shallow as you like to pretend you are." When Drew looked at him sharply, Nick laughed. "You're not the only one who notices things. So you take him to dinner a few times, maybe a play or a movie, throw him a quick one, and go your separate ways."

"You wouldn't mind?" Drew said.

Nick knew he was wavering. "You'll be kind to him. If I can't fuck him, I want someone I can't hate doing it."

Drew reared back. "That's really kind of creepy, you know."

"Okay, so that was pretty blunt, but it's basically the truth. We don't poach, you and I," Nick said. "We never have."

"So I'm supposed to take him off your hands like he's some kind of used car?" Drew said skeptically.

"No, I told you, you're helping me get over him, and helping him get over me by removing him from the field of play," Nick said.

"Assuming he's into you. He might not be," Drew said, reasonably sure Morgan was but unable to let a chance to needle his friend go by.

"Oh, he's into me," Nick laughed. "If you'd seen some of his antics, there'd be no doubt. Actually, if you'd seen some of those antics, you wouldn't be fighting me on this. He's incredibly good-looking and apparently willing to tease."

"Someone's got a positive self-image," Drew said snidely.

Nick made a face at him, but he knew Drew was basically his. "So you'll do it so I can get my mind back on the job where it belongs and stop violating all those professional ethics?"

"Don't forget preserving your dignity," Drew said.

"That's long gone," Nick sighed.

"Fine, give him my number," Drew said. "But just remember, you owe me."

"Put it on my tab," Nick said.

"Darling, you're so far in arrears that I don't know why I even bother keeping track."

"You said 'rear'," Nick snorted, trying to irritate Drew.

It worked. "Grow up."

ENERGIZED, Nick swung into action. He had his plan, his plan to protect his lie. *God, you're pathetic*, he told himself, steering his car onto CalPac's posh campus.

Part one of the plan was Drew, and he had Drew committed. Actually, Nick thought *he* should've been committed, but he shoved the voice of reason aside. Why start listening to it now?

Part two was Morgan, and to get Morgan on board required strategy. To that end, he made rare use of his adjunct-faculty parking permit. He could tell which were the cars belonging to the other adjuncts and assorted part-timers because they were all basically slagheaps on wheels like his. The tenured faculty drove nicer cars, and an invisible line divided the faculty floor of the main parking garage.

Since Nick had access to his athletes' schedules, he knew where Morgan was supposed to be and when. Assuming Morgan hadn't skipped class, which was unlikely, Nick knew he could "accidentally" bump into the younger man on purpose.

He checked his watch. Morgan had another ten minutes in his art lab, which meant that Nick had another six or seven minutes to get into position. Fortunately, Nick's long legs allowed him to cross CalPac's small campus in a hurry.

Nick felt like a pervert crouching in the bushes as he checked his watch, but it was all about the plan, the plan and the lie. Another minute….

The doors to the Arts Building swung open as students exited their classes, laughing and talking. Nick ignored them, intent on just one student, the one student among the few thousand at CalPac who set his heart to racing.

Nick spotted Morgan. His mouth went dry. Morgan really was that striking—muscular without being chunky; handsome, chiseled features without looking American generic. All the other students vanished from Nick's awareness. For that moment in time, it was just Morgan and Nick. Then the reality of what he was up to intruded and made him queasy. But he had to do it.

Nick drew a breath and strode out onto the sidewalk, running straight into Morgan, whose mind was elsewhere. He must've hit Morgan harder than he'd intended, because the clipboard he carried to look official went flying, and Morgan almost fell over. Nick grabbed quickly and found himself holding the man he could not get out of his head. Both of them were stunned, and all he could do was stare into Morgan's eyes, lost in the feeling of holding him.

"Coach Bedford?" Morgan said, making no move to free himself.

"Morgan! I'm so sorry! I… I didn't see you," Nick stammered.

"What're you doing on campus? I didn't think you made it in here much," Morgan said. He had a dreamy look on his face, held in his coach's arms.

"I don't," Nick confessed.

"Then why are you here?" Morgan said.

Nick realized he still had Morgan in his arms. He forced himself to let go. "The athletic faculty had a meeting this morning."

Morgan handed Nick his clipboard. "The Athletics Department is on the other side of campus."

"I get so turned around here," Nick said, blushing.

They stared at each other a moment longer.

Morgan scratched his head. "I… uh, should let you go or something."

"Wait!" Nick said. "Can I buy you coffee or something? To apologize for knocking you over?"

"Yeah, that'd be nice," Morgan said softly.

"Cool," Nick said. "Lead on. I obviously don't know where I'm going."

Morgan laughed and led him across campus to the student-run coffee house.

"NICE," Nick said, looking around the airy structure of exposed girders and industrial lights.

A faint whiff of the bean tugged at Morgan's nose in that antiseptic coffee house, but nothing more. He shrugged. "I liked the old, dim coffee house better. It was cozier, and you could actually smell coffee when you walked in. This one looks like a car showroom or something. But the student body voted, and you can't stop progress."

"Or something," Nick said. "What'd you want? My treat."

"Cool, thanks," Morgan said, smiling back. He'd have been happy with a Stop 'n' Rob if his coach were there with him. Yep, still crushing hard.

They placed their orders, and after picking them up, they found a table in a quiet corner, well away from groups of students chatting quietly or solo studiers.

"So," Morgan said. He'd started grinning sometime between the collision outside the Arts Building and placing their order and couldn't seem to stop. "Here we are."

"Here we are," Nick said. They drank their coffee in taut silence for a few minutes, each man nervous and excited by the presence of the other. "I have to confess," Nick said finally, "it wasn't just a meeting that brought me to campus. I needed to talk to you away from the boathouse."

"Really?" Morgan said.

"Yeah, remember that Saturday night a few weeks ago when we ran into each other at that bar?" Nick said.

Morgan smiled some more. "I remember," he said softly, sure his coach was about to 'fess up, sure he was about to get his wish.

"Remember that guy I was with?" Nick said with straight-guy enthusiasm that sounded homophony to Morgan's wishful-thinking addled ears.

Morgan nodded, puzzled.

"Turns out," Nick said conspiratorially, "he's totally into you."

"Oh," Morgan said, hoping the hurt didn't come through in his voice.

"Oh, yeah. He's spent the last two weeks pestering me for information about you. I mean, jeez, Drew, hire a private detective already, but I guess he doesn't feel the need to, since he's got me and all."

Morgan didn't want his coffee anymore. It pooled in his stomach with his disappointment and shame. It made him sick. He'd hoped…. "He was… cute?"

"Drew's a hottie," Nick laughed, "or so he tells me. You know, if I were into guys. Anyway, he really wants to get to know you better. Here," he said, pushing a piece of paper at Morgan. "Here's his number. You should call him."

Morgan swallowed the lump in his throat, humiliated from his toes to the roots of his hair. His coach didn't want him, after all. "He… wants to go out with me?"

"Hell, yeah. You're all he talks about," Nick said, smiling.

Morgan thought his coach's smile looked a little sickly around the edges, but he was feeling a little sick himself just then so he wasn't sure. He didn't want to go out with Drew. He wanted to go out with Nick Bedford (and in and out and in and out…), but it didn't look like that was going to happen.

"Please?" Nick begged when Morgan didn't answer right away. "He's relentless. Do your coach a favor? Go out with him so he'll leave me alone?"

"When you put it that way…," Morgan said. He forced himself to smile. He didn't want to smile. He wanted to gather up what was left of his pride and leave and pretend he'd never had a schoolboy crush on his coach. But he couldn't just ditch Coach Bedford like that. "You can give him my phone number. I guess."

"Thanks, Morgan. You won't regret it. They don't come any better than Drew St. Charles. I'll see you at practice this afternoon."

For his part, Morgan wasn't sure what to think as he tried to go back to his daily routine after his improbable meeting with Coach Bedford. He looked at the phone number of a stranger and then put it into his wallet. He couldn't have his coach, but could have his friend. From what he saw, the other man was certainly attractive, even if he wasn't Nick Bedford. He could settle for second best. Settling wasn't something Morgan was used to, but in emotional affairs, he was learning, what he wanted and what he got were sometimes wildly divergent.

"HAS he called yet?" Nick demanded as he and Drew settled in for a casual dinner. He still felt like he'd kicked himself in the nuts, setting up Drew and Morgan. He kept telling himself it had to be done, but somehow that didn't help.

"Somehow, when you called and invited me to dinner, I expected more than an interrogation," Drew complained.

"What're you talking about? I don't see any rubber hoses or bright lights," Nick said.

Drew held his hands up in front of him. "Hey, whatever you're into is none of my business."

"Ha ha," Nick said. "I just want to get this nailed down before it gets out of control."

"Interesting choice of words," Drew said. "And I'd say it's already out of control."

"You know what I mean," Nick sighed.

"I know, and I'm doing you a huge favor, darling Nicky, so I get to be as difficult as I want to be," Drew said.

Nick made a face. "You know I hate that."

"I know, but what can I say? They had a sale at Cheap Shots 'R' Us, so I stocked up. Besides, that's one of the things you love about me," Drew said. "Admit it."

"I guess it is," Nick said, smiling despite himself.

"And I know how much this is distracting you," Drew said. "And him, I'd imagine."

"If it is, it hasn't shown up in his rowing. I can't say anything about his academics, because they don't notify me until it gets really bad, and I wouldn't stoop to looking it up on my own," Nick said. He smiled at the recollection of Morgan's rowing. Morgan's stroke only grew more and more fluid and graceful. If the tension between the two of them was a distraction, he rarely let it show. Nick admired that.

Then something occurred to him. What if Morgan wasn't distracted because it—he, Nick—didn't matter enough to distract him?

Drew held his hand out. "In fact, I'll call him right now. Give me his phone number."

Nick called up Morgan's information in his phone's address book and handed it to Drew, who punched the digits in. "Hello, Morgan? It's Drew St. Charles… yes, that's right, Nick Bedford's friend…."

DREW pulled up in front of the apartment complex where Morgan lived. He shrugged. Not bad. Student digs could've been a lot worse. Someone's parents must have money. Scholarship students tended to be more frugal. At least, he always had been when he'd been spending his scholarship money back in the day.

He caught himself checking his hair in the mirror and smiled. Old habits died hard, and that particular habit was still in its vigorous prime. He was just supposed to show Morgan a good time and distract him, not sweep him off his feet. It didn't matter if his hair wasn't perfect. Still, if the boy liked gym queens, they might nonetheless have a bit of fun.

Drew took the stairs up to Morgan's apartment two at a time and knocked on the door. Almost immediately it opened, and Morgan appeared. Drew had never had a thing for tall guys per se, but he easily understood what Nick saw in Morgan, at least physically. The kid was hot, even though when Drew dated, he gravitated toward endomorphs, beefy guys who had to be careful they didn't turn into fat ones. But Morgan's intellectual appeal? That remained to be seen, but fools usually failed to turn Nick's crank.

"Hi, you must be Drew," Morgan said. He extended his hand awkwardly.

Remembering at the last minute that he was supposed to be head over heels for this guy, or at least in lust with him, Drew pulled him in for a hug. "Yes, and you're Morgan. It's so nice to see you in good light."

A smaller man stuck his head out the door. "What, no flowers?"

"Stuart!" Morgan yelped. He let go of Drew and turned around to push his roommate back inside.

"What—what are your intentions—hey, that hurts!—towards my roommate, Mr. St. Charles?" Stuart called as Morgan gave him a final shove and slammed the door.

"I bet he's trouble," Drew laughed, as much at Stuart's antics as at Morgan's mortification.

"I sure am!" came a muffled reply.

"Yes, and he'll be dealt with as soon as I come home," Morgan hissed.

Drew arched one eyebrow. "Ought I ask him about your curfew?"

Stuart cackled from behind the door but had the decency to stay put on the inside.

"Can you please just get me out of here?" Morgan whimpered.

"He's protective," Drew observed. "This is a good quality in a friend."

"It's a good quality in a dog. Him? He's just a pain in the ass," Morgan sighed.

"And not in the good way, from the sound of it. Let's go. I've made dinner reservations at Le Crepe en Haute, and it doesn't do to be late. The maitre d' has a similar personality without any of your roommate's charm," Drew said.

Drew used the remote on the key-fob to unlock the car.

"Niiice," Morgan said when he saw which car chirped its response.

Drew shrugged and had the good manners to blush as he opened Morgan's door for him. "It's advertising."

"Oooh," Morgan teased. "All those muscles and a BMW. I can't wait to see what's for dessert."

Drew's eyebrows went up. This was Nick's shy young athlete? "I'm a real estate agent, among other things, and a good car tells clients I'm a successful one, that I'll earn my commission."

"I'm just teasing you," Morgan said, buckling up.

"And you're so good at it," Drew said.

The banter continued as they drove to the restaurant. Drew discarded the notion of using the valet service. The restaurant was expensive enough, and he was taking Morgan out, not trying to buy him.

"Thanks for going out with me tonight," Morgan said once they'd been seated.

"It's my pleasure," Drew said. "When Nick said he knew the guys he'd seen at Aspects…."

"You just had to meet me?" Morgan said with a twinkle in his eyes.

"Something like that," Drew said, rolling his eyes. Then he caught himself. He was supposed to be nuts about this guy. As reluctant as he might've been to participate in this charade, he'd told Nick he'd do it, so he'd better act like his heart was in it. It was time to pour on what his older brother referred to as "the patented St. Charles charm." Drew smiled his big, warm, sell-this-house-on-the-first-day smile. "So Nick's apparently told you about li'l ol' me, but I know next to nothing about warm and wonderful you. So tell me, who's Morgan Estrada?"

People always froze when they had to talk about themselves, but Drew'd found over the years that "active listening" warmed them up fast. Drew leaned forward, making sure he looked rapt as Morgan stammered his answer.

"Oh my God, I have an older brother too!" Drew squealed. "Not three, that must've been a trip. So were they the overprotective sort, or the beat-you-to-a-pulp sort? Because I had the latter, and let me tell you, that's so not fun."

As he listened, Drew had to admit that Morgan wasn't what he'd expected. Morgan might be a good seven or eight years younger than he and Nick were, but he was far from the socially inept youth that Drew remembered being at that age. Someone had clearly taken some pains with the home training with this one. No wonder Nick was so smitten.

"They didn't!" Drew gasped when Morgan told him about the time his brothers grilled his first boyfriend. That certainly explained Morgan's horror about his roommate's antics.

Drew mentally wrote it all down. Anything he learned about Morgan could be funneled right back to Nick—for a price. It might be cruel to make Nick dance, but it'd be amusing payback for making Drew do his dirty work.

"You know, I have to admit, hearing you call him 'Nick' sounds so strange to me," Morgan said. "He's only ever been 'Coach Bedford' to me."

"Whereas since first impressions are lasting impressions, in some ways, he's still Nick Bedford, geeky freshman, to me," Drew said, "despite all the water under the bridge, as it were. I have no idea who 'Coach Bedford' is."

"But I've seen you at regattas, at least the local ones," Morgan said.

"He's my best friend," Drew said, "not my coach."

"You go just for him? You're a great friend. My non-rowing friends sure don't bother," Morgan said.

Oh, darling, if you only knew what a good friend I am, Drew thought. He laughed, his laugh a little more musical than usual. "Nick's good enough not to hold the memory of me as a freshman over my head, and I'll always love him for that."

"Is that when you met him?" Morgan asked, smiling back at Drew.

"Yes, freshman year at UC San Diego. You should've seen us," Drew laughed. "Actually, no, it's a good thing you didn't…."

They continued the introductory chatter through dinner, mostly discussing Nick, their one clear point in common. Drew grew bored as Morgan's relative inexperience became more and more obvious, his patented St. Charles charm increasingly forced. Drew found Morgan to be polished for his age, but the vibe was a bit off. He'd never particularly fancied younger men, and this only confirmed it. And as much as he loved Nick, talking about him all evening without actually revealing anything juicy proved to be tiresome and more work than anticipated. Drew was constantly on his toes as they finished dinner and left the restaurant.

Drew wasn't exactly angry with Nick, but there was something about what Nick had asked him to do that didn't sit right with him. So in a fit of pique, Drew had bought tickets to a production of *Cyrano de Bergerac*, since it spoke to their situation. Instead of an ugly but brilliant man wooing a beautiful woman by using a handsome idiot as a puppet, Nick avoided wooing a beautiful man by using another beautiful man as a dodge. Or something. Thinking about it too long made Drew's head hurt.

Then Drew noticed something. Morgan seemed like he was having a good time, a really good time. He smiled at Drew. He touched Drew's arm to illustrate points. Morgan turned to face him as he drove and then blushed before looking away quickly.

Drew grew suspicious as they took their seats in the theater. He told a lame joke, the dumbest one he knew.

"Drew, no! That's too funny!" Morgan guffawed.

And that's when it hit Drew. Nick might've been more right than he knew—and more wrong. Morgan really looked like he was smitten by him, so maybe those looks Nick thought he saw were just his horned-up imagination and wishful thinking. What if Morgan really was interested in him?

Fortunately, the lights went down, and Drew breathed a sigh of relief. He could let his guard down for a little while.

Drew excused himself at intermission for a quick trip to the bathroom. Locking himself in a stall, he whipped out his cell phone and fired off a text to Nick. *You owe us both big time, you son of a bitch. This kid may be falling for me, and if I have to break his heart, I'll never forgive you. Or myself.*

But Nick didn't get the text.

Chapter
SIX

NICK was at home, where he often spent his Saturday nights. Usually, he studied and read. But that night, he knew what was going on across town. He hadn't even asked Drew where they were going. He didn't want to know. He didn't want to be tempted to interrupt. To fall to his knees at Morgan's feet to confess his lie and beg for a chance.

But he knew that somewhere, the man he wanted to call his own was being wined and dined, and not by him, and he hated it. He'd never been so uncomfortable in his own skin. He felt twitchy and irritable, like he had an itch that couldn't be scratched. He didn't know what he feared more, that Drew and Morgan wouldn't hit it off… or that they would. Whatever happened, Nick just knew it couldn't end well, at least not for him. No, he thought, getting up from his desk to pace around his apartment again, this evening had regret written all over it.

Nick looked at the clock on the microwave in his kitchen. Nine p.m. "Damnation," he said, knowing full well what he was about to do.

He stomped off to his bedroom, shedding his sweats as he went. Ass-Pecs was just getting going, and the best way to get over someone was to get under someone else. He kept telling himself that as he put on a shirt so tight it looked like he'd sprayed it on. That and jeans so low his pubic hair would've peeked over the top if he hadn't trimmed it made it clear he had an eight-pack, that he'd earned his muscles through sport and fitness, not by haunting a gym. They also made it clear what he was looking for.

He sprang for a cab. He didn't intend to be in fit state to drive home. Fifteen minutes later, he was at the bar, surveying the room through his first shot of tequila, the first of many.

"You drink like a man who's serious about it," a voice rumbled in his ear.

Nick glanced over, and next to him was a man he hadn't noticed before, about his height, with close-cropped blond hair and ice-blue eyes.

"It passes the time," Nick said.

"Maybe I can help you pass it better."

Nick raked the man with his eyes and liked what he saw. He had the tightly leashed look of power Nick associated with military men, a man with a body to match his own and, with any luck, the will to use it and him. Oblivion was oblivion, wherever it came from.

Nick passed the bartender money to cover his liquid dinner and then some. Then he stood up and smiled. "Lead on."

Nick's quarry stood and smiled like a predator, and Nick smiled right back, already buzzing like a hornet's nest. The man matched him inch for inch, muscle for muscle, and, Nick discovered on the dance floor, move for move.

They settled into the beat like they were made for it. Nick didn't waste any time. When the man looked at him with ravenous eyes, Nick grinned right back and moved in closer.

When the man moved to unbutton his shirt, Nick let him. When the man ran his hands over his chest, Nick raised his arms overhead to give the man room to play. He closed his eyes and tried to lose himself.

People stared, but Nick didn't care. Let them stare. He was nothing. His best friend was out there somewhere, romancing the man he wished was touching him, and nothing else mattered. When the beat changed and the muscular blond man turned him around to dance front to back, Nick wasted no time in making his wishes known. He ground his ass against the man's crotch and felt the answering hardness press back.

This was what he wanted, Nick told himself. What he needed. So when the man's hands found their way to the button fly of his jeans, he gyrated harder and let him pop the first few buttons.

Nick closed his eyes again, allowing himself to think that it was Morgan's hands on him, that it was Morgan who reached around to take him in hand. Strong fingers wriggled their way to his cock, smooth palms sliding over taut flesh.

Nick's eyes jerked open. Smooth palms. There were no calluses, no rough spots created by the friction of the oar handles. He was suddenly as cold and sober as if he'd taken a bucket of water to the face.

He pulled away and turned to face the man, frantically buttoning up. "I'm sorry. It's just… you're not him."

For the second time in as many months, Nick fled the bar.

MORGAN didn't want to hurt Drew's feelings. Dinner had been delicious, even if the restaurant's name made him giggle, and the play was hilarious and touching. Drew had gone to some effort to make the evening memorable, and Morgan appreciated that. For his part, Morgan had pulled out his best "first date" game. He related amusing anecdotes without monopolizing conversation, laughed at Drew's stories without guffawing, and tried to keep his galloping nerves from carrying the evening away with them. He threw a little flirting Drew's way and meant it. Flirting was fun, and Morgan had always enjoyed it. He even did that "lean in and touch his date's arm" he'd seen in a romantic comedy once.

But after dinner, Morgan's worries set in, and by the play's intermission, he was almost scared. What if Drew took his flirting seriously? Morgan didn't think he was prepared to fuck the guy just for consistency's sake. But he knew he couldn't pull back all of a sudden either, not without hurting Drew. Drew was a nice guy, easy on the eyes, and his personality glittered. He'd be a real catch… just not for Morgan.

"Nightcap? Late dessert?" Drew suggested after the play.

"Let's just talk," Morgan said with a slight smile.

Despite the late hour, plenty of people still strolled the boulevards, taking in the mild spring evening. So Morgan and Drew joined the urban excitement.

"That sounds nice," Drew said. His eyes darted this way and that, taking in the sights walking by.

Morgan caught it. Then he thought about it. Even at dinner, Drew had glanced at people, sometimes lingeringly. *If he's so hot for me, why's his head swiveling every time some hot guy walks by?* Morgan wondered.

The more he thought about it, the more his bullshit detector went *ping!* Pieces fell into place, and Morgan connected the dots in an intuitive flash. Something about the evening screamed "put-up job." He might be barely be twenty-one, and he might lack Stuart's cynicism, but he wasn't a complete fool either.

Now Morgan had a theory to test. He wanted to see if there was any chemistry on Drew's part. He'd just ruled it out on his own part.

By this time, they'd settled on a bench underneath some trees in a large park. The trees had little white lights woven through their branches, making a very romantic setting. For someone, Morgan thought, but not for them.

Tilting his head slightly, Morgan moved in for a kiss. He startled Drew, but then the other man returned the kiss, lips touching his.

Nothing. Nada. Zilch. Nothing but skin moving on skin. They might as well have been shaking hands.

Morgan broke the kiss and looked Drew right in the eyes. "This whole thing's a load of crap, isn't it?"

Drew sputtered but gave up quickly. It wasn't his lie he was protecting. "How could you tell?"

"You just admitted it," Morgan said with a vulpine smile. "Also, it was like kissing my brother. Now spill it."

Drew considered it for a moment. "You know, I think it'll be better for all concerned if I end my involvement in this charade right now, because you're right. It's a put-up. But Nick Bedford needs to be the one to tell you why."

Morgan looked at him with dark, wounded eyes, eyes that were bright under the moonlight. Somehow, despite his own lack of investment in the date or in Drew and his relief at not having to follow through with the flirting, it hurt.

"I'm really sorry, Morgan," Drew said. He went to comfort him, but Morgan batted his hand away.

The two men sat in silence beneath the trees, white lights twinkling above them, people around them heedless of Morgan's turmoil.

"I know I'm younger than you guys," Morgan said finally, his voice thick, "but that doesn't mean I'm stupid."

"No, it certainly doesn't," Drew said softly. He wondered if he'd ever do anything to deserve the depth of feeling Morgan held for Nick. "I'll take you home now."

Morgan said nothing as they headed in the direction of Drew's car.

MORGAN took the stairs to his apartment two at a time without turning to wave at Drew. He didn't have it in him to be civil right then. Drew might not have been the author of his current humiliation, but he was an accomplice. The lion's share of his rage was reserved for Nick.

"Damn him!" Morgan screamed as he slammed the door shut hard enough to rattle windows. He looked around the darkened living room and realized it was later than he'd thought. Confirmation came a few moments later when Stuart, clad only in pajama bottoms, padded out from his bedroom. "I'm really sorry, I didn't think—"

"So I'm guessing it didn't go so well?" Stuart yawned, absently scratching at the ginger fur on his chest.

"It was all a set-up," Morgan said.

"Uh… yeah," Stuart said. "I thought you knew that from Coach Bedford saying a *friend* of his wanted to go out with you."

"He tried to shove me off on his best friend! What the fuck!" Morgan shouted, angry all over again.

"Keep your voice down," Stuart said.

"Don't tell me to be quiet," Morgan hissed.

"I didn't tell you to be quiet, I told you to keep your voice down. Unless, of course," Stuart replied, "you want the neighbors to have a front-row seat to your relationship troubles."

That got Morgan's attention. He got up and headed for the kitchen and the coffee maker, telling Stuart about the disaster of a date.

"Hmmm," Stuart said after Morgan had finished and returned with the coffee.

"What?" Morgan said, suddenly on edge. Stuart was wilier in the ways of men than he and just generally more cunning.

"Coffee's good," Stuart murmured.

Morgan rolled his eyes. "Yeah, back to me."

Stuart set his mug down. "Morgan, sweetie, it's always about you."

"No, it's not," Morgan said, crossing his arms as if they'd ward off Stuart's comment.

Stuart looked at him like he was simple, staring at him until he squirmed. "Is it really?" Morgan said.

"Don't worry about it. It's terribly complicated being you, I'd imagine," Stuart said. "Come to think of it, most of you are this way."

"Most of us?"

"You freakishly large giants I spend my time herding. You're all high-maintenance."

"I prefer the term 'finely calibrated'," Morgan said primly. "So other than storming in to the boathouse and kicking Nick Bedford in the shins, any suggestions?"

Stuart didn't say anything for a while, thinking about it. "I've had my doubts about Coach Bedford for a while. What he told you versus what I've seen since you two had your little chat after that night at Aspects... well, I think he's full of shit."

"You think he's really gay? That he was just bullshitting me?" Morgan said.

"The evidence sure points in that direction," Stuart said. "First of all, there's Drew St. Charles. No het man would be entirely comfortable having Tinkerdrew as a best friend, let alone dirty dancing with him at a gay bar."

Morgan snickered. "He's not that bad. He's just comfortable with who he is."

"And who he is, is a gay man who needs flame-retardant underwear," Stuart said. "Moving on, there's also everything that's been going on between you two."

"Tell me about it," Morgan said. "It's driving me insane. On the one hand, I want to tell him to knock it the hell off. On the other hand—"

"You're fueling his jerk-off fantasies with your antics," Stuart said.

"I am not," Morgan said.

"Please, Morgan, I'm not stupid. I can't say you're going out of your way to do it, but you're doing it. It's actually a lot of fun to watch."

"There might be a little deliberate teasing there," Morgan said, smiling. "Just a touch."

"Yeah, it's the touching that gets him," Stuart snorted. "So here's what I think you should do. Crank it up. Coach Bedford's gotta be gay, he's avoiding you for some reason despite obvious mutual interest, and he tried to shove you off on his friend. So reward him for it. Flush him out of the bushes. Make him at least 'fess up."

"I'll have to be careful," Morgan mused. "The last thing I want is a long explanation to the rest of the team. Can you imagine what Brad Sundstrom would make of it?"

"You let me handle the rest of the guys. Sundstrom's all talk anyway, and jealousy issues aside, he might surprise you. No, don't get mad, get even," Stuart said, a twinkle in his eyes.

THE week after Drew's date with Morgan had been pure hell for Nick, utter and absolute hell. To begin with, Drew was pissed at him. Nick understood why, but he'd hoped Drew would've tried harder to understand his motivations. It wasn't like the date had been some lark Nick had dreamed up to make everyone's lives more interesting. But his best friend was mad at him, and that meant Nick had some serious make-up work to do.

By itself, that wouldn't have been so bad. Nick still had his coaching and would've put Drew out of his mind when he was on the water. Unfortunately, coaching and rowing were at the heart of the matter, and he was reminded of the entire mess and his starring role in it every time he went to work. He'd added afternoon practices to their workout regimen three days a week too, which meant twice-daily torture, for him at least. Morgan didn't look like he was suffering.

Actually, Morgan looked like was having a fine time, and therein lay his problems. Morgan was having a fine time, all right, but Morgan was stalking him, Nick was sure of it. Every time he looked up from rigging the boat, there was Morgan, staring at him with his hot, dark eyes. Every time Nick looked at his rowers in the boat, his five-seat wore skin-tight clothes if it was cold in the morning and next to nothing during afternoon rows. The first time Nick had glanced at Morgan on the water, he'd almost driven his launch aground at the sight of so much skin. Every time Nick tried to lead his athletes in post-row stretches to increase flexibility and prevent future injuries, there was Morgan, displaying like he'd starred in *Yoga Sluts III* or something.

Life with Morgan in it was now a torment for Nick, and there was nothing he could do to change it, not if he wanted to keep his job. Whether or not he'd be able to salvage what little was left of his dignity and self-respect remained an open question. Nick had long since abandoned telling himself he wouldn't even look at Morgan. He'd have to blind himself, given Morgan's current campaign. That's what it had to be too—a deliberate campaign. He'd caught Morgan and Stuart looking at him and snickering more than once. It was yet another reminder of the gulf that separated him from Morgan. Those guys might be in their twenties, but they still acted like kids on occasion. It just made him paranoid, and he'd taken to glowering when he caught them at it. That only made it worse.

So that Friday after practice, nearly a full week after Nick's ill-considered plan to set up Drew and Morgan, Nick was working on one of the junior varsity racing shells. The CalPac rowing program was too small to support a full-time boatman, so Nick was happy to split repair duties with the other coaches.

Nick sighed and looked up from the seat track he'd been tweaking. Morgan lingered on the other end of the boathouse after the other rowers had left, intent on some equipment chore of his own. Allegedly.

Nick returned his attention to the task at hand, but he was preternaturally aware of the other man, could almost feel him moving just beyond the edge of his peripheral vision.

He looked up, and Morgan was closer, much closer. He was still busy with something that looked entirely legitimate, but Nick wasn't stupid. Something was up, and he felt hunted, like a stag, and like a stag, he tried to put as many obstacles as he could between himself and the hound.

Trying to look casual, Nick fled to the other side of the boat to work on another seat's rigging. He might as well as have just dropped everything and run. He chanced a look up, and Morgan was almost on him.

Nick quickly looked back at his work. The oarlock he fiddled with became the focus of his world, but he still knew Morgan stood right there, separated from him only by the width of a boat, two scant feet of carbon fiber. He could reach out and touch the man who'd consumed his thoughts. That man could reach out and touch him.

Rationally, he knew Morgan was only standing there for a few moments, but to his tortured mind, it felt like forever. Unable to stand it any longer, Nick looked up. "Oh, hey, Morgan," he said, trying to play it cool. He cringed. It even sounded lame to him. "Working on something?"

Morgan stared at him with his deep, dark eyes, serious, even grave in his stony face. "You lied to me. I know you're gay."

"What are you talking about?" Nick said, trying to save the whole sorry situation.

"I can see it in your eyes every time you look at me," Morgan continued. He looked down. "And in your shorts. You probably shouldn't wear tight shorts if you're going to throw wood when you stare at your rowers."

Nick shifted, trying to hide himself. But the only way to do that was to press himself into the shell, which would've moved him even closer to Morgan. He flushed, his cheeks burning like the Olympic torch. He laughed, or tried to. "It happens. Mind of its own. You know what it's like."

"What would you do if I reached out and grabbed that hard cock through your shorts? What would you do if I came over there and yanked those shorts down and buried my face in your sack?" Morgan taunted.

Nick swallowed audibly.

"I know I'm just a dumb jock, so it took me a little while to figure out what was going on. If you didn't want me, just say so," Morgan said flatly.

"No, it's... I.... What do you want from me?" Nick demanded, anguished.

"Be honest with me," Morgan said, no longer the victorious hunter but only a man whose feelings Nick had hurt. "For the first time since spring break, be honest. What do you want?"

Nick looked at Morgan, at this man whom he'd realized he wanted not just in his bed but needed in his life, and was afraid. The stakes had never been higher. He'd never wanted anyone so much, never felt the need for a relationship with someone so strongly it made him ache. What if his own desperate denials had so angered the younger man that he now had only hatred and contempt for him? He'd run and run and tried to hide, but it hadn't worked. He was still cornered in his own boathouse by one of his rowers, and all his stratagems had accomplished only their mutual misery.

"You."

Morgan glared at him for a moment, his lips pressed into a tight, flat line. "Me. You could've had me months ago," he said, not recognizing his own hard, sharp-edged voice. "Instead, you've been eye-fucking me every chance you got, distracting me, staring at me. Setting me up with your best friend?! Do you know how messed up that is? And lying to me. That's what pisses me off the most. You've been lying to me, Coach."

"I'm… sorry."

"You're sorry," Morgan repeated. "You sure as fuck are. You're acting like one sorry piece of work. That's not who I thought you were."

"You want the truth?" Nick demanded, finally angry. "I'll give you the truth. The truth is, I can't get you out of my head, no thanks to those antics of yours. You're what I think about all day. I think about you as I go to sleep at night, when I sleep, that is, when I'm not tortured by visions of you. I wake up thinking about you. I… I spend hours wondering what you feel like, what you taste like, what you'd look like in my arms.

"And because I'm your coach, I can never find any of that out," Nick said, low and furious, his voice thick with pent-up emotions.

"I… what?" Morgan said.

"You heard me. You're one of my athletes. Do you know how many regulations I'm breaking—hell, shattering into a million pieces—just by having this conversation? Right now, some enforcement official from USRowing has just bolted wide awake in bed, seized by the knowledge that somewhere, some coach is crossing the line that we can't cross," Nick rasped.

"So yeah, I lied to you," he continued, lowering his voice. "Coaches can't date athletes, period. The NCAA says so, USRowing says so, every governing body of rowing and sport in general says so, and I love my job. So I lied to protect my job, my future."

"I—" Morgan started, but Nick cut him off with an angry gesture.

"No, you'll hear me out," Nick spat. "After the little game you've been playing, you owe me that. You want honesty? Fine. I've done everything I could to get you out of my mind, yes, including setting you up with my best friend, even lying. I lied to protect you too, you know."

"Me?" Morgan said, skepticism plain on his face.

"Yeah, you. I'm trying to protect you from accusations of favoritism by your teammates, from being put in a position you may not be ready to cope with, from being taken advantage of by an older man."

"From what!" Morgan laughed. "You're not even ten years older than I am!"

"Doesn't matter. The very nature of the coach-athlete relationship presumes asymmetry—an inequality of experience, influence, and power. Never mind the handful of years, the very fact I'm your coach means we're not on a level playing field, you and I. The fact that I'm your coach means we start with the presupposition that I am firmly in control and can unfairly influence you," Nick said. "It goes downhill from there."

"Firmly in control? You're hiding behind a boat," Morgan pointed out. "You're not in control of anything. Really? USRowing and the NCAA? Is that the best you can do? Do I look like I'm being taken advantage of?"

Clutching his adjustable wrench like a talisman, Nick slowly shook his head.

"Then get this through your thick head, Coach Nick Bedford," Morgan said softly. "I get that there are codes of conduct, but they only bind you. I get there are things you think you can't do, but what is that to me? I'm a person too, and I can make decisions for myself. I'm an adult, and I want you. You're not a creepy old man chasing his young athlete; you're a hot guy a few years older. You're someone I want to get to know, maybe, hopefully, more. So before you go making any more non-crew decisions that have anything to do with me, you check in with me. Communicate with me, yeah?"

As Morgan spoke, he slowly walked around the boat until he was face to face with Nick. "You think you can remember that?"

Nick gulped and nodded. His emotions were a whirlwind, and he didn't trust himself to speak.

"Good," Morgan breathed. He tilted his head and leaned in. Nick responded in kind, their lips just brushing.

"Hey, Estrada, hurry up already!" came Brad's raucous call, accompanied by a fanfare on his car horn.

Nick blinked as Morgan broke their kiss.

"We're not done, you and I, not by a long shot," Morgan said over his shoulder as he picked up his duffle bag and walked out the door.

NICK didn't remember driving to Drew's house, but he must've, because he was on the doorstep. That was fine. It was where he needed to be. He needed his council of elders, even if Drew was the only counselor and they were the same age.

He knew Drew was home too. The garage door was up, and his car was in the garage. Otherwise, Nick wouldn't have been sure, because he knew Drew was pissed too. He had a whole slew of unanswered calls, emails, and text messages to prove it. He deserved it.

He'd handled this whole situation poorly from the very beginning. But how could he make it up to his best friend if Drew wouldn't answer the door?

Nick rang the bell again and followed it up with a good pounding on the door. "I know you're in there, Drew! You left the garage door up. Can you at least give me a chance to explain…? C'mon, Drew! I really need to talk. He cornered me in the boathouse this afternoon, and I don't know what to do…. Drew? I've got a spare key, you know. Don't make me come in there after you… Drew?"

Nick's shoulders slumped. Drew must be extra-special pissed. He turned to head back to his car. Despite his threat, he wouldn't go in there after Drew, not if he really didn't want to talk. Nick knew he deserved the cold shoulder.

And there Drew stood, dressed for gardening with a large-brimmed hat and long baggy sleeves made of some God-mocking synthetic.

"You look like a bee-keeper," Nick said before he could stop himself.

"You can't be too careful about sunlight. The way I see it, I need to get another forty to fifty years out of this hide, which means minimal UV," Drew said. "Did you come over to insult my gardening wardrobe, or did you have an actual purpose?"

Nick sighed. It was going to be one of *those* encounters. "Well, if you'd answer emails, calls, or texts, I wouldn't have to storm over here, now would I, princess?"

Drew almost smiled. "I suppose you won't quit that infernal racket until I talk to you. C'mon back. My roses need attention, as, apparently, do you. I await your lavish and groveling apology for putting me in the horrible position you did."

Nick knew he had him then. "Did you listen to the voice mails or read the emails and texts? Because it's all pretty much in there."

"But live theater is so much better, don't you think?" Drew called over his shoulder.

Nick waited until Drew was through the gate and then ran past him and fell on his knees, sliding the last few inches. Skinned knees were worth a friend like Drew. He grabbed Drew's hand and pressed the gardening glove to his lips. "Please, please, please, Drew St. Charles, find it in your heart to forgive me for setting you up with the world's hottest rower. While well-intentioned, it was also cruel to someone I love more than life itself and someone else who I hope to love that way."

"Well," Drew said, "you do say the sweetest things."

"And if you don't, I'll tell your parents just what happened during spring break of our junior year."

Drew reared back like he'd been slapped. "You wouldn't!"

"Probably not, no," Nick admitted. "Besides, there's got to be some kind of statute of limitations. But c'mon, buddy, I need you."

Drew gestured to a lawn chair and went back to work on his roses. Some time after they'd graduated, Drew had grown obsessed with gardening, probably about six months after he'd bought his house, Nick thought.

"So tell me what's the latest dire happening down the CalPac Crew's boathouse."

"Your chilly demeanor this past week tipped me off, but Morgan saw through the ruse and called me on it," Nick said.

"Good," Drew grunted. "He's not stupid, Nick."

Nick smiled. "No, he's not, is he?"

"Come back to Earth, please," Drew said. "While roses need acidic soil, I'd prefer it not be from me vomiting because of your treacle. So tell me what this development is before I lose interest altogether."

"He's been stalking me."

"What!" Drew dropped his cuttings basket and peered over his sunglasses.

"Sorry, not that kind of stalking. But before, we'd each get caught looking, but now he just stares. He's practically naked at practice, and I swear some of his stretches come from the Kama Sutra."

"Go on," Drew said. "I find myself intrigued despite my pique."

"Today, after this afternoon's practice, he cornered me. He knows what's up, he knows I'm hot for him, and I finally snapped—"

"Yeah!" Drew squealed, hopping up and down and clapping. "So how was it? What was the kiss like? Is he big?"

"I said I snapped, Drew, not that I fucked him," Nick sighed. "He wanted to know what was up. I told him."

Drew looked crestfallen. "Oh. What else?"

"I also told him that because I coach him, I can't get involved with him," Nick said.

"And?"

"He basically laughed me off. That's why I need your help, Drew. What am I going to do?"

Drew sat down next to Nick. "I've heard your dreary arguments about USRowing and the NCAA, but tell me what he said."

Nick repeated Morgan's words as best he could remember them. He remembered them well. He should, as they were practically etched in fire in his memory. "So what do I do? He's the one I want, but because I coach him, he's the one I can't have."

"Very interesting. He's got a point, you know," Drew said. "Yes, you're the coach, and you're not supposed to fish in your own pond. Ever. This has been tearing you up because you're an honorable man who believes in the rules, and it's that quality along with so many others—to say nothing of that smokin' hot bod of yours—that's attracted Morgan. That said, as much as I can see the potential for abuse, let's be honest. People don't make rules for things that aren't issues. They just don't. The rules exist because this happens. Maybe one of the reasons coach-athlete relationships happen is because the athletes have agency too."

"But—"

"No buts, babydoll. Morgan's over eighteen, and he's hardly an innocent. The rules may be the rules, but he gets a say in this too," Drew said.

"I want this… want him, God knows I do, but can I trust myself? It's all just so convenient. Coach gets boner for jock, jock gets one right back. Coach docs nothing, jock corners him. Coach gets the jock in the end. What could be simpler? But what if my lust is just blinding me, and I really am taking advantage of him?"

"I want you to know just how strongly I'm resisting the urge to smack you right now," Drew said. "He offered, if that's the right term, to yank your pants down and blow you. After months of this, he got tired of it and took the bullshit by the horns. He's not a child, he's a man, and he made his desires known."

"I just wish I could be sure," Nick sighed.

"Don't we all?" Drew said. "There are no guarantees in life or in love. But really, how much more of a message do you need?"

Nick regarded Drew for a few moments. "How'd you get so smart about all this?"

"I grew up reading advice columns like Ann Landers and Dear Abby. Those old gals taught me a lot about life," Drew said with a shrug. "Besides, it's not my life we're discussing. So call him."

"You really think I should?" Nick said, chewing his lip.

Drew slapped Nick. "I couldn't resist any longer."

Nick rubbed his cheek. "Ouch! That hurt! What'd you do that for?"

"Nicholas Bedford, you've driven the three of us nuts for a couple of months now. It's time to be a man. It's not that hard, babydoll. He's told you what he wants. It's you. Do you accept it or not? If not, man up and end it cleanly, because like it or not, you're already involved. If you accept it, then be a man and treat him right."

"You're so good to me. Thanks for sticking by me," Nick said, sniffling.

"I know. But you've been there for me," Drew said.

"And if you ever slap me again, I'll drop you like a bag of wet cement," Nick said, suddenly looming over Drew in his lawn chair. Then he kissed the top of his friend's head and jogged to his car. He had a call to make.

DREW'S buck-up of Nick's courage lasted until he got home and looked at his telephone. Wow. He was really going to do it. He was going to follow his heart, even as his head shrieked that it was a mistake.

No, he was going to do it. Right after he cleaned up from practice and then sliding on Drew's lawn. With any luck, this would be the start of a fresh chapter in his life, a man like Morgan Estrada in his arms and in his heart. He should be clean.

He managed to draw cleaning out far longer than usual. Then he fumbled around, looking up Morgan's number, and then spent more time simply staring at his telephone, benumbed. He was going to do it. He really was.

Nick picked up the phone and punched the numbers with a shaking hand. Before it could ring, he hung up. He wiped sweating palms on his shorts.

He reached out to pick the handset up again and then jerked his hand back like he'd touched the stove burner. This was harder than he'd thought it would be.

Groaning, he got up and paced around the living room, pummeling the air with his fists, anything to break the tension and just do this thing. Christ, he was a fool. Morgan had practically thrown himself at him right there in the boathouse, and he was loping around his apartment like a caged wolf.

Nick sat down, picked up the phone, and stabbed the numbers into the keypad. His chest felt like it had steel bands around it. He couldn't breathe.

"Hello," Morgan said.

"Hi, Morgan, it's Nick."

"Coach Bedford! I'm really sorry about earlier. I was totally out of line. I—"

"No, it's Nick. Call me Nick," he said softly.

Chapter
SEVEN

NICK and Morgan played the calendar game and settled on a dinner together the next weekend. It was the longest five days of Nick's life. He alternated between giddy anticipation and abject terror at the thought of what he was doing. He couldn't ever remember working himself up like this over a date before, even a first date. But then, none of them had been Morgan.

Nick fidgeted in his living room, peering out the window, waiting for Morgan to arrive. First-date jitters, to be sure, but he was also worried that the ghost of that sham date with Drew would haunt this date too.

"I'll drive," Morgan had said, "so we avoid Stuart. I've no idea what he's planning, but based on his antics when Drew picked me up, I'm sure it's complicated and embarrassing."

"I can only imagine," Nick had groaned.

Nick sprang off the sofa when he saw Morgan pull up. He didn't know what kind of car Morgan drove, but he sure recognized the driver. He was actually relieved to see it was a Civic. CalPac was a private school and as such sported more than its share of rich assholes. A late-model luxury car in the hands of an undergraduate didn't necessary imply assholery, but it certainly seemed to. A newer—but not new—Civic meant prudence, not privilege.

Nick stood on the front steps and waited for Morgan to park. He waved hesitantly.

Morgan rolled the window down. "Hi."

Nick swallowed his butterflies and walked over. "Hi. Thanks for picking me up."

Morgan smiled back up at him. "You're welcome. Are you ready?"

Nick drank him in. Morgan was so handsome. His classical features and fair skin now tanned somewhat with the afternoon practices made him look like a catalogue model, attractive but not too pouty or pretty. Despite the difference in their ages, which wasn't too terrible to begin with, Morgan was clearly a man. It reassured Nick. He wasn't a cradle robber.

When Nick just stood there, Morgan said, "Do you maybe want to get in? So we can get dinner?"

Nick started and then turned scarlet. "Sorry," he mumbled.

"No worries," Morgan said as Nick got in and buckled up. "It's kind of cute, you getting all flustered. It makes you look human. No more big, bad Coach Bedford. Now it's Nick Bedford, my date for the evening. I like those pants. You look great. Sorry, I guess talk a lot when I'm nervous."

"No worries. It's kind of cute," Nick said, grinning.

They stared at each other for a moment, then laughed at themselves, and the tension was broken.

"So, where to?" Morgan asked.

"And once again, here I am, giving directions," Nick laughed.

"Yeah, but I'm not the coxswain, so it's totally different," Morgan said.

"Thank God. No offense to Stuart, who's a great guy and a hell of a coxswain, but he's not who I want to eat dinner with. Speaking of which, how do you feel about Salvadoran food?"

Morgan thought about it for a moment. "I'm not sure I can say I've ever had it. Where is it?"

"Near State, and far enough out of the way that we won't run into anyone from CalPac." Nick gave him directions, and in twenty minutes, they were seated in a restaurant so tiny there were fewer than ten tables. Nick had eaten there a few times and could only describe the décor as intense.

"Wow," Morgan breathed, looking around. "It's really…."

"Catholic?" Nick said.

"Yeah, like my grandmother's house, only more so." Morgan nodded. "It's kind of… wow."

There were crucifixes everywhere made of every kind of material, from plastic and wood to pounded tin and glass, and most of the interior lighting came from candles placed everywhere without plan or reason. Stalactites of wax dripped down in profusion, and when one candle died, another was simply set in place.

"Too much?" Nick said, suddenly panicking. "We can go somewhere else. Get take-out and head back to my place, even—"

"No, it's fine," Morgan said, a little abstracted.

"It reminds me of part of Baz Luhrmann's *Romeo + Juliet*, the one that came out in '96 or so," Nick said.

Morgan nodded. "I think I remember that one. Very romantic."

They ordered, and while they waited, started getting to know each other.

"Okay, so I have to ask," Morgan said. "When did you get into coaching? As near as I can tell, you're less than ten years older than I am."

"I'll be twenty-nine this summer," Nick sighed. He looked at Morgan. "That too old?"

"No," said Morgan, who'd found that he preferred his men to be a bit more mature than the usual run of college-age guys, "definitely not." Then he thought for a moment. "So you must've gotten into coaching pretty quickly after college?"

"Right after. A few years after I graduated, I started as an assistant coach even while I was working in finance. Turned out, I liked one a whole lot more than the other. So I bounced around for another year or two, then got really lucky to get this job. That it was a small school with a lousy record helped," Nick said dryly. "So what about you?"

"What about me?" Morgan said. "I'm twenty-one but still a junior thanks to crew's time demands. I'm majoring in comparative literature, but you probably knew that from our school information."

Nick nodded. "But coaches aren't supposed to go on fishing expeditions in student records. I really don't know a whole lot more about you than that, not the interesting parts."

"Oh?" Morgan said, loading the single word with a wealth of meaning.

"Yeah, like why comp lit? I'll ask the inevitable question… what're you going to do with it?"

"I chose comp lit because I found I learned a lot about the human condition from the literatures of multiple cultures, not just one, and since I really can't imagine being a professor, I plan to get a teaching credential to teach high school English," Morgan said.

"Really? That's fascinating. I'd love to hear more," Nick prompted. He listened, rapt, barely tasting his food. He was struck by Morgan's ideas and opinions, which were older than his twenty-one years. Sure, he could be silly at times, but he also came across as clear-eyed and steady with firm plans for the future. Nick hadn't been that together at twenty-one. No, Morgan had plans, plans Nick hoped he could fit into.

He'd had first dates before, but none he'd wanted to last forever the way he wanted this one to.

AFTER dinner, they wandered to a nearby ice-cream parlor for dessert and then to a small park. It was only twilight, but even so, the landscaping and streetlights were on, and children still played on jungle gyms and a wooden fort. Nick and Morgan walked for a few minutes before settling on a bench.

Morgan sat sideways on the bench, one knee tucked under him. He was torn. He'd had a wonderful time thus far, but he kept thinking about Nick's attempt to avoid him by setting him up with Drew. They'd talked it out a bit that day in the boathouse, but there was more to say. Just… not then. The sham date still bothered him, but he wanted to enjoy the rest of the date with Nick. He made a conscious effort just to feel what he felt that night. The past was the past, and he'd deal with it later.

Morgan faced Nick, as interested in watching him talk as what he said. When he'd first seen Nick back when he was a novice, those thoughts of getting closer to Nick had spurred him to make the varsity boat his second year at CalPac. His fascination with his coach had grown, and now they were on a date.

Nick enthralled him. Whether it was some anecdote from his own collegiate rowing years or a story about his childhood, Morgan lapped it up like a cat before the cream. If asked later what he himself had shared, he'd have been hard-pressed to recall, despite his claim that he chattered when nervous. But then, Morgan wasn't nervous anymore. He just listened, mentally tracing the lines of Nick's strong jaw, wondering what the dark stubble would feel like under his fingers. On his lips.

Morgan looked around, noticing that the park had emptied, that it was well and truly night, that he and Nick were alone on a bench in a pool of light. It registered, but no more. He was fascinated as the blanks were filled in about his coach, the little details of the person behind the persona. No, not the coach, he corrected himself. Because he was pretty sure this would be more than just a one-off date. He wanted to know everything.

Morgan looked at the now-deserted playground. "Let's swing."

Nick shrugged. "Sure, why not? Want me to push?"

"You have no idea," Morgan breathed.

Nick cocked one eyebrow at the innuendo. "I have no idea what you're talking about," he said loftily.

"Of course not," Morgan laughed and sat in the swing. "Now, push."

"So you're one of *those*, are you?"

"I really can't imagine what you mean," Morgan said.

Nick laughed and gave Morgan a solid push, but not too much.

They talked as Nick pushed Morgan on the swings, but less intensely than on the bench. One person oscillating back and forth made deep sharing difficult, and when Nick grew tired of pushing, he sat on the next swing while Morgan lazily pumped his legs to keep moving.

Eventually Morgan's swing wound down, and the two sat next to each other talking about the inconsequential things that two people can share when comfortable with the other's presence.

Morgan wrapped his arms around himself to stay warm, shivering a bit in the cool spring night. He felt as much as saw Nick stand up and move behind him. Nick hesitated behind him, but then Morgan felt strong arms wrap around him. Morgan sighed and leaned back against Nick, who tightened his embrace.

The feeling of Nick against his back blew Morgan away. There was nothing sexual about it, but he was swamped with such feeling and emotion that he struggled to breathe. No lover's touch in the moment had ever done this to him, and here he was, leaning into his coach. When Morgan leaned his head back, it felt like a key fitting into a lock.

It was pure heaven as Morgan felt an electric tingle like none other racing from him, through Nick, and back into him, growing and reinforcing. Not even the first time he'd kissed another man had felt like that. All his senses flared, and he pulled Nick's arms tighter. It was what he'd always wanted but hadn't known until that moment.

Morgan raised his face just as Nick leaned down, and somewhere in between, their lips met. Morgan reached back and up to hold the back of Nick's head as Nick leaned in. The gentle pressure filled both men with warmth as each reveled in soft skin against soft skin. Then the kiss deepened, and Morgan knew what Nick's beard felt like as

Nick moved to devour his mouth and they lost themselves in each other.

THE first date left both men floating through their daily lives and looking for reasons to be together. They saw each other at practice every day, but it wasn't the same. For one thing, Nick was at work and was still himself unsure how to act towards Morgan in front of the rest of the crew. For his part, Morgan still had rowing on his mind when he came to practice each day, since the competitive spirit that drove him to the varsity team during his second year in college hadn't gone away just because he went on a date with his coach. That didn't mean they weren't thinking about each other every available second.

One afternoon in the middle of the week after their date, one of the days the crew didn't have supplemental afternoon workouts, Morgan dropped by the boathouse. Coach Bedford—Morgan tried to keep in the habit of calling him that when they were at the boathouse— made it clear his athletes were to work on their fitness even when there was no scheduled practice, but he also made it clear to his varsity rowers that they could use the ergometers in the boathouse any time by giving them all keys and the alarm code. To drive the point home, he also emailed weekly "optional" erg workouts. Since Morgan had a free block of time that afternoon, he planned to use the team ergs rather than hit the on-campus student recreation center. Besides the hoped-for presence of Nick Bedford, Nick took better care of the team ergs than the maintenance people at the rec center.

But when he arrived, Morgan discovered that the boathouse was open, both the door and the large bay door that rolled up like a garage door, and a gentle breeze was coming in off the water.

Nick—Coach Bedford—stood beside a boat overturned in slings, gently rubbing the hull. "Oh, hello, Morgan," he said, smiling.

"Hey, Coach, how's it going? That's not our boat, is it?" Morgan asked.

Nick laughed. "No, it's one of the novice boats. See?" he said, pointing out the name on the bow. "I wouldn't make you row this unless I was punishing you for something. I've already repaired the hull. Now I'm just polishing it." He paused for a moment. "It sounds kind of funny."

"What does?" Morgan said, cocking his head to one side. He liked this side of his coach. Without the pressure of practice and training, his coach was more like his boyfriend should be—gentle, easygoing, humorous.

"Hearing you say 'Coach' now," Nick said.

Morgan shrugged. "It's kind of weird for me too. I mean, I go home, we call or email, and it's Nick. At practice it just seems like it's best to keep calling you 'Coach'."

"We're not at practice now," Nick said softly. He crossed to where Morgan stood and gave him a gentle hug. He kissed Morgan's cheek. "Hey."

Morgan kissed him back, and for a moment, it was just the two of them in the spring breeze off the water, surrounded by the apparatus of the sport that was central to both their lives.

"This is nice," Morgan said after they stopped, "but I came here to work. I've got this tyrant of a coach who keeps sending me erg workouts to do."

"That bastard," Nick hissed. "Tell me who he is and I'll beat the crap out of him for you. Or at least give him a nasty look."

"I happen to like my coach," Morgan laughed as he headed for the locker room. "A lot."

"I THINK I might be jealous," Nick sniffed. "Just lock up when you're done. I have to leave in a half-hour or so." He smiled and went back to work on the boat, one of the beaters the novices trained in. He wouldn't put his varsity oarsmen in one like this, if only because their bitching would scorch his ears. All the talk in the world about how it was "the rowers, not the boat," and they were still convinced they couldn't row except in the latest carbon-fiber miracle from Vespoli or Hudson. No, it was a good old boat and had a few miles left to row in it. These boats were like people, he thought. They were made of many layers of different materials, and when you treated them right, they'd last a long, long time, and like people, you had to know how to handle them to get the best out of them. It was something he struggled to keep in mind each day as coach.

Coach. Nick found it ironic, sometimes humorously, sometimes grimly so, but coaching was at the center of it all. If he hadn't taken the job of pulling CalPac's crew up out of the sewer, he would never have met Morgan. If he weren't Morgan's coach, he'd be free to date him and trumpet it from the rooftops. He didn't want to be "the coach" if Morgan was there to see him, but on the other hand, one of his rowers was there to train, not canoodle, and he needed to respect that. It was all so complicated, a precarious balancing act that one wrong move would upset, hurting Morgan and him in the process, a balancing act that he worried about maintaining.

So Nick went about his business while covertly watching Morgan out of the corner of his eye. Morgan got an erg out and did some light rowing interspersed with some hard strokes for about ten minutes before getting off to stretch out. Good. It made Nick happy when his athletes took him seriously, and he'd said time and again that stretching when cold was like pissing in your pants. It might feel good momentarily, but it was pretty much self-defeating. It was stretching when the muscles were warm that prevented injuries and increased flexibility. After a good stretch, Morgan went to work on the day's assigned workout, and Nick continued to watch him, prepared to make mental notes of any potential issues. But Morgan was there to work out on his own, and Nick didn't feel like being "the coach" right then.

Once Morgan was into the workout hot and heavy, Nick abandoned the pretense of polishing the repaired hull and just watched. Seeing him erg was totally different now that they were honest with each other about their feelings. It was no longer a torment or a test of his self-control or even a chance to store up material for his spank bank, and the man actually wore less now that the weather had warmed up. He felt that actually acknowledging their attraction had drained off the sketchy parts. Nick watched Morgan and appreciated both the technical form and also the physique of his… boyfriend.

It hit Nick then. He had a boyfriend. Only instead of an awkward, cringe-inducing hard-on, he sported a goofy smile.

"SO HOW was your day?" Morgan asked. He didn't have all that much to say, but that wasn't why they'd been on the phone for close to an hour. It was the kind of purposeless phone call meant to perpetuate and prolong contact rather than convey information. He was on his bed, feet resting on his pillow, head where his feet should be.

"You know you saw me today, right?" Nick said. He stood in his kitchen, pretending to make dinner. Mostly he just leaned against the counter, enjoying the sound of Morgan's voice. He could read the telephone book aloud and still sound sexy, Nick thought.

"Yeah, but that was this morning at practice. That's been *hours*," Morgan protested.

"We'll return to double days every day for the final push for the PCRCs, then you'll see me twice a day," Nick said.

"That doesn't count, it's practice. Besides, you'll probably get sick of me," Morgan said.

That is so not going to happen, Nick thought. Then he wondered what would happen if he told Morgan that. Maybe it would make up for that set-up with Drew. He coughed. "Not possible."

"I'm sorry, what?" Morgan said, not sure he caught what Nick said but praying he had.

"I said," Nick repeated softly, blushing even though they were miles apart, "that it's not possible, that I won't get sick of you."

Morgan couldn't breathe as his heart swelled in his chest. "I… really like you too."

"I meant it," Nick said.

"I know, and it makes me feel really special," Morgan said. It was funny, but in talking to Nick, he felt the distance separating them as much as he felt the words and emotions pulling them together. His eyes stung.

"You are." Nick sensed the vulnerability on the other end of the line. "I wish I could hold you right now."

"That'd be nice," Morgan sniffled. Damn it, he told himself, he was not crying. He would not choke up.

"Hey now, are you okay?" Nick said helplessly. "I didn't mean to make you sad. Oh, God, I'm sorry, Morgan. I just thought—"

"No, you didn't do anything wrong. That was so nice. It's just that you're there and I'm here, and right now, that sucks," Morgan said, drying his eyes. He glanced at the clock. "Shit, is it that late? I should go to sleep. I have to get up early tomorrow."

"Yeah, me too," Nick said, smiling despite his concern. "You going to be okay?"

"I'll be fine. I just got all girly for a moment," Morgan said.

"Being emotionally vulnerable doesn't make you 'girly'," Nick said. "It makes you someone I wish I could kiss goodnight right now."

"Me too," Morgan said.

"Goodnight, Morgan. Sleep well. See you in a few hours."

"See you soon, Nick. Sweet dreams."

Then they'd have to be of you, Nick thought as he hung up the phone. How was it that he felt more alone than ever now that he had a boyfriend? There had to be some way for them to see more of each other.

A solution to their problem came to him the next morning during practice. As soon as he had everything put away, he fired off an email to Morgan. It was perfect.

In less than an hour, Morgan called him. Nick liked that. Unlike some, Morgan wasn't so far gone into technology that he communicated entirely by text messages or chat windows.

"So you said you had a solution to me pining away?" Morgan said. Then he cringed. Too needy too early? He really had to learn to filter everything. He hadn't gone all chattery on Nick too many times, but there was no point in scaring him off this soon.

"Yeah, I do, as a matter of fact. You're busy, I'm busy, but...." Nick hesitated, worried he might come off as too pushy. He had to be careful of that, particularly since he was still Morgan's coach. "Um... do you want to study at my place? With me, I mean?"

"Study? I guess I could," Morgan said, thinking that of all the things he wanted to do to and with Nick, that wasn't one of them. "Sounds kind of dull for you, doesn't it? I s'pose you could watch TV or something. I can concentrate through almost anything."

"No, silly," Nick laughed. "We study. Together. I'm in school too, you know."

"I... you're what?"

"I'm taking classes at State," Nick said, laughing again. "I told you that.... I'm working on my MS in kinesiology. It's a condition of my continued employment—graduate work in some kind of exercise science. Most collegiate coaches have that kind of qualification. Nothing but the latest scientific findings for you dogs."

"If you did, I'd forgotten," Morgan confessed, feeling kind of stupid that he hadn't known this basic fact about not only his coach but his boyfriend.

"Yep, I've got reams of photocopied articles to catch up on, to say nothing of grading and my own research," Nick said. "So... you wanna?"

You have absolutely no idea, Morgan thought. "Yes, sure, that'd be great."

"Great," Nick said, echoing him. "How about tonight after practice?"

"Damn, I can't! I've got a study group for a physics class. We're all humanities majors, and we're all lost in this stupid general ed class. Why can't they leave us alone to stew in our ignorance?" Morgan said.

"How about tomorrow night, then? I'll make us something simple for dinner, and then we can get to work," Nick suggested, thinking that what he really wanted to get to work on was Morgan.

"Six o'clock work for you?" Morgan asked.

"It'll be perfect."

Nick hung up the phone in his office and sat back at his desk with a smile on his face that only gradually faded. The next day and a half would drive him crazy with waiting.

NICK stood before his bathroom mirror, trying to make sure he looked casual enough to look like he hadn't dressed up just to study. Because that would be silly. Polo shirt tucked into jeans he knew made his ass look great, or pulled out? He left it out, a part of his mind supplying the hope that Morgan's hands might find their way under it.

Dinner was an apparently artless risotto with a salad and mineral water. No wine; they were studying. Coaches ate like that all the time, right?

There was no help for the fact that Nick had scrubbed his apartment down to the floorboards, but at least dinner's aroma masked the scent of the organic cleaning agents he had splurged on.

Hair? Check. Outfit? Check. Environment? Check. Dinner? Check. Well, almost. There was a bit of work left to be done. Homework and reading? Check.

Nick glanced at the clock. Just a bit before six. He had time to spare.

Then the doorbell rang. Nick's place wasn't that big, and he made it to the door in record time. "Hi," he said, opening the door to Morgan, who'd never looked so appealing. Cargo shorts hung low on his hips topped by a Hawaiian-print shirt with the top three buttons left undone.

"Hi," Morgan said back, shy smile on his lips.

"Come in. It's not much, but it's home," Nick said, sweeping his arm to encompass the living room.

Nick stood aside and Morgan came in, trying to see everything without looking obvious about it. He dropped his backpack by the door, then winced. "Laptop. Damn."

"Ouch. You can use mine if you need to. Make yourself comfy while I finish dinner," Nick said. "Hungry?"

"Yep, and it smells delicious," Morgan said, following Nick into the apartment's tiny kitchen. "What can I do to help?"

"Actually, it's all pretty much good to go, I just need to finish the risotto, and there's not a lot of room for two people to cook," Nick replied.

"Got it, but just one thing first," Morgan said. He came and stood behind Nick, enfolding him from behind and kissing his neck. "Hmm, you smell good. What is that?"

"Tea tree oil. I use it after I shave," Nick said, kissing him back over his shoulder, absently stirring.

"You shaved?" Morgan said, eyebrow arched.

Nick blushed. "Maybe."

"So did I," Morgan confessed. *But I'm not telling you what or where.* He released Nick before he embarrassed himself with his rapidly growing erection. Something about pressing himself up against Nick like that made him want more. He retreated from the kitchen to lean against the wall just outside the zone of action. Besides, watching the man cook was pretty sexy too.

Back at the stove, Nick was just glad that stirring risotto was a mindless mechanical task. After an initial moment of surprise at feeling Morgan behind him, Nick had fought to keep his knees from buckling. Morgan was just enough taller that they seemed to line up back to front in all the right ways. Fortunately, the stove hid his reaction. But cooking with gas? So not the place for a hard-on attack.

A few minutes more, and dinner was ready. Nick set it on the table, then fetched the salad and fizzy water from the fridge. In short order, they sat down to a light supper filled with small talk and the accidental-deliberate bumping of knees under the table, followed by shy smiles. By the time they were done, each man's knees rested against the other's, the feelings of skin and warmth and contact vying with the olfactory and gustatory sensations of dinner. It was heady and intoxicating in the way that it could be only at the start of a relationship, when everything was new.

When they both admitted that this could go on all night and that their schoolwork wouldn't read itself, Nick sent Morgan into the living room while he cleaned up. When he finished, he found Morgan already deep into a book, laptop open on the coffee table before him.

"Did it live?" Nick asked, nodding at the computer.

"What? Oh yeah," Morgan said.

Nick pulled a textbook out of a stack on the floor next to the sofa, along with a large stack of paper. "Photocopied journal articles," he explained in response to Morgan's quizzical look. "I have to keep up on the latest in a lot of areas of human performance for school and coaching."

Morgan shook his head. "I can't believe I didn't know you were in school too. That certainly explains what you do between practices. Kinesiology, you said?"

"Yeah. It dovetails nicely with coaching, and if coaching ever blows up in my face, I figure I can go back to school and become a physical therapist," Nick explained.

Morgan felt a chill. "You might not coach?"

"It's not the most dependable job in the world," Nick said with a shrug, "starting with the fact that I only work when school's in session. I pick up odd jobs coaching learn-to-row camps at local clubs and work for Drew's home-reno business, but that's not much. Then, too, to get a 'promotion' I pretty much have to move on to bigger and better schools, but that depends on whatever program I'm with doing well, and it depends on my education, which in turn includes continuing coaching education with USRowing. CalPac only required a level one coaching certificate to start, but I've been working on my level two on top of everything else."

"So the training plan…," Morgan said, nodding slowly.

"Comes right out of this stuff. The periodization, the gradual ramping up of the intensity followed by a break, then another cycle of intensity? Yeah, that's all this sciency stuff," Nick said. "But you know what the best part is?"

Morgan shook his head. "I don't know; grad student poverty keeps you slim?"

"No, since I know how the body's put together, I give dynamite massages, or so Drew tells me," Nick laughed.

"Hmmm, I'll keep that mind," Morgan said, blushing as he remembered the dream. Something told him the real deal would be even better.

"So you said you majored in comp lit," Nick said.

"Yes, much to the delight of my parents, I might add. Comp lit these days is more accurately comparative cultural studies, I guess," Morgan said, "but in some ways, trying to define it is like nailing Jell-O to a wall. Most of what I've read has been in translation, although I can read German reasonably well and one or two other languages with work. If I go on to grad school, I'd have to focus down on just one other cultural-linguistic group, but I'm just not sure I'm that interested."

"But you said you wanted to teach," Nick said.

"Yes, I think so. The comp lit department's advisors keep telling me what good prep comp lit is for just about everything, but since I haven't taken a lot of science and math, and since I can't stand blood, medicine's right out," Morgan said dryly. "And I don't think I've got the temperament for law school. I did some internships as a classroom aide last year and really liked them, so that's the direction I'm headed."

"What's that there?" Nick asked, genuinely interested in what his boyfriend thought about. His own bachelor's degree was in economics, and he'd done a lot of catch-up work in biology and chemistry at community colleges before starting his master's work in kinesiology. The humanities were the one area he'd never given much thought to.

"Reading for a term paper," Morgan said. "A comparison of the novel in history."

"The novel in history," Nick echoed. "I can't say I've really thought about that. I mean, I guess I thought novels just were. You know, so long as people have thought and written about things that never actually happened...."

"Actually, no, novels are definitely historically bounded," Morgan said. "They really start with Murasaki Shikibu's *Tale of Genji*, the story of—you know what? I don't want to talk about that right now."

"What do you want to talk about?" Nick said, looking deep into Morgan's eyes.

"This," Morgan said. He reached over and pulled Nick to him, then kissed him.

"That's one of my favorite subjects," Nick said a few moments later when they came up for air. He looked over at Morgan, still not quite believing he was this lucky, but there Morgan was, in the flesh, and right then, it was the flesh that interested Nick the most.

As far as Nick was concerned, that Hawaiian shirt was an open invitation to explore, and so he did, kissing Morgan's lips for a few minutes before making his way along one side of Morgan's jaw, kissing and nipping his way toward one ear. That earned him a low moan and an exposed neck as Morgan unconsciously tilted his head to give him greater access.

Nick took full advantage of it to continue his assault of lips and teeth down Morgan's neck, made easier by the loose shirt. He pulled the shirt aside to expose a bit of neck and started sucking. It'd leave a mark. He knew he should stop. But damn—

Nick gasped. There was a hand under his shirt. So intent had he been on Morgan's neck that he hadn't noticed at first. Then Morgan found one of his nipples, the left one, the one with the piercing.

"What's this?" Morgan whispered. "A ring?"

"Yeah," Nick panted.

"You must take it out at when you're kicking our asses on the ergs. Does it do anything?"

"I think you found what it does. Ahhh," Nick moaned. "Oohhh."

Morgan's hand left the ring and moved south, heading for Nick's waistband. The part of Nick's brain still able to think froze. Was this where they wanted to go? Because that was where they were headed. Nick was hard as a rock and leaking like crazy, and he was sure Morgan's underwear would show a similar wet spot. Not that Nick was going to look, not right then.

It was the hardest thing he'd ever done, but Nick stopped Morgan's hand. "Not like this."

"Wha—?" Morgan said.

"Not like this," Nick repeated, his mind clearing the fog of lust Morgan had raised. Nick kissed him, but on the lips, and gently. "Not like this, Morgan. I want our first time to be deliberate, special even. Not just groping on the couch like horny teenagers."

"You don't want to?" Morgan said, hurt rising in his eyes.

Nick had to act fast to salve Morgan's pride. "That's not what I said." Nick kissed him again, gently, holding his face with both hands. "You have no idea how much self-control that took. You have no idea what you do to me. I'll show you, but not now. I want to, more than I've ever wanted to before, but not on my sofa."

"You want it to mean something?" Morgan said, faintly mocking.

Nick looked him right in the eyes. "Yes, I do."

"Oh," Morgan said. He looked down, cheeks coloring. He smiled a little. "I do too."

"I want it to be special because I think you're something special," Nick said, pulling Morgan to him. "When we... when we're intimate...." He tried again. "You're not a quick fuck, Morgan. I could have that at the bars any time I wanted it, and so could you. I don't want that. I want you, and when we have sex, no matter how down and dirty it is, I want it to be worthy of the kind of man I think you are."

"I don't know," Morgan said with mock-seriousness. "It could get pretty dirty. You don't know what I'm capable of. You don't want to know what I'm going to do to you."

Nick opened his mouth, then closed it, nonplussed. "I look forward to finding out," he said, pulling Morgan forward to kiss his forehead.

"Yes, Daddy," Morgan said.

"So *that's* how it is, huh?"

Morgan shrugged. "That's for me to know and you to find out."

Nick smiled and pulled out an article. Morgan picked up his book and settled back against his boyfriend. Nick liked the feeling of Morgan cuddled up against him. It felt good. It felt right. Like something he hoped would never end, even though he knew it must if Morgan wasn't going to spend the night.

And so they passed the next few hours, until close to eleven, when Morgan yawned and stretched against him. "Is it really that late?"

"I'm afraid so," Nick said. "I've got to hit the hay if I'm going to be worth anything tomorrow morning."

"I guess I should go," Morgan said, gathering up his books and laptop.

Nick looked down. He didn't want Morgan to go. "You could maybe spend the night," he said quietly, looking everywhere but at Morgan.

"Do you mean that?" Morgan asked.

Nick looked at him. "I know I said I want our first time to be special, but I don't want you to go." *Ever*, he added silently.

"I don't want to go, either," Morgan sighed. Then he looked down. "I have a confession to make."

The bottom dropped out of Nick's stomach. "What is it? What do you mean?"

"I've got a duffle bag in my car with a toothbrush and some workout gear for practice in the morning."

Nick stared at him for a second and then burst out laughing. "What're you waiting for? Go get 'em."

"You don't mind? I didn't want to seem pushy or something," Morgan said.

"I understand, but I don't think either of us is ready to call it a night, yeah?" Nick said.

Morgan shook his head. "I like being with you."

"Same here."

"I'll be right back," Morgan said with a grin, and he went to get his things.

It was a bit awkward, at first, as they undressed in front of each other. Morgan thought it was silly; they'd both changed in locker rooms many times, so why should this be different? But it was.

"What?" Nick asked when he saw Morgan pause, shirt off.

"I feel funny changing in front of you," Morgan mumbled.

Nick rolled his eyes but took his T-shirt into the bathroom. "I sleep in my underwear," he called. "I hope that's all right."

"Same here," Morgan replied, coming into the tiny bathroom as Nick finished changing.

They stood shoulder to shoulder in front of the mirror, looking at each other's reflections. Morgan was a little taller, Nick's shoulders a little wider, his chest more solidly built.

"We look good together," Morgan said, "but you're hotter."

Nick blushed and looked away. "Stop talking about yourself."

Morgan kissed Nick's cheek but didn't say anything else.

They got on with their bedtime preparations, the small things that measured familiarity between two people, each trying with mixed success to stay out of the other's way.

Nick nudged Morgan with his elbow. "Hey. I'm glad you're here."

"Yeah?"

"Yeah. I'll… um, be right out," Nick said, nodding at the bathroom door.

"You're—?"

"Uh-huh. Pee shy. I'll never be able to go with you staring at me," Nick said.

"You're so cute," Morgan said, closing the bathroom door behind him.

When Nick got out, he found Morgan sitting on the edge of the bed. "What's wrong?"

"I don't know where you want me," Morgan said.

Nick thought of his heart. "Right here seems pretty nice," he said. He drew back the covers and got into bed, holding the blankets back for Morgan, who climbed in somewhat diffidently, like he was unsure he really belonged there. It was awkward, but not the clumsiness of long legs and arms. Morgan just didn't know what to do.

"What's wrong?" Nick asked, feeling the tension radiate off Morgan's body.

Morgan thought of the last time he'd been in bed with Nick. It had been in his dreams. Only now, he was really there. It still didn't seem real to him. "I just don't want to mess this up."

"So long as you don't wet the bed, we'll be fine," Nick joked.

But Morgan didn't laugh.

Nick reached out and pulled Morgan to him. "Is this okay? Because if it's not, we don't have to do this. I'll go sleep on the couch."

"No, stay. Who'd have thought sleeping next to someone was harder than having sex with him?" Morgan said. He rested his head on Nick's chest, hearing the other man's breath and heartbeat. He inhaled, smelling Nick through the faint scent of his laundry detergent. It was a clean scent, redolent of his after-shave, and under that, something that could only be Nick. It soothed him, somehow.

I'll show you "hard" this weekend, Nick thought, but held his tongue. The younger man was obviously struggling with something.

Maybe he found the emotional intimacy implied with sharing a bed for the night more difficult than the physical intimacy of sex. Nick didn't know, just as he didn't know Morgan's sexual history. But another man loving Morgan was the last thing he wanted to think about. Instead, he gently kissed Morgan's curly hair.

"Would it be easier for you if I didn't hold you?" Nick said, holding his breath. He didn't want to let go now that he finally had Morgan in his arms and in his bed.

Morgan thought about it. "No, I don't think so. I like your arms around me. It's where I've wanted to be for a long, long time."

"If I want you here, and you want you here, then this is where you must belong, at least for now," Nick said.

"Yep," Morgan said. He settled into the other man, letting his body's rhythms lull him to sleep.

In the morning, before they left for practice, Nick said, "Do you want to come over after practice Saturday morning? We could spend the day together, and then the night?"

"The night or 'the night'?" Morgan asked.

"Both," Nick said, shooting him a look that made his pulse race.

Chapter
EIGHT

SATURDAY morning dawned sunny, and if the wind off the water was any indication, the day would be a warm one. Despite the promises of the next twenty-four hours, Nick had a job to do, and he did it well. None of his athletes would suffer for his involvement with one of their number.

The practice was a good one. Good practices always filled Nick with satisfaction. It meant his plans for their development were working. It meant they took his coaching seriously, both on and off the water. It meant they might pose a threat at the PCRCs. It meant he might have a job that fall.

By the end of practice, most of the guys had stripped down, including Morgan. They often did, but for some reason, the fact that Morgan rowed with his shirt off that morning, sunlight gleaming from the rivulets of sweat running down his back and between his pecs, struck Nick. They were going to take their relationship to another level today. It sounded corny when he thought about it, but he still watched Morgan, captivated by the sheer aesthetic beauty of that particular body in motion. Nick knew he was a lucky man. He only hoped Morgan felt that way.

Nick guided his launch up against the dock with scarcely a bump as Stuart did the same with the varsity boat. "Good practice, guys. Great work," he called to his rowers. "I'll email you the usual postmortem, but in general, I like where we're headed."

Then Nick met Morgan's eyes, and they had one of those movie moments. Everything disappeared but the two of them. Nick was entranced, drinking in every detail of Morgan's face and body, and from there, seeing Morgan's personality writ plain as day. Morgan might be younger than he, but he was no boy, no innocent ingénue. He was a man who knew what he wanted and, Nick suspected, was used to getting it.

Morgan smiled, then, not a big smile, just a hint around the eyes and slight curve of his lips. His smile held a promise, but a hint of challenge too, and Nick's throat went dry. He knew that this step was it, the one step from which there would be no return, because if he gave himself to Morgan it would be all or nothing. He'd tried nothing and had failed miserably. It was time to try all, to jump in with both feet. He smiled back.

Morgan nodded as if satisfied with what he'd seen. That only made Nick more nervous as he wondered *what* the other man had seen. Suddenly he couldn't hold Morgan's gaze any longer and had to look away, but not without smiling himself.

But now he couldn't be in the boathouse with Morgan, not with everyone else there too. His feelings were too new, too raw, too overwhelming for him to hide much around Morgan. To be in Morgan's presence at that moment would be to trumpet his feelings to one and all, and he wasn't ready for that.

"All right, you dogs, enough dawdling, let's get this boat out of the water," Stuart barked.

Nick suddenly found the fuel supply for his launch's engine engrossing as Morgan's attention was pulled away by the coxswain's demands.

"You were brutal out there, you damn vicious leprechaun," Brad groaned. "I thought Coach said it wouldn't be that hard a row, Cockring."

"For the last time, stop calling me that!" Stuart grated.

"With your red hair and green eyes, there's a fairy in there somewhere, Cockring," Brad laughed. "Maybe you should check the family tree for what they found in the woodshed."

Stuart smiled, long and vicious. "Ten boat-ups, boys. Be sure to thank Brad. Ready, and up!"

Groaning, the rowers pressed the rowing shell—all fifty-five feet and two hundred pounds of it—over their heads and down to their shoulders, up and down, ten times. Nick watched as Stuart counted out the reps. This was between the coxswain and the rowers, and he wasn't going to interfere unless it jeopardized the equipment. Besides, if Brad hadn't learned to keep his trap shut by now, there was no hope for him. Perhaps his teammates could teach him. But "Cockring" for Cochrane? Nick hadn't heard that one before.

Morgan groaned along with the rest of them. Practice had been long enough, with enough high-intensity work that he knew he'd feel it later.

Later. Just the thought made him shiver. He'd liked what he'd seen in Nick's eyes a moment before. Too bad he couldn't savor it.

After the boat was on the racks and wiped down, Stuart dispatched the rowers to various clean-up chores while he and Morgan fetched the oars from the dock to the oar locker. Then they made a show of putting the oars away properly, in pairs, while the other guys drifted out of the boathouse.

Finally, Stuart and Morgan were alone in the boathouse. "Are you sure this is what you want?" Stuart asked.

"Yeah, it is," Morgan said, a soft smile on his face. Dating Nick Bedford was the fulfillment of a fantasy he'd had since freshman year. Nick was handsome and strong and smart. And gentle. Morgan liked that best of all.

"Coach'll give you a ride home tomorrow?" Stuart said.

"I'm hoping he'll give me a ride while he's home tonight," Morgan smirked. Stuart actually blushed. Morgan hadn't thought he knew how. "He will," Morgan said.

At last, Coach Bedford came up the dock, lugging the gas tank for the launch. He put it in the fuel depot located just outside the large bay doors, peering into the boathouse as he closed and locked the fuel away.

Stuart handed Morgan his car keys. "You might as well go get your bag while I put the cox box away."

But as Morgan headed to the parking lot and Stuart's car, Stuart ignored the small cylinder that powered the boat's speakers. He placed himself squarely in his coach's way.

"You ran a good practice," Nick said. "I've got a few comments for things I'd like you to watch out for, but I'll include those in a separate email for your eyes only. No sense in making them more paranoid than we have to."

Stuart nodded. "Yeah, whatever. Listen well, because I'm only going to say this once, and then we'll pretend this conversation never happened. Take care of him."

"I'm sorry?" Nick replied, unsure of just how much his coxswain knew about his involvement with his five-seat.

"Don't hurt him again," Stuart said quietly.

"What do you mean? I'd never—" Nick said.

"That 'date' with Drew," Stuart hissed, his voice as quiet and lethal as a guillotine's blade.

Nick closed his eyes, his shoulders slumped.

"If you hurt him again, I'll make you regret it. Morgan's something special. I know he seems like he's bold as brass and tough as nails, but there's another side to him, and I'm very protective."

"I can tell. I'll make it up to him," Nick promised.

Stuart nodded. "I hope so," he said as Morgan walked up, bag slung over his shoulder.

"Are you ready?" Morgan asked Nick, loading a world of meaning into that question.

But Nick was. He over-thought things, he knew that. But not this. "Yeah, just let me get my things from my office."

"Cool," Morgan said softly. He followed Nick, not even looking back at his roommate.

"See you guys. I've got some stuff to do with the cox boxes." Stuart sighed and turned to the bank of cox boxes, red LEDs blinking their charge status. The boxes were fine. The reality was that he couldn't bear to see them together, not just then, not like that. He was happy for Morgan and knew he'd never had a chance with the man, but it still hurt to watch them leave the boathouse together.

NICK and Morgan drove back to Nick's place in silence, each nervous and trying not to show it. Morgan didn't have much success with that. He bounced his left leg up and down, sometimes in time with the songs on the radio but often not. Nick reached out and put his hand on Morgan's knee. "You okay?"

Morgan stilled his leg. "Just nervous, I guess."

"Wasn't there a movie called *Relax… It's Just Sex?*" Nick said.

"Yeah, but it's not *just* sex, it's sex with *you*," Morgan said softly.

Nick quirked a smile. "We don't have to, you know."

"I want to, it's just… it's you," Morgan said, turning to look at Nick.

Nick glanced at him, both hands on the wheel. "I know. I feel the same way."

They drove in silence the rest of the way, and Morgan wished Nick's hand still rested on his knee. When they reached his door, Nick opened it and let Morgan precede him. "I've got big plans for our date weekend. I thought we'd get cleaned up and then grab a late breakfast somewhere, maybe take in the farmer's market, and see where the afternoon takes us. But one thing first."

"What's tha—?" Morgan started to say, but Nick's mouth cut him off. The kiss started chaste enough, but Morgan liked Nick's priorities and sighed into the kiss, wrapping his arms around Nick's waist, and when Nick's tongue teased his lips, he opened and took Nick's tongue in.

Then Morgan pulled back, breathing heavily. "I want you."

Nick kissed him again, frantically this time, pouring out his soul through his mouth. All the words he longed to say but was afraid to, and afraid of, he said with his kiss.

The feeling of Morgan against him, the feeling of the other man under his hands, the smell of his sweat from a workout that he, Nick, had engineered, combined and went straight to his groin.

Morgan made needy sounds, little groans that told Nick loud and clear what he wanted. "Bedroom? Please?"

After a final hungry kiss, Nick broke away and pulled Morgan with him. He couldn't wait any longer. He dragged Morgan to his bedroom.

Kicking the door shut, Nick grabbed his sweatshirt and started to yank it off, but Morgan stopped him. "I want to do that. I want to see you. All of you."

Nick forced himself to slow down. "All right, you take the lead."

"I will," Morgan said, arching one eyebrow. He ran his hands under Nick's sweatshirt, feeling the play of the muscles under the T-shirt. He grazed his hands across Nick's pecs and flicked the nipple ring, smiling at the hitch in Nick's breath. Only then did he take the hem in his hands and pull it up and over. Nick obligingly raised his arms, and Morgan took shameless advantage of his helplessness to suck on his neck.

"Hey, that's not fair!" Nick yelped from inside his sweatshirt.

"What? I can't hear you," Morgan said, moving to a new spot. "The sweatshirt's muffling your voice."

Unable to do anything else, Nick let sensation overwhelm him. Morgan's tongue on his sensitive skin, thrilling, tickling, followed by the rough scrape of Morgan's teeth, then the soft caress of his lips, all combined to pull Nick into a haze of pleasure.

Then Morgan stopped and pulled the sweatshirt free. Nick shook his head to clear it. "You will pay for that."

"Yeah? How, tough guy?" Morgan said, grinning.

"Like this," Nick said, launching himself at Morgan and pushing him onto the bed. Before Morgan could do more than squirm, Nick grabbed his hands and pinned them by his shoulders, sitting on his chest.

Morgan fought, but not much. This was what he wanted. His coach on him, over him, hopefully in him. There were other things he wanted, but this was enough for now. More than enough.

"You like it like this, don't you?" Nick growled.

Morgan could only gasp, "Uh-huh," as Nick launched an assault of his own on Morgan's neck. Morgan liked it. A lot. He struggled a little, but it could've been writhing in pleasure.

Nick kissed and bit his way around Morgan's jaw, then repeated the operation on his neck. Then he continued down Morgan's chest, the kisses perforce rougher through the fabric of the technical-fiber shirt he'd donned after practice. He nibbled on one nipple gone erect and hard. "Niiick…," Morgan whined.

Then Nick sat up. "Shirt off. Now."

Nick got off of Morgan. He looked down at the erection straining against Morgan's shorts and grinned. "I like that."

"So do I," Morgan growled. He sat up and tugged at his shirt but then stopped, riveted at the sight of Nick. He'd suspected and fantasized that Nick would be beautiful up close, but he had no idea how. Somehow standing next to him in the bathroom that first time they'd spent the night together hadn't been the same, and seeing him in the locker room after his shower that day didn't count. While Nick was shorter, his shoulders were broader and tapered nicely down to a trim waist and a treasure trail that disappeared into his underwear. Seeing Nick, before they did what they were about to do… that was totally new and different.

Morgan stood up. He had to touch. He ran his hands across the chest, just enjoying the other man's skin. Nick had a faint farmer's tan, but Morgan could tell he tried to keep the sun off him during practice. From chest down to the defined abs and that treasure trail, and then on down to what was behind door number one.

Morgan unbuttoned Nick's jeans and pulled them down. "You did say you had big plans for me, all right," he said, palming Nick's cock through his boxer-briefs, already spotted with precum.

Then Morgan pulled the jeans the rest of the way down, and Nick stepped out them to reveal strong quads—a bit larger than one might've thought, but that was a byproduct of the rowing.

He stood before Morgan, arms spread wide, clad only in his boxer-briefs. "Here I am."

"And you're all mine," Morgan breathed.

"And you're wearing too much," Nick said. He pulled Morgan's shirt over his head, resisting the temptation to trap him. There were other things he wanted.

"Oooh, I do like a hairy man," Nick said, smiling at what he saw. Morgan was nicely furred without looking like a yeti. "I'd never noticed that. I guess I can't see it from the launch."

Morgan blushed and tried to cross his arms, but Nick stopped him. "What's wrong?"

"I get teased sometimes," Morgan mumbled. "At least I did growing up. None of my brothers are this hairy, and I started early."

"I said I liked it," Nick murmured, kissing Morgan's neck again and smoothing his hands down Morgan's torso, feeling the six-pack under his thumbs, "so no hiding it from me, okay?"

Nick took his time exploring. Seeing Morgan from the launch was one thing, having him up close and under his hands quite another, and he intended to enjoy the discovery.

Morgan's shoulders and back and legs were developed from rowing, the rest from cross training. He was tan, but not enough to raise thoughts of unhealthy solar exposure, and the glow contrasted with his tighty-whiteys in a way that made Nick's knees weak.

"You're beautiful," Nick breathed before he ran his tongue down between Morgan's pecs, "and I'm going to make your body sing."

Morgan threaded his fingers through Nick's hair as his eyes half-closed. Then Nick was turning him around and then pulling his briefs off.

"Wow," Nick sighed.

"What?" Morgan said, opening his eyes and looking back over his shoulder.

"You. Here. Just… wow."

Morgan blushed and turned away.

"No, I'll show you," Nick said. He pulled his underwear off and kicked it away, standing behind Morgan, his now-painfully erect cock pressed into Morgan's sculpted ass. He closed his eyes and steadied himself as pleasure lanced through him. He allowed himself a slight snap of his hips, sending another wave through him. But that was all. This was about Morgan.

Nick wrapped his arms around Morgan's waist. "Yes," he said, kissing the back of Morgan's neck, "beautiful. I thought you were cute when you first showed up as a walk-on at a recruitment event—and yes, I remember you—but the man you've become…. You're amazing. Just seeing you row…."

"I've seen you watching," Morgan said. There was no challenge, just a hint of pride that he was worth watching.

"Wouldn't you look?" Nick breathed into his ear. As he had earlier, Nick smoothed his hands down Morgan's chest, then sides, and finally his back, just exploring with his hands this wonderful body before him.

Nick exhaled some of his pent-up tension and leaned into Morgan's back again. His hands moved down the contours of Morgan's abs to his lower belly and around his groin to meet between his legs. Morgan groaned as Nick's hands neared but didn't touch his cock, furiously hard and bouncing with his pulse. Nick's hands circled closer and closer, brushing his sac, only to move away again.

Morgan moaned, and Nick relented, slowly moving his hands up from Morgan's pelvis down to his rock-hard cock. Morgan sighed and shuddered. "That what you wanted?"

Morgan nodded, and Nick stroked him gently for a few moments, just long enough to smear precum leaking from the head down the shaft to slick it. But then he moved his hands away, and Morgan whimpered in protest.

But then Nick was back, biting and sucking at Morgan's neck, and that was good too. Nick made his way down Morgan's broad back, sometimes kissing or licking, sometimes just running his stubbled cheek across the soft skin, ending up on his knees.

Then Nick kissed the top of Morgan's ass cheeks and caught a whiff of his scent, musky and sweaty and all man, and groaned himself. He had to stop himself from biting and biting hard, but damn, it made him burn. He'd been hard, but now it hurt. He wanted to throw Morgan down and slam into him over and over, just to feel it.

Instead, Nick licked the top of Morgan's cleft. When he felt Morgan shiver underneath him, he said, "Is it okay? Can I…?"

"No one's ever done that," Morgan said.

Nick couldn't believe that, not with the incredible smells coming from Morgan's ass and groin. "Spread your legs."

Nick barely waited for Morgan to comply, kissing his way down Morgan's crack, stopping just above his puckered hole. He stopped to inhale, letting the pheromones, the male musk, overwhelm him. The rush made him dizzy. Nick loved to rim. It drove him crazy and never failed to reduce his partners to moaning, begging, needy things desperate to be fucked.

Moving slowly, as much to give Morgan a chance to object as to draw out the pleasure for him, for them both, Nick kissed his way around Morgan's entrance, delicate little things like the brush of a butterfly's wings, no more than glancing touches of his lips.

"Wha—? Ohhh," Morgan moaned.

Then Nick leaned in, kissing harder, interspersing the kisses with bites. When his tongue glanced over the puckered opening itself, a shudder wracked Morgan's body, and Nick smiled. He reached a hand up to stroke Morgan and found that his cock was juicing precum in a constant trickle.

Then he licked Morgan, right on target, just running his tongue around and over the tight, clean opening. He gave Morgan a chance to get used to that and then stabbed his tongue in, hard. Then again, over and over, flat-out fucking Morgan with his tongue.

"Nick!" Morgan cried. He staggered forward but braced himself on Nick's bed.

But Nick showed him no mercy as he thrust his tongue in and out, slicking Morgan up. He pried Morgan's cheeks apart to rim deeper, dragging his stubble across the tender flesh of his ass, driving Morgan insane. That Nick could do that turned him on like few other things.

"Please, Nick. Now," Morgan begged. Morgan was gasping, and Nick's own breath was ragged. It was time.

Nick staggered the few feet to his nightstand on his knees and pulled out condoms and lube. He squirted a healthy amount of the cool liquid into his palm to warm it and then slicked Morgan up. Morgan was pretty open from the rimming, but the more lube the better.

"Yesss," Morgan hissed as Nick pushed lube into him. He rocked back and forth, fucking himself on Nick's fingers for a moment.

"Sorry, I need both hands for the next part," Nick said as he took his fingers away. He could tear open the condom wrapper with one hand and his teeth and lube himself one-handed, but he didn't want Morgan going off too soon.

Suited up, Nick said, "Are you ready?"

"Jeez, yeah, will you hurry up and fuck me?" Morgan said breathlessly.

Chuckling, Nick stood and lined himself up against Morgan's hole, feeling it twitch around his finger. Then he pushed his cock home. He took it slowly, partly to drive Morgan insane but partly to give him a chance to get used to it.

But Morgan had other ideas. He slammed himself back onto Nick's cock with a harsh cry.

Nick's head swam as the pleasure flooded out from his groin. Then Nick slowly began to fuck Morgan, and the tight, wet heat threatened to snap his fragile self-control as Morgan clamped down on his cock. "Ah, Jesus, Morgan," he gasped. "So good."

Morgan grinned as he arched into the pleasure filling him, and he rose up, leaning back into Nick. Nick grabbed him with one arm, holding him across his chest, and Morgan held onto him, reveling in the feeling of strength coming from behind him, filling him up and holding him up.

Nick sighed and closed his eyes as he rode one of his favorite sensations in the world: the feeling of another man's ass against his groin. Each slide into Morgan brought him up against Nick; each moment of contact sent shockwaves through him, making him tingle all over. He could've come just resting up against Morgan, but that wouldn't have been fair.

Morgan reached out to jack himself, but Nick reached out with a slick hand and batted his hand away. "Mine," he growled in Morgan's ear and started stroking him.

Nick fucked up and into Morgan for a while and then bent him over, pushing him onto the bed. Without missing a stroke, he increased the tempo, fucking him harder. The feeling of Morgan's broad, strong back and incredible ass on the front of his body sent wave after wave of electric thrills ripping through his body, from his cock pistoning in and out of that incredible ass to his sensitized nipples. It was like he was fucking him with his whole body. It was a paradise he never wanted to end, one that couldn't end fast enough as his hips snapped, thrusting in and pulling back, thrusting and pulling.

As Morgan fell forward he almost blew his wad right then, and still Nick kept drilling into him. Then Nick shifted slightly and Morgan cried out, grabbing at the sheets, Nick's hands atop his, as each punishing stroke nailed his gland. No man had ever made Morgan feel like this. Then Nick's fingers interlaced with his, Nick's arms atop his, and it was all Morgan could do not to cry from the feeling of being covered and protected and loved.

But even as Morgan hurtled towards the edge, Nick pulled out, leaving him feeling empty and cold. "Wha—"

"I want to see your face when you come," Nick rasped.

Nick rolled Morgan over and lifted his legs. He pushed in again, filling Morgan back up. As Nick grabbed his cock again, Morgan clamped down again, and Nick's eyes almost rolled back, but he forced himself to stay present. This was for Morgan, and he wouldn't come until Morgan did. He'd waited a long time for this and didn't want to miss a single moment or nuance.

Nick looked deep into Morgan's eyes, stroking him in time to his own thrusts.

"Nick, close," Morgan panted.

"Give it up," Nick breathed. "Do it."

And then Morgan did. He cried out as spurt after spurt covered his chest. The sight of the thick white jism splashing on Morgan's abs was all it took, and seconds later, with a final snap of his hips, white-hot light rose up and Nick shot so hard it almost hurt, blast after blast filling the condom. "Morgan!"

Spent, suddenly boneless, Nick leaned over Morgan, resting on his forearms. Winded, he felt his pulse racing in the aftermath. He still kissed Morgan long and lovingly. "Wow. You're amazing."

Morgan just smiled but didn't—couldn't—say anything.

Still inside Morgan, Nick bent down and licked some of Morgan's cum off his pecs, shivering at the taste of him. Then he licked more, cleaning what he could with his tongue.

Morgan's arms encircled him. "You... you're... damn, Nick. Just... damn."

They rested like that for a few moments until Nick felt himself softening. Reluctantly, he broke their embrace, and holding onto the condom, he pulled out. Taking it with him to the bathroom, he said, "I'll be right back."

And very soon Nick returned with a washcloth and towel. "How are you?"

Morgan smiled and stretched, long and lazily. "Never better. Better than I ever dreamed."

Nick kissed him as he carefully cleaned Morgan and dried him with the towel. Tossing them to one side, he held the covers back for Morgan and then climbed in next to him. He held out his arms, and Morgan curled up against his side, head resting on his chest as sleep claimed them both.

Chapter

NINE

MORGAN'S rumbling stomach finally roused them both midmorning. "Hey, you've got to feed me. I'm a growing boy," he said.

Nick chuckled and reached for Morgan's cock. "Doesn't feel like it yet."

Morgan swatted his hand away. "C'mon, I'm starving. You want a repeat? Feed me."

"Yes, sir," Nick said, rolling over. "Why don't I fix you a sandwich or something while you shower, just something to tide you over until we're both dressed, then we can go grab lunch somewhere, maybe hit the farmer's market if it's still open, or maybe the flea market."

"That sounds nice," Morgan said, smiling. "Did my bag make it in before you waylaid me?"

"I think it's in the living room," Nick said.

So while Morgan showered, Nick fixed him a snack and then cleaned up himself. Thus fortified, they ventured forth to enjoy the rest of their Saturday.

"I don't eat out a lot," Nick said as he drove, "but I get tired of my own cooking once in a while."

"I can't see how. The dinner you made me was incredible," Morgan said.

"Thanks. I might've been trying to impress you. Just a little," Nick admitted with a smirk.

"Mission accomplished," Morgan said. He looked over at Nick and grinned. He just couldn't get enough of Nick's company, and they had the whole weekend together, or close enough. "So you like to cook?"

Nick thought about it. "No, I like to eat, but I have really high standards."

"I can live with that," Morgan said, hoping that meant something for boyfriends too. He put his hand on Nick's leg, and Nick smiled.

"Anyway, I thought we'd go someplace for lunch, and then I'll cook tonight, if that's okay with you," Nick said.

"Whatever you want is fine with me. I'm just happy to spend time with you," Morgan said. "Maybe later I'll feel like opinionating, but for now? Lead on."

"That works for me," Nick said. Then he shot Morgan a sly look. "Actually, I'm kind of looking forward to it."

"I can't imagine what you're talking about," Morgan said, trying to keep a straight face.

Then they burst out laughing. Finally they just smiled at each other, each with the sunny bonhomie of one freshly fucked by someone he cares about.

AFTER lunch, they wandered through a farmer's market, where Nick picked up a few things to include with dinner.

"I had no idea you were such a foodie," Morgan said.

"I'm not, really. But why buy pesticide-laden produce at the supermarket when it's fresher and cleaner here?" Nick said. "Besides, you're worth it." He put his arm across Morgan's shoulders and pulled him in for a kiss. Morgan stiffened but then kissed him back.

"That okay?" Nick asked.

Morgan smiled. "Of course. You just surprised me, is all. You didn't strike me as the publicly demonstrative type."

"Surprise!" Nick said, grinning. To be honest, he surprised himself too, but it felt right. But ever since he and Morgan had started dating, and now the real deal instead of eye-fucking each other every time they were in the boathouse together, he didn't have to protect the lie anymore. He had a boyfriend, and what a boyfriend he had. He'd never felt like this about another man and wanted people to know. Somehow, the lie didn't seem as important as it had before.

They spent the afternoon wandering among shops and galleries and the farmer's market without the proverbial care in the world. And then something happened that brought the precariousness of his situation rushing back to Nick.

They had just finished selecting the last thing Nick needed to make dinner when Morgan looked up. "Hey! I'll be right back," he said, and he took off.

Nick paid and looked around for Morgan. He saw him fifty or so feet away, chatting with a blonde woman his own age. Morgan looked back over his shoulder and then beckoned Nick over.

"Nick, this is Matilda. She was my freshman year roommate's girlfriend. He was a total douche, but—"

"I dumped the douche and kept Morgan," she said. "Best decision I ever made."

"They called us Eminem," Morgan laughed. "Remember that?"

"How could I forget? They thought we were—"

"I know," Morgan groaned.

Nick listened as they burbled on, faking interest in their frosher shenanigans. Then he shivered. What if this woman had been on the women's crew? What if she'd been one of his rowers? Granted, the guys weren't likely to be trolling a farmer's market for fresh mushrooms, but still. Morgan and Nick were out in public together, and being seen "together" was a risk Nick had never considered.

Morgan snapped his fingers in Nick's face. "You in there?"

"I'm sorry," Nick said, smiling weakly. "Just thinking about cooking, I guess. It was nice to meet you, Matilda. You ready to go, Morgan?"

After that, Nick tried to get back into the spirit of things, but the shine was definitely off the afternoon. They wandered among shops and galleries, but Nick glanced over his shoulder the entire time, the opposite of cruising. The goal was not to be seen, rather than to attract attention.

"We should probably head home if I'm going to get dinner on the table," Nick said, making a show of checking his watch.

"I've got some reading I could be doing," Morgan said. "Home," he'd said. Morgan knew it was far too early in the relationship to think about things like that, but home and Nick in the same thought filled him with longing.

With a silent sigh of relief, Nick steered Morgan back to the car and safety.

"SO WHAT do you want to do tonight?" Nick asked as they ate. He'd shelved his freak-out for the time being, but he knew he'd have to deal with the issue sooner or later. It was a minefield he didn't want to cross. He wasn't ashamed of himself or Morgan, but his own circumstances demanded discretion. He felt like every time he turned around he realized anew just how precarious the balance required was.

You, Morgan thought. Aloud he said, "What're my options?"

"Studying, television, movies," Nick rattled off. "Uh…."

"What about dancing?" Morgan said, eyes lighting up. "That sounds like fun. I've got a hot new boyfriend to show off."

Nick groaned inwardly. Shaking it on the dance floor with Morgan wasn't particularly discreet, but there was no easy way out without faking a limp he hadn't had moments before. "Okay, dancing it is. Which club?"

"Aspects. They've got the best DJ on Saturday nights," Morgan replied without hesitation. Then he grinned. "You know. You've been there before."

Then Nick remembered what had happened the last time he went to Aspects and wanted to kick himself. He'd tried to put it out of mind, but the alcohol-hazed humiliation simmered just below conscious recollection, and Morgan's choice brought it rushing back to the surface. *Sorry, but I make a complete fool of myself every time I go there, and the last time I flushed dignity down the toilet, along with my self-respect, by nearly having sex in public with a stranger, so can we please go somewhere else?* Nick cringed at the thought. "What about Wonderland?"

"Too 'stand and model'," Morgan sniffed.

Growing desperate, Nick said, "Buckaroo?"

"A country and western bar? Are you serious?"

"No, not really," Nick sighed.

"Look, if you don't want to go dancing with me, just say so," Morgan snapped.

"Morgan, no," Nick said, pretending he didn't feel the sick feeling in his gut. But without an explanation, he couldn't very well shoot down Morgan's choice. He pasted on his best fake smile and said, "It sounds like fun."

MORGAN quickly forgot the weird vibe from Nick about the selection of Aspects for the night's entertainment. They spent dinner staring into each other's eyes, candles the only light in the room. If he'd seen it from without, it would've made him gag, but living it was something else.

Morgan hadn't really planned on going dancing. Now that he thought about it, he hadn't really planned anything at all as to how the evening should play out. Fortunately, the pants he'd brought weren't too dire, and he scrounged a nice shirt from Nick's closet. "Hey, if I can't steal your clothes, whose can I steal?"

"Just be glad we're close to the same size. If you were dating Stuart, you'd be shit out of luck," Nick laughed from where he brushed his teeth in the bathroom.

Morgan, balanced on one leg while putting the other in his pants, almost fell over. Was Stuart out to their coach? He didn't think so and wasn't sure. Still, it was something he'd better take up with Stuart before he let anything slip. "Uh… yeah, that'd be awkward, all right."

Nick left the bathroom, tucking in his shirt as he walked. "Are you ready?"

"As ready as ever I'll ever be," Morgan said, smiling.

THEY got to Aspects at just the right time, when it was busy enough to be an attractive destination on a Saturday night but not yet so packed that they couldn't find a table. "You hold down the fort while I get drinks."

"Just beer for me," Morgan said.

"Thank God," Nick breathed as he made his way to one of the bars. He loved Drew like a brother, but Nick always worried about spilling those sticky drinks Drew favored, especially as the bar filled.

A few guys tried to catch Nick's eye, but he ignored them. He considered himself off the market and was pretty sure Morgan felt the same way. Aspects might not have been crowded, but men and women lined the bar. He waited patiently for the bartender's attention.

"Hi," a guy sitting near him said.

Nicked nodded politely but didn't take the bait.

"Got a name?"

"Nick."

"Just Nick?"

Nick nodded. When the bartender asked for his order, he said, "Two beers."

"You're here with someone," the man said.

"My boyfriend," Nick said, handing over the money and taking the beers.

The man raked Nick with his eyes. "He's a lucky man."

"I'm the one who's lucky," Nick said. He indicated the table where Morgan sat with his chin.

"Looks like someone else is trying to get lucky," Nick's admirer laughed.

Nick looked over, and sure enough, some guy had slid in where he'd been sitting.

"I'm not worried. He knows who he's going home with," Nick said. But just because he knew it rationally didn't mean his lizard brain wasn't hooting and hollering and itching to respond to the threat.

Nick walked back to their table just a little quicker than he'd left it.

"I told you, my name's not 'Fuckdog'," Nick heard Morgan say, his voice flat and edged with anger.

"But it will be, and I'll make you howl too," the interloper said.

Nick frowned. The voice sounded familiar.

Since the interloper had taken his seat, Nick moved around to the other side of the table.

And almost dropped the beer on the floor.

It was him. The reach-around. If they'd bothered to exchange names, Nick had been too drunk to remember it.

"Is there a problem?" Nick asked Morgan. He just prayed Reach-Around left without saying anything.

"Just you," Reach-Around laughed. "You had your chance. Get lost."

"My boyfriend and I are enjoying ourselves. You need to leave," Nick said. "Now."

Reach-Around looked at them speculatively. "You're both pretty hot. How 'bout a three-way?"

Morgan's jaw dropped, and Nick knew he'd better do something fast before this got further out of hand.

Nick stood up. "How about you leave before the bouncers throw you out?"

"Some boyfriend, if you have to rely on the bouncers to do your dirty work," Reach-Around snorted.

"You're not worth an arrest record," Morgan said.

"It's time for you to go," Nick said. He raised his hand and caught the attention of one of the bouncers by the door.

"You'd have sucked, and not in the good way," Reach-Around said, slinking away.

Nick saw that Reach-Around was well and truly gone and then sat back down. "I'm really sorry about that."

"It's okay," Morgan said softly, smiling a lopsided smile.

"No, it's not, not if you're upset," Nick said.

"I'm okay, really. I've been hit on before, but… he wouldn't go away. Most guys leave you alone if you tell them to," Morgan said, "but he wouldn't."

Nick put his arm around Morgan. "Do you want to go home? We don't have to stay here."

"My hero," Morgan said, resting his head on Nick's shoulder. Nick made him feel safe. Protected. Wanted, desired, even, but in the good way, not in the creepy way of that asshole.

Then something occurred to Morgan. That asshole seemed to know Nick. Or had at least met him. Morgan raised his head to look at Nick. "What did he mean, 'You had your chance'?"

Nick started to reply, then stopped. "What'd you mean?"

"He said you'd had your chance. What did that mean?" Morgan demanded.

Nick closed his eyes for a moment. This was exactly why he hadn't wanted to go to Aspects that night. Whatever the odds were, his number had come up. He should've bought lottery tickets.

Nick looked at Morgan. Still handsome, but the man was whip-crack smart, and he wasn't going to let this go. Nick thought about bullshitting Morgan. It wasn't like they'd been dating when his night with Reach-Around (what was his name?!) went down. In fact, quite the opposite. Nick had done everything he could think of to avoid dating Morgan. That alone provided a legit reason to chalk this up to a jealous ex-boyfriend and move on.

But now Nick was dating Morgan, and there was something in Morgan's eyes, something begging for reassurance, something vulnerable that melted Nick's heart. There could be no secret shame staining their young relationship.

Nick looked down at the table, marshalling his courage. "This has to do with the night of your date with Drew. Are you sure you want to hear this?"

"I don't know… do I?" Morgan said.

"It's not bad, it's just not…." Nick sighed. "It's not bad, but it's not very flattering, either."

"What is it?" Morgan asked, worried as well as curious.

"Not here," Nick said, suddenly desperate to be anywhere but Aspects. He got up. "C'mon, we're going somewhere else. You won't want to dance afterwards, anyway." *Hell, you may not even want to date me, but I owe you the truth*, he thought.

Nick didn't say anything as he dragged Morgan out into the cool night air. He didn't say anything to Morgan as he drove them away from the bar. Not really thinking about it, he ended up driving them back to the park where they'd first kissed, as if subconsciously he sought the positive association. But when he turned the car off, he didn't get out. Some conversations were meant to happen in the dark.

Nick turned to face Morgan, whose face, half lit by the orange light of the street lamps, displayed a mixture of concern and anger. "Out with it already," Morgan said tightly.

It felt to Nick like his lungs had quit working, locking his breath in his chest. Closing his eyes to block out the sight of an angry Morgan, Nick said, "The night you went out with Drew, I couldn't stand it. I wanted it to be me."

"It *is* you," Morgan said, "but this build-up is driving me crazy."

"I wanted it to be me then and knew it couldn't. So I did what I never do. I went to a bar, got raging drunk, and let myself get picked up by a stranger. Or maybe I picked him up. I can't really remember very well," Nick said, frowning, "but it was that guy who tried to pick you up while I got our beers."

"That doesn't seem so bad," Morgan said cautiously.

"The dancing got pretty heavy," Nick continued, ignoring Morgan. He had to. If it turned into a conversation, he'd chicken out. "I tried to pretend it was you, but when he reached down my pants, I knew it wasn't and couldn't be."

Morgan wrinkled his nose. "Do I want to know this?"

"His hands were smooth," Nick laughed. He reached over and took Morgan's hand, turning it over to run his fingers over the palm. "See? Calluses from the oar handle and the erg. He didn't have them."

"It could've been worse, I guess. We've all done things we're not proud of," Morgan said gently.

Relief flooded through Nick. "Yeah?"

"Yeah," Morgan said. "Then what happened?"

"I ran screaming out of the bar and into the night."

"No shit, really?" Morgan laughed. "No wonder you were lukewarm about dancing."

"I was right, wasn't I?" Nick said. He didn't bring up the other, bigger reason for his reluctance.

"It's just dumb luck that he came back to haunt you," Morgan said, still chuckling. Then he grew serious. "That's not the part of that evening that bothers me, anyway. What I want to talk about," he said, pulling his hand back, "is that 'date'."

"Oh," was all Nick said, slumping in his seat. The date. There were two injured parties in that particular farce, and he'd apologized only to one of them. It was time to pay the piper.

"At first, I was confused," Morgan said. "I thought you were gay. You explained it away, although of course we both know that was a lie."

"I explained that—"

"I'm not done," Morgan said. He paused, choosing his words carefully. "It was flattering, though. Drew's good-looking and a smart guy. He was a fun date. Or would've been, if we'd actually been interested in each other."

"I'm sorry," Nick said quietly. "I thought I was doing the right thing, and instead I hurt two people I care about a lot."

"That's the part I don't get—how this charade was the right thing. I thought I was fine with it, but I'm not. Really, Nick, what the fuck?" Morgan said, all the pain and confusion flooding back.

"Again, I'm really sorry for the deception. I thought I'd made that pretty clear," Nick sighed.

"I know what you told me," Morgan said, "but I still don't get why."

"Because I felt I had to. Because of the ethical problems this poses. I know you don't appreciate those, but they're there and they're very real," Nick said. "In a way, it's like being out in the military. I risk my job—my career—every time we go out."

"I guess I don't see it that way. I just don't see how rules can trump feelings. We were both feeling it," Morgan said, "and you know it. But instead you concocted this bullshit story and dragged me and Drew into it."

Nick wanted to crawl under the floor mat. "Rules don't trump feelings, Morgan." When Morgan didn't say anything, Nick reached out and gently put his hand on his chin. "Look at me. They don't. We're here, aren't we?"

"Yeah, I guess," Morgan said, voice thick with all the things he wanted to say but couldn't.

"We're here because yeah, I am feeling it and I hope to hell you still are, but that doesn't change the fact that by all the ethical guidelines and codes for coaches, what I'm doing—I, not you—is wrong," Nick said. He felt like he was drowning, and he clawed at the water to stay afloat, to keep this relationship afloat. "But the responsibility for that is mine. None of this changes how I feel about you or makes me any less sorry for the chickenshit thing I did. I hope I didn't kill this before we even had a chance, and I hope you can try to see my side to know why I did it, but I'm still sorry I hurt you, and I always will be."

Morgan didn't say anything. He sat next to Nick in the car, but to Nick it felt like he was a thousand miles away, mulling over what he'd been told. Nick waited in taut silence, kicking himself over and over. It all started with the lie, the idea that he had to play it straight to coach collegiate athletics. Times were changing, but perhaps not as fast as they could, and maybe he did have to go back in the closet. At the time, Nick thought it had been a price he was willing to pay. He loved crew, he loved coaching, and denying a little bit of himself had seemed worth it, but now he questioned that choice, because the lie had certainly demanded more than a little bit of himself. At some point, it had taken over, and Nick hadn't even noticed.

Nick's mind bristled with roads not taken. He could've found some other way to earn a living so he didn't have to bolt from business to coaching. He could've gone directly to PT school and coached on a casual basis for a club that'd be happy to have him. If he hadn't cocked this up, if Morgan forgave him, he still could. The realization scared him. Chucking it all was more than he wanted to face at that moment, so he put it carefully away. But he determined then and there that if he still had a chance with him, Morgan would never be one of those roads not taken. Nick wasn't letting him go without a fight.

"Morgan? What're you thinking?"

"I still just don't get *why*," Morgan said.

Nick groaned and leaned forward, resting his head on the steering wheel. "You had to be off-limits. I mean really off-limits."

"More off-limits than all those rules and regulations?" Morgan said.

"Yeah. I figured if you were dating Drew, I could get over you. It made sense at the time, but now it just sounds crazy," Nick said.

"You're kidding." Morgan laughed in spite of himself. "That's… I don't know what that is."

"It's pretty messed up," Nick sighed, realizing again how the lie had distorted his thinking.

"What am I going to do with you?" Morgan said.

Nick looked at him, a shy half-smile on his face. "Keep me?"

Morgan rolled his eyes and shook his head ruefully. "Take me home."

"Home… to your place?" Nick said quietly.

"To your apartment," Morgan said. "I'm suddenly tired."

SOMETIME after midnight, Morgan woke up in Nick's bed. They'd come back to Nick's apartment after the emotionally exhausting trip to the bar and gone right to bed. Sometimes, sleeping on something really did make a difference. When he'd gone to sleep, he could barely think clearly, offering Nick no more than a grumbled "goodnight" before they'd turned the lights out.

But now, in the dark of the wee hours of the morning, Morgan understood his feelings. He knew that one day they'd laugh about the previous night's encounter in the bar. He already thought it was kind of funny. It had certainly ripped the scab off that "date" with Drew. Yes, the deception had hurt, and Morgan hadn't realized how much until last night. But he also realized he had no idea what it must be like for Nick, either, torn between desire and the realities of life. On some level, Morgan knew he'd led a reasonably privileged existence, free of want or work. Going to a private school like California Pacific skewed his perspective in a number of ways, but on an intellectual level, he realized most people didn't attend plush private colleges. Most people had to work for what they had.

Morgan rolled over and looked up at the ceiling as he thought. The comfortable existence was the least of it, however. When he thought about it, he realized he'd always been out. When his friends had noticed girls, he'd noticed boys, and his family had noticed his noticing. Little was said about it not because it was shameful or because his family had assumed he'd hide it, but because there were more important things to talk about. The youngest Estrada boy was gay. Big deal. One of his cousins was an ass about it, but the one time he'd said anything, Morgan's three older brothers had flown at him like the Furies, and that was that. Morgan was gay, and heaven help anyone who said ill of it. In that, Morgan knew he was very lucky indeed.

Morgan knew Nick well enough by now to understand that Nick's biography was very different. Where Morgan's coming out had been pro forma and met with a collective yawn, Nick's had occasioned frigid silence that lasted for months, and his family hadn't entirely thawed, even still. Where Morgan pursued a degree in the gay-friendly arts, Nick had gone first into finance and then into athletics, and Morgan knew first-hand what jocks could be like on the gay issue. He himself had felt the barbs of "Dude, that's so gay" flung by unthinking teammates over the years. Even when followed by a "Sorry, bro, I didn't mean you," they still stung. Morgan tried to imagine hearing that and having bills to pay. He failed, which told him everything he needed to know. While Nick had gone about protecting himself in a totally ham-handed way, Morgan had no business judging him for it.

Rolling over on his side to face Nick's broad back, Morgan tried to picture lying to protect himself. He tried to imagine going back in the closet in the important areas of his life to continue leading life as he knew it. He came up blank. Sighing, he admitted to himself that he was just that naïve. Nick was enough older, had enough experience on him, that Morgan was just going to have to give him the benefit of the doubt, and when it came down to it, that was exactly what he wanted to do. He looked not for an excuse to go but for a reason to stay. Life with Nick was better than life without Nick, and if he let his anger over the date with Drew become a deal-breaker, that was what Morgan would have—life without Nick.

That decided, Morgan snuggled up against his boyfriend and fell asleep.

Chapter
TEN

SOMETIME during the night, they must've rolled over and switched positions, because when Morgan woke up again, he had Nick pressed against his back. And Nick's morning erection pressed against his ass. He liked that. He liked that a lot.

Then Morgan remembered the rimming. He was no slut, but he'd had a few boyfriends, including one who'd taught him a thing or two, but no one had ever rimmed him. His other sexual partners—he wouldn't call them lovers, not even that one serious boyfriend—had clearly robbed him of something. The memory of Nick's flicking tongue made his hole twitch and his dick harden. The thought alone of the pleasure as that tongue set the nerves around his hole to sizzling was enough to make him beg. He wanted it again, just as he wanted to be filled by Nick all over again. The feeling of Nick holding him tight even as he filled him with his cock had made him soar like nothing ever had.

But as much as Morgan wanted a reprise, he also longed to do something for Nick, to share some sexual secret like the one revealed to him last night. He didn't know what Nick might have in his repertoire, but Morgan had another side to show his new boyfriend—a naughty side.

Morgan folded the comforter down and then gently rolled Nick onto his back. Nick stirred but stayed asleep. No matter, Morgan thought. He'd soon take care of that. They'd both been so exhausted last night that they'd stripped down to their underwear and gotten into bed, too tired to do anything else. But Morgan had rested well, and it was time.

He knelt down and gently peeled Nick's briefs back. He took Nick's penis, already reasonably hard, into his mouth. He sucked gently, moving his tongue lazily along the shaft as it stiffened further in his mouth. As Nick grew harder and larger, Morgan took him in as far as he could and used his hands on the rest, gently stroking the shaft while he focused elsewhere.

Morgan ran his tongue over the head, tracing a figure eight with his tongue for a few moments. Then he teased the slit before he licked down the underside. Ever so gently, he sucked first one ball, then the other, into his mouth, warming and wetting them before he moved farther south. He buried his nose under Nick's sac, breathing deeply. He groaned as Nick's scent filled him, but he fought down the need to rush, to wake Nick up and demand he fuck him. The delicious torment of waiting would make it so much better for them both, so Morgan returned to the top, once again taking Nick's cock in as far as he could, sucking and licking and stroking.

Nick woke up with a groan, his hips already thrusting. "Morgan? Ohhhhh…."

Morgan looked up. "Good morning, sunshine!" he said before diving back in.

"No fair," Nick growled. He fought to clear his head, but Morgan's attention to the other one kept foiling his efforts. "I can't kiss you down there. Come up where I can reach you."

"You'll reach the interesting parts soon enough," Morgan said.

"Is that a promise?" Nick said, fully awake and definitely into it. He reached for Morgan. "Or a threat?"

"Both," Morgan said, grinning wickedly. He surged up from Nick's groin, grabbed his arms, and pinned him to the bed, climbing on top of him.

Nick's desire flared hotter, and he strained against Morgan's grip, just so it didn't look like he'd surrendered too fast. "Damn," he breathed. "I'd cut back on your weight training, but the results are too nice to look at."

"Wouldn't do any good," Morgan said, his breath quickening. "I'd still have you. I've got something you want."

"Yeah? And what would that be?"

Morgan didn't say anything. He just ground his ass against Nick's cock. "Yeah, right there," Morgan moaned. "God, I want you."

"I can do something about that," Nick said, tensing to roll Morgan off, but Morgan tightened his grip.

"I don't think so. I don't remember telling you that you could do that."

"You… oh, so that's how it's gonna be?" Nick said. "I think I like this side of you."

"I'm going to let go for a moment, and you will stay put," Morgan said.

"I will, huh? I mean, I will, sir?"

"And don't you forget it," Morgan said. He climbed off Nick and sauntered to Nick's closet. From it he pulled several silk neckties. "Is it okay to use these?"

Nick's eyes grew wide. "Wow. You always seemed like such a good boy."

"I'm a very good boy," Morgan said, "and you'll see just how good very, very soon."

"What're you going to do?"

Morgan stared into Nick's eyes, dark and hungry. "I'm going to tie you down, take you some place you've never been. Then you are going to fuck me until I scream your name and you lose the power of speech."

But Nick already was some place new. If he wasn't careful, he knew Morgan would own him outright, and knew he didn't care. He'd gladly take what Morgan offered and die a happy man.

Morgan watched Nick intently as he bound first one wrist and then the other to slats in the headboard with his own neckties.

The bindings weren't that tight, but that wasn't the point, and Nick knew he could free himself. His throat went dry anyway.

Morgan leaned in and kissed Nick tenderly on the forehead, then down one cheek and over to his lips. Nick was already breathing faster just from the anticipation. He closed his eyes, reveling in the kiss. When he opened then, he saw the tie in Morgan's hands.

"I'm going to blindfold you. I want you to react, not anticipate. I'll control what you feel, and that's all I want you to do, just feel," Morgan said.

Nick nodded as Morgan covered his eyes. "Don't be nervous. I'll be right here, and I won't leave you. Even if I don't say anything, I'm still here. Do you have any questions?"

"This… wow, this is heavy," Nick said, suddenly nervous, even a little scared.

"No, I'm not into heavy, just a little fun to heighten the sensations," Morgan said. "I don't like the heavy stuff, just fantasy and control. No gags, no safe words, no real restraints."

"Have you ever done that?" Nick said, wondering at this new side of Morgan.

Morgan nodded. "Just once. It was enough to know I didn't need to do it again. Once a philosopher, twice a pervert and all that. Now hush, no more words."

Nick lay there, his hands by his head, his eyes covered with a blindfold that was soft against his skin.

"Relax," Morgan whispered from near one ear. "You're not in control for once. Let go, and let me make you feel good. Do that for me. For us."

And suddenly, Nick found himself wanting to let go, just a bit. He nodded.

"Good," Morgan said.

At first, Morgan just touched Nick. Starting at his pecs, Morgan's fingers caressed his body down to his feet, just rubbing and smoothing Nick's skin. "You are so beautiful," Morgan whispered. "The more I see, the hotter you look."

Morgan carefully avoided Nick's cock, still hard from the blowjob, but even so, Nick grew even more aroused, and his cock started to buck.

Morgan chuckled a little. "See? It knows what it likes, even if you're unsure," he said. Then he pulled his hands back, waiting.

But before Nick could wonder too long what would happen next, Morgan was back, breathing a trail across his body, hot breath that raised goose bumps and shivers as Morgan moved above him. Sometimes the breath was gentle, nothing more than an exhalation, just enough to stir the hair on Nick's body. Sometimes the breath was focused, making the muscles ripple under Nick's jaw as Morgan worked his way up and down his lover's body.

"How did I get so lucky, having such a pretty, pretty toy to play with?" Morgan said before pulling back again, and then Nick gasped as Morgan nipped the sensitive skin inside his thighs, making his hard dick jump and dance. But just as quickly as the bite had come, Morgan soothed it with lips and tongue, leaving behind warmth that quickly cooled before moving on. Nip, kiss, lick, all over Nick's body, and it left him shaking with need.

"Oooh," Nick breathed as Morgan trailed the narrow end of another silken necktie across one nipple. It hardened instantly as Morgan traced Nick's name over it, the silk fabric of the tie now an exquisite torture. When Nick's breath came in short gasps, Morgan licked the nipple lazily, again changing the stimulus.

When Nick could do nothing but shake, Morgan decided it was time. Reaching into Nick's nightstand, Morgan pulled out the condoms and lube. He eased a generous amount of lube inside himself, and then again. It felt good, but it was like artificial sweetener: a poor substitute for the real deal.

"Are you ready?" Morgan asked Nick.

"Uh-huh," Nick rasped.

Morgan tipped the bottle of lube over Nick's cock and slowly allowed one, two, three drops to fall on the head. Then he rolled the condom down the shaft, giving it a few light strokes.

"Yeah, do that, again," Nick said.

"I've got something better," Morgan said. He climbed over Nick, slowly lowering himself down to Nick's waiting cock. He reached down and guided Nick in until the head just poked into his channel, resting on his knees, facing Nick in the cowboy position.

Morgan paused there, just feeling. He breathed deeply, willing his muscle to relax and let Nick in. He felt Nick straining beneath him but waiting for Morgan to take the lead. The initial stretch shot a red lance of pain through him, but it faded quickly, replaced by a lingering warmth and heat.

With a sigh and a shiver, Morgan slowly lowered himself down, inch by delicious inch. The movement of Nick's hard cock past his muscle and up the chute made Morgan gasp. He closed his eyes and rode the wave of pleasure that rippled out from his entrance as Nick stretched and filled him and passed over his gland.

The fullness made Morgan sigh, quite apart from the pleasure of the fucking itself. Holding his lover inside him was something special, and that feeling of closeness combined with the emotions Nick raised in him made him feel like nothing and no one ever had.

Morgan looked down at Nick and smiled at the sight of his lover stretched out beneath him. Nick strained against the silk ties binding his hands, just enough to provide some tension. He bucked slightly under Morgan. "Please," he begged.

"Soon," Morgan whispered, cherishing the sight. Nick might be the top, but Morgan was firmly in charge, pinning him to the bed with his body, dominance through submission. He knew he could make Nick cum just by sitting there and rocking his pelvis slightly, but that would deprive them both. Nick was heading for paradise, and Morgan guided the way. He was the bottom, but he called the shots.

Slowly, Morgan raised himself up, enjoying the slide, letting all thought leave him. Then, just as slowly, he dropped down, fucking himself on Nick.

On the next stroke, Nick took over, thrusting in and out with a flick of his hips, and Morgan let him. He cried out wordlessly as Nick gave him what they both wanted. Nick filled him and then pulled back, almost out, leaving him empty and wanting, only to ram his cock home again.

Morgan rested on his knees, head thrown back as Nick fucked him, in and out, empty and full. Nick's hands were bound, and Morgan didn't touch himself. He'd pop too quickly. He wanted this to be all Nick.

He stroked Nick's chest, grooving on the muscles flexing and straining beneath him. When Morgan touched Nick's nipples, Nick shook his head. "No… I'll cum too soon. You're… incredible."

Then Morgan grinned and clenched his muscles, clamping down on Nick as he fucked him. Through his own rising climax, Morgan managed to time it just right, tightening up as Nick thrust up and in, relaxing slightly as he pulled back and down.

Each time Nick thrust into him, he nailed his prostate, and the light of a thousand ecstatic suns exploded in Morgan's mind. "Nick!"

"Wanna… wanna see you," Nick panted.

Morgan pulled the blindfold off, and Nick stared up at him with eyes wide and dark, almost gone in pleasure.

"So close," Nick breathed, looking into his eyes. "So… beautiful."

That was all it took, and with Nick's next thrust, Morgan's orgasm ripped out of him. "Nick!" he gasped, shooting his load up Nick's chest, coating his pecs.

"Oh… oh… oh, my God!" Nick grunted, and he came, his vision narrowed. All he could see was Morgan's face, and all he knew was that he'd brought Morgan off without touching his cock.

"You saw him too?" Morgan murmured, still riding Nick's wave. He leaned forward and kissed Nick, untying his hands at the same time.

Nick wrapped his arms around Morgan, holding him tight, pulling him down. Morgan wriggled his arms under Nick, holding on tight, heedless of his own load cooling between them.

"You… I… that was…," Nick struggled to say.

"Told you," Morgan gloated. "Told you I'd make you lose the power of speech."

Nick just held him tighter. He breathed in deeply, taking in Morgan's scent. His chest tightened. He could fall so hard. Was falling.

Morgan smiled and closed his eyes. Nick was still inside him, still hard, and he was secure.

Nick sought out Morgan's mouth. He kissed him slowly, leisurely. There was no hurry now, no urgency.

"You were right," Nick whispered. "I couldn't even remember my own name, but I never forgot yours."

Morgan smiled and pulled himself up. He wiped himself off Nick and then cleaned himself up while Nick dealt with the condom.

They spent another lazy hour holding each other before Morgan made Nick breakfast. After that, they dressed, and then both had homework demanding attention. Before they knew it, the day had passed, and it was time for them to part company.

Chapter
ELEVEN

AMONG all the coaches at the CalPac boathouse, Nick drew the short straw and so again drove the powerful but slow truck carrying the boat trailer up to Lake Natoma for the Western Intercollegiate Rowing Association's spring regatta. Once again, Nick was grateful that CalPac was so close to one of the best courses in the west. The WIRAs were a huge competition, drawing crews from all over the western United States, and since they were held a few weeks before the Pacific Coast Rowing Championships, Nick thought it a good gauge for his team's progress. Drew thought it was a good reason to get out of town for the day and so joined him.

"It is always this windy for this race?" Drew asked as another gust buffeted truck and trailer.

"No, this is something special they've dialed up for us," Nick said, hands steady on the wheel. "The course is one of the best in the country. The lake's behind a dam, and the dam operators are very obliging about adjusting the water level for races, but the wind? Nothing they can do about it. The course runs mostly east to west, but the winds'll be out of the north or south. The crews'll just have to cope."

"But they'll still be wearing Spandex, right?"

Nick just shook his head. "Yes, and since they launch by wading out into the lake—there's no dock—you'll get to see more leg than usual."

"Then I'm good."

They puttered along in the interstate's slow lane, waving in response to the occasional honk from cars or vans transporting other crews to the race.

"Let me know if you spot the CalPac vanpool," Nick said as they pulled into the state park that held Lake Natoma. "The crews should be here by now."

"So that's where Morgan is," Drew said, eyeing Nick.

"We thought it'd be too obvious if he suddenly started driving everywhere with me," Nick said. He avoided the little voice at the back of his mind that suggested that hiding like this just perpetuated the lie. "Besides, he has some studying to do and figures he can get more done in the van than in here."

Drew laughed. "Remember when we studied in front of the television? Some things never change."

"Now it's all I can do to read in a quiet apartment or library," Nick muttered.

"You're getting old," Drew said helpfully.

"We're the same age, you know."

"Yeah, but I was smart enough not to go back to school." Then Drew smiled. "You two can't keep your hands off each other, can you? I bet that's the real reason."

Nick glared at his friend. "I'd like to think I'm professional enough not to molest my boyfriend at a regatta, and that he's a serious enough athlete not to be distracted by my mere presence."

"A hit! A very palpable hit!" Drew cackled.

"Thank God we're here. Why I ever thought you were good company, I'll never know," Nick muttered good-naturedly.

Drew just laughed.

No sooner had Nick turned off the engine than Stuart and the coxswains from the other crews descended on the trailer and started barking orders like the diminutive drill sergeants they were.

Nick ignored them. They knew their jobs and how to get the rowers to do theirs. Now it was time to do his. He picked up his battered briefcase and got out of the truck. "Come on," he said to Drew, "you can help me check in."

Drew, who'd been more interested in checking out the eye-candy, said, "Do you actually need help checking in?"

"Not really, but if Stuart catches you lazing about, he'll put you to work. Idleness at a regatta offends him, for some reason."

"He wouldn't," Drew said. Then he looked at where Stuart had his rowers swarming over the trailer like monkeys. "Would he?"

"Do you really want to find out? C'mon, I need to check in and find out where we're supposed to put our boats. If I make Stuart wait, he'll make me regret it, I'm sure," Nick said.

"You're not actually afraid of him, are you?"

"Do I have to answer that?" Nick said.

"Did you just whine?" Drew said.

Nick didn't reply as he led Drew off to the pavilion housing the race officials to check in, submit his athletes' waivers, and, of course, find out where to berth their shells.

After checking in, Nick headed off to tell his rowers where to go, leaving Drew to trail along behind him. He was clearly in his coaching headspace and left Drew to his own devices. Drew didn't mind. He'd been to many regattas and didn't need anyone to hold his hand, although there were a few specimens of collegiate manhood roaming the venue Drew wouldn't have shot down if they tried.

Drew also didn't feel like re-rigging the racing shells, and despite Nick's assessment of Stuart as a martinet, Drew would've felt guilty for not helping the guys out. He knew enough to help but wasn't experienced enough to work at a reasonable pace. If they really needed him, Nick would ask, and otherwise he'd only be in the way.

So Drew just wandered through the race venue, enjoying the sights. There were so many things to see at a collegiate regatta, but mostly the acres and acres of man flesh, and all of it wearing Spandex.

It was good to be Drew that day, and he was glad he wore dark sunglasses.

But while the regatta afforded many opportunities to see beef on the hoof, Drew kept watching Nick's rowers as they re-rigged their boats and then warmed up before their races. He ignored the junior varsity squad because most of them looked like they'd barely cleared puberty. But one of the varsity rowers caught his eye and held it, and this guy looked like he'd started shaving in grade school. Drew liked that.

So he watched the CalPac men warm up for a while but mostly stared at the big lug. He'd long ago perfected the art of looking in one direction while staring in another, tangential direction out of the corner of his eye. He'd hit puberty late and hadn't really bulked up until college, and this was how he avoided getting the snot beaten out of him on a regular basis.

"So who're you looking at?" Nick asked, settling in beside him on a bench.

"That double handful of big mook you've got on your team," Drew said.

Nick frowned, trying to think of who that described. "Brad Sundstrom?" he yelped.

"Could you be a little louder?" Drew hissed. "I think he almost heard you."

"That guy there, the one carrying four oars at a time?" Nick said, more quietly this time.

Drew allowed himself to look openly. "Yep, that's the one. See how nicely his muscles bulge when he lifts heavy things?"

"He looks like that all the time," Nick sighed. "I think he must live at the gym when he's not at the boathouse. I kind of wish he wouldn't. All the muscle isn't light, and there are ways to build strength without all that bulk."

"Who asked you, Coach Comedown? Let me live in my dream world, will you?" Drew said.

"Enjoy the view, but don't get your hopes up. He's straight as an arrow. Also, he's kind of dim," Nick said, grinning spitefully at his friend.

"I'm not daydreaming about the conversational possibilities, thank you very much," Drew said. He made a show of checking his watch. "Shouldn't you be delivering some kind of inspiring pre-race talk or something?"

Chuckling, Nick stood up. "Yeah, probably, since communication is one of the things I harp on. They've all heard it before, but it seems to make them happy. Or maybe it gives voice to their anxieties and allows them to focus on the race if I remind them of their training and skills."

Nick took his leave to give his pep talk while Drew enjoyed the view. Then he shivered, suddenly cold, and he went to the truck to get his windbreaker.

NICK stood on the shore, lips pressed tightly in a grim line. A cold wind blew right in his face, heavy with the smell of coming rain. Storms were rare this late in the spring, but not unheard of, and despite sunny forecasts, the weather had turned to crap in the middle of the regatta.

"Why don't you wait in the truck? There's no sense in us both being cold and wet," Nick said to Drew, who huddled next to him, hunched over in his windbreaker.

"I've never been a fair-weather friend, and I won't start now. Besides, when your boys come off the water, they're going to need all the help they can get," Drew said.

Nick nodded, knowing Drew was right. His crew was out practicing, but they'd be starting soon. The wind came from just the wrong direction, enough of a headwind to make rowing hard, enough of a crosswind to make it very unpleasant on top of that. Add to that the fat drops of rain already spitting out of the sky, and it was going to be a death-race to the finish line. Even Drew could tell that the crews presently racing were struggling.

"Won't this wind make it hard to row?" Drew asked.

"It'll make the whole thing hellish, from lining up at the start to getting the boat out of the water," Nick said. "Stuart's going to have his hands full. The boats line up along a starting platform, and they all have to be aligned in their lancs before the race can start. If he gets there too soon, the rowers will get cold. If he gets there too late, they'll be rushed and may panic. It'll take constant adjustment and work on his part, and if he loses his cool, the rowers'll lose theirs."

Drew nodded in understanding. "But if he keeps his cool, the rowers will keep theirs too, right?"

"We can only hope," Nick said, checking his watch. He held up a pair of binoculars. "They're entering the starting area. Lane three," he said, handing the binoculars to Drew.

"Is that a good one?" Drew asked hopefully, looking at the CalPac Crew, searching out Brad in the six-seat. The hulking oarsman slowly pulled on his oar in response to a command by Stuart.

Nick shrugged. "It's no worse than any of them. The course is pretty exposed."

Loudspeakers in the observation area, along with a Jumbotron monitor, brought the action right to them, although Nick preferred to use his binoculars, even if he had to wipe rain off the lenses with increasing frequency.

The six boats sat in their lanes, with the rowers at the ready, the blades of their oars in the water, their legs coiled and ready to propel the oars through the water and crank the boats into motion.

Even as a gust of wind blasted across the course, hands from the boats shot up. While some of the smaller boats had bow-seated coxswains, the bigger eights were exclusively steered from the stern, so Stuart sat in the rear of the boat, face-to-face with the rower in the pace-setting stroke seat. His hand was in the air as he commanded the pair of rowers in the bow to adjust the shell's position with minute movements of their oars. Other coxswains and rowers did likewise in their own shells.

"We have alignment. No hands will be recognized," came the starter's voice over the loudspeaker.

Drew watched on the monitor and Nick through his field glasses, and even before the race started, the rowers looked miserable.

"Three... two... one! Go!"

And the rowers commenced their fight, for a struggle against the elements it was, as the crews fought for each stroke against wind and rain.

The race was two thousand meters, and the crews clawed for every meter of water. While Stuart and his rowers started in the head of the pack, they soon fell behind, and by the halfway point merely battled to stay out of last place. Even if Stuart alone could see the course, the rowers sensed the boats passing them by.

By the time the CalPac Crew passed the fifteen hundred-meter mark, they were clearly visible without need of binoculars or monitors. The cold turned their skin red, and rain soaked their unis and slicked their hair. They were a portrait of misery.

Nick's lips were pressed even tighter, and even Drew could tell something wasn't right in the shell. "Nick...?" Drew said.

"They've given up. The wind and the chop and the rain, and they just gave up."

"It's gotta be hard going today," Drew said, trying to defend Nick's boys against his words.

Nick shook his head angrily. "Of course it's hard. We don't always get flat water. What're they going to do, go belly up every time there's a breeze? That's bullshit."

They watched the final moments of the race in silence as the CalPac Crew limped across the finish line in fifth place.

They paddled out beyond the finish line for a minute or two. Then Stuart called, "Weigh enough!" the traditional call to stop rowing, and the eight rowers dropped their oar blades flat on the water in disgust.

Brad at six-seat flopped back, sides heaving, only to struggle up and lean over the gunwales. Drew flinched as he puked his guts out.

Behind him, Morgan sought out Nick's eyes and mouthed, "I'm sorry." Nick just nodded and then turned his head.

When Brad had finished, Stuart called them up again, and they slowly paddled to shore. Just as they weighed enough, the skies opened up and the deluge started in earnest.

Nick toed off his shoes and then stripped his pants off to reveal his own racing shorts. He waded out to steady the boat as his athletes struggled to get out of the shell. He had a few things to say, but not just then.

Drew watched Nick and then took one look at Brad. He kicked off his designer track shoes and rolled up the legs of his expensive jeans as far as he could and then waded out into the frigid water. He took oars from rowers so dazed with fatigue and lactic acid they barely nodded their thanks.

Drew held six oars in his arms, sticking out every which way, and tried to make his way back to the shore. But the oars were twelve feet long, and he didn't have the knack of carrying them. The rain also made the sleek shafts very slippery, and he struggled not to drop the entire mess.

Brad looked up and sighed. He jogged up the beach after Drew to help. "You don't have to do that," he rasped.

Drew gulped. "I want to."

"Yeah, but you suck at it," Brad said. He took the oars from Drew and leaned them up against a picnic table to get them out of the way while they pulled the boat out of the water. Other crews waited to launch, and they had to hustle.

Tongue-tied, Drew didn't say anything. *I want to*, he thought, watching the giant trudge back to the boat through the rain.

Brad turned around. "Hey… thanks for trying."

Drew shrugged, smiling shyly.

Back at the boat, Nick helped Stuart guide the boat up and out of the water. "Get it de-rigged and on the trailer, and then get warm and dry. We'll go over the race later, but I think we've all got things to say."

The rowers moved to obey, but slowly. No one was really happy, least of all Nick, who was torn between ripping into his rowers for letting the conditions throw them and rushing over to Morgan with a blanket, a towel, and hot cocoa.

Even as the rowers disassembled their shell, the rain tapered off, the late-spring storm ending as quickly as it had begun, leaving only wind and cold, wet oarsmen in its wake.

NICK slammed the truck's door closed and started the engine. Even before he pulled his hand back from the ignition, Drew reached over and cranked the heat up as high as it could go. "Thank you," Nick said through chattering teeth.

"You did very well back there," Drew said, rubbing his arms vigorously. Nick looked at him, and he continued, "You wanted to rip those boys new ones, and you held it in."

"You don't know that," Nick protested.

"Please. It'll probably make your face break out later, but you kept it in check."

Nick snorted. "Barely. But if I start in on it now I'll never shut up, and I think you've about hit the saturation point for rowing babble."

"Good, let's talk about me," Drew said. Nick looked at him askance, a look Drew returned with wide-eyed innocence. "You said he was a big jerk, but he seems nice."

"Give it up, sugartushy," Nick laughed.

"I'd sure like to," Drew muttered. "Damn. Just… damn."

"Brad doesn't bat for our team. And he's kind of a pain in the ass."

Drew brightened, but Nick added, "Not that way."

"Killjoy. You got a rower. I don't see why I can't have one." Drew slouched in his seat.

"Because he's straight," Nick repeated.

"Do you know that for a fact?" Drew countered.

"Well… no, but he's only ever bragged about 'banging chicks', I believe is how he puts it. Besides, Morgan would've said something if he'd ever batted for the other side," Nick said.

"Neither you nor Morgan are out, so why assume Brad would be?" Drew countered.

Nick blinked. "Brad's never indicated differently."

"That doesn't mean a thing, and you know it, and that means there's hope," Drew said rebelliously.

"Yeah, and it was the last thing left in the box before Pandora slammed the lid back down," Nick said, "so don't get your hopes up."

"Pandora?" Drew asked, one eyebrow arched.

"I took a classics class once." Nick hunched his shoulders defensively like he always did when Drew teased him about his intellectual side. "I just don't want to see you get hurt, okay?"

"I know you don't, but I'm a big boy," Drew said.

"That's not how I remember it," Nick snickered.

"Bitch. This is the thanks I get for listening to all your whining about Morgan?" Drew said. A few minutes later, "So how's the sex?" Drew asked.

Nick grinned. "Unbelievable."

"Best ever?"

"Best ever," Nick said, his blush obvious even in the quirky light of the dashboard.

"So have you fucked him over a boat yet?"

"Drew!"

Drew was quiet for a moment. "Has he fucked you over a boat yet?"

"We are so not talking about this," Nick said, switching the radio on and tuning into the alt-rock station. They drove in silence for a while; then Garbage's "#1 Crush" came on.

See your face every place I that I walk in. Hear your voice every time that I'm talking....

The confession of love and desperate obsession, the willingness to do anything to stay together, the low, near-orgasmic moans, all of it hit Nick right between the eyes.

"That's it," Nick breathed, and it was. He knew it was true. Thinking about it later, he was lucky he didn't drive the truck and trailer off into a ditch. But it was true. That was how he felt, that and more. Stumbling blindly, he'd landed in love. He loved Morgan. He smiled, and it suffused his face with radiance. "I love him, Drew. So… this is what it is. I never knew."

"I'm happy for you, Nick. You deserve this," Drew said, putting his hand on Nick's knee.

Nick smiled at him, all talk of Brad forgotten.

Chapter
TWELVE

LIFE and school continued after the disappointing performance at the WIRAs. Coach Bedford, as Morgan tried to think of him in reference to rowing, had said a few choice things, but the last stroke—and race—was history. Learn from it, move on, and Morgan sure as heck did so. On some level, he knew the Pacific Coast Rowing Championships, the PCRCs themselves, were just around the corner, but his coursework demanded his attention in the form of a major term paper.

So late on the Wednesday after the WIRAs, Morgan and Stuart stuck a match to the midnight oil lamp to light up the night. "You're going to have to remind me what you're writing on," Stuart said, rubbing his eyes.

"I'm comparing the notion of the quest in *Don Quixote*, *Candide*, and *Robinson Crusoe*," Morgan said, eyeing the tarry remnants in the coffee maker with suspicion before dumping the sorry mess in the trash and starting over. "My thesis is—"

Stuart waved his hand in the air. "Yeah, yeah, whatever. If I can't tell what you're arguing from reading it, then you're in trouble. So where is this masterpiece of comparative literature?"

"On my laptop."

"'On my laptop,' he says," Stuart muttered. "Like my eyes aren't tired enough as it is."

Stuart dragged Morgan's computer over to him and started reading. "Uh… Morgan? This doesn't look like your paper. It's a spreadsheet."

"Huh?" Morgan poked his head around the corner from the kitchen. "What's on it?"

"Looks like schools, but I didn't know you were thinking of going into physical therapy. That's kind of a stretch from comp lit."

Morgan sat down and took the computer back from Stuart and looked at the document in question. "I'm not." Morgan looked at the result of his searches in the school's career center. He planned to enroll in programs that would allow him to earn a master's degree along with a teaching credential.

But driven by some itch, he'd been spending time at the career center again. He told himself it was just idle curiosity, but he'd started researching which schools that had MA/credentialing programs also boasted PT programs. He'd also created a list of institutions with PT programs within twenty-five miles of schools he planned to apply to.

"Morgan?" Stuart prodded him.

"I'm not interested in physical therapy, but Nick is," Morgan said quietly. "It's his back-up plan if coaching ever goes blooey. In any event, it'd be a logical extension of his current graduate work."

Stuart sat back and looked at his roommate. He could usually read Morgan well enough, but right then, Morgan was closed up tight. "So what's this mean?"

"I guess I'm planning for the future, a future with Nick," Morgan said.

"Do you love him?" Stuart asked softly.

Morgan thought about Stuart's question. It was one he'd asked himself too. "I don't know," he said with a frown. "I like Nick. I like him a lot. I like being with him."

"But do you love him?" Stuart pressed.

"I don't know," Morgan said with some irritation. "I just said that. I don't know. I find myself wanting to be a better person when I'm around him." He paused, thinking harder. "I like myself better when I'm with him, too. It sounds funny when I say that out loud, but it's true."

Stuart didn't say anything, waiting for Morgan to keep talking. Morgan thought about it more. He gestured towards his laptop. "I'd even sacrifice my own happiness for his. Not all credentialing programs are created equal, but I'd go to a worse one if Nick needed to go to a PT program there." He looked at Stuart. "So tell me. Is this love?"

"I wish I knew," Stuart said. He gestured to his textbooks. "The answer's not in here, I know that much." He touched his chest. "It's in here, but only you can answer it."

"I wish I knew too, because Nick's amazing. He's everything I thought I wanted, but jeez, Stuart, I'm only twenty-one. What do I know about it?" Morgan said.

Stuart shrugged, but, lost in his own thoughts, Morgan didn't notice. He hadn't contemplated his relationship with Nick to any great extent, content to take things as they came. But at some point, he had stopped thinking of the future in terms of "I" and started to use "we." But he didn't know if that meant love. He just wished he could be sure. In a few short weeks, they'd be done for the summer, and some of the pressure would be off, since they wouldn't have to hide as much. But Morgan had another year of school, another year of Nick as his coach. Was what he felt strong enough to complicate his senior year and jeopardize Nick's career?

AFTER what he considered a disastrous and unacceptable performance at the WIRA races, Nick took to kicking up a nasty wake in front of the boat. He called it the WIRA drill. The rowers found it rough going, but it taught them to keep it together despite the chop. At least, that was the theory. Nick didn't care. He had a job to do, and if generating choppy water was what it took, he was happy to do it. His rowers had already taken to calling it the Maytag drill, because it felt like they were in a washing machine.

Friday morning after practice, Nick took his time cleaning up. He had a class to teach, but not until later, and a lab of his own that afternoon, and a lot of the equipment needed his attention. So he planned a leisurely morning at the boathouse, letting his hands follow well-worn pathways and freeing his mind to think about Morgan. Since his realization about what he felt for Morgan after the regatta, thinking about Morgan invariably provoked considerable anxiety.

They hadn't seen much of each other outside of practice lately, and practice hardly counted. That produced in Nick a peculiar feeling of restlessness. He'd had a major realization about his feelings for his boyfriend, and he longed to share it, even as the thought scared the piss out of him. What if Morgan didn't feel it too?

Nick didn't get very far with his plans for the morning, however. He looked up as Morgan came back into the boathouse, still dressed in his workout clothes. "Hey," Morgan said, his voice loud in the now-deserted boathouse.

"Oh, hey," Nick said, looking up from the rigging he'd been adjusting. "I was just thinking about you."

"Yeah? Good thoughts, I hope," Morgan said. He walked across the boathouse to Nick, stopping right in front of him.

Nick smiled. "Only good thoughts," he said, figuring that spilling his guts about his nervous insecurity or blurting out declarations of love wouldn't be a good look.

"Cool," Morgan said, smiling back.

They smiled at each other for a moment and then both started laughing.

"I'm glad you're here. We haven't seen much of each other outside the boathouse lately, have we?" Nick said. "And here we are… in the boathouse."

"I know, end of the semester stuff," Morgan said. "I'm really sorry."

"Hey, you're a student, that's why you're here," Nick said. He smiled again. He just couldn't help it.

"No, I'm here because I've got some free time—no classes at all today—and I want to see my boyfriend," Morgan said, putting his arms around Nick.

"Boyfriend. I like the sound of that," Nick said. *The man I love. I like the sound of that even better… but if he doesn't love me back….* He left the rest unthought. "You want to help me with some of this? It'll go faster, and then I can goof off for a while."

"Or you could just goof off," Morgan suggested. He pulled Nick in close and kissed him.

"In theory, but here, in the boathouse, when the rigging needs to be checked, I probably can't, not and give you my full attention. I'll be thinking about what I need to get done," Nick admitted. Worrying about whether or not Morgan might love him back made him edgy enough, but physical displays of affection in the boathouse… he just wasn't sure about that yet. He hoped Morgan hadn't caught on to his edginess.

"That makes you a really good coach and kind of a lousy boyfriend," Morgan laughed, but when he saw Nick's face fall, he said, "I'm kidding. I just miss you is all."

"I miss you too," Nick said, quirking a smile. He swallowed, trying to stifle budding panic.

They puttered around on the varsity crew's primary racing shell, Morgan handing Nick tools and Nick making minute adjustments to the oarlocks, his discomfort at not speaking up turning to dread and his dread growing with each passing moment. "I…," Nick started, then stopped.

"Yeah?"

"Uh… can you hand me that level? I need to check the pitch on this oarlock," Nick said.

Morgan gave him a funny look but handed the small level over.

Nick made a show of the adjustments, looked up to find Morgan watching him, and then gulped.

"Is everything all right? You're kind of antsy today," Morgan said.

"I… uh… yeah, everything's fine," Nick said, kicking himself mentally for his cowardice.

Morgan gave him a skeptical look but let it slide.

Nick fussed at something that didn't need it for another moment, berating himself for his nerves and cowardice. "I… that's not true, there is something I want to tell you. It's just difficult."

"Then let's go sit down somewhere," Morgan said, swallowing. "The water looks peaceful. How about the dock?"

They walked in silence down to the dock. It had dried since practice ended, and they kicked off their shoes and sat at the end of it, dangling their legs in the water.

Nick looked at Morgan and smiled nervously. He flushed and looked away. "I've got something I want to tell you, but it's hard for me. I… it's just hard."

Morgan took his hand and held it, waiting as patiently as he could. He was dying to know what was eating Nick. He didn't think he was about to be dumped. Nick had been too happy to see him, smiled too genuinely, to be working on growing a set just to dump him.

Nick inhaled and exhaled noisily. "We've been spending a lot of time together lately… okay, not lately, but you know what I mean. The time with you has become really special to me, and I…." He swallowed the lump in his throat. "I've come… I, uh—" He started to speak and then stopped again. He took Morgan's hand. "It's hard for me to say this. I've never said it to anyone, and I'm a little afraid of it, but I love you."

"Oh," Morgan said softly. He was touched. Touched, and a little scared. No one had ever told him that before. He sat back, hand still in Nick's. He took a deep breath. "I… I don't know if I can say the same right now."

"I…," Nick said. He'd half expected this. He breathed deeply, cramming his disappointment down, trying to keep it from crushing him. Morgan was in many ways mature beyond his years, but he was still young and inexperienced in some ways. "That's okay. You don't have to say it back if you don't mean it or if you don't feel it. But I feel it, and I wanted you to know."

"It's not that I don't feel it, Nick," Morgan said quickly, genuinely sick at heart at not being able to say it back. "It's that I don't know if what I feel for you is love or not. I like you a lot, I feel more strongly about you than anyone else I've ever been with, hands down. I want to be with you. I want to keep seeing you, see where this goes. I just hope you can be patient."

"I'll wait as long as I have to," Nick said. It stung, but what could he do? It didn't count if he had to force Morgan to say the words back.

"Thanks," Morgan said. "I hope I'm worth it."

"Oh, you're worth it," Nick said. "You're worth it."

"Something kind of funny happened the other day," Morgan said. He could see the hurt Nick tried not to show and was desperate to salvage the situation. "Stuart saw a spreadsheet I made of the teaching credential programs I plan to apply for. I correlated them with a list of PT programs."

"Really? That's cool," Nick said. Hearing that helped. Morgan might not know whether he loved him or not, but he was obviously thinking of the future.

Morgan looked at Nick for a moment, chewing his lip. "Can I ask? How'd you know? That you love me, I mean."

Nick explained "#1 Crush" and how it had hit him right between the eyes. "We should rent the movie it's from this weekend, *Romeo + Juliet*."

"Celebrate new love with doomed love?" Morgan said. "Sure, why not?"

New love. He'd said "new love." Nick kissed Morgan again, chastely at first, but with growing heat. They both realized more or less simultaneously that it'd been too long.

"Are we going to?" Morgan breathed.

"I sure hope so," Nick said, calculating whose apartment was closer. "Where?"

Morgan pulled back, grinning. "The locker room."

"We can't!" Nick gasped, shaking his head. "You're insane."

Morgan nodded, his eyes dancing. "We can."

Nick shook his head again, but Morgan could tell he was weakening, perhaps because of the hand working at the growing bulge in his pants. "We shouldn't."

"We're going to," Morgan said, his voice throaty. He grabbed Nick's hand and pulled him up.

"When did you get all alpha male?" Nick said.

"I've always been one," Morgan said, his lip curling. "You just haven't been paying attention."

Nick had a decision to make. He could pull back and demand they go someplace private, or he could go for it. He didn't want to pull back. He didn't want the lie to win, and if he refused to kiss Morgan publicly, it would. He grabbed onto Morgan, grinding against him. "I like the sound of that. Are you going to dominate me?"

"Do you want me to?" Morgan asked, even as he pushed Nick up against the outside wall of the boathouse.

"Uh-huh," Nick gasped, hoping he didn't sound whiney and needy, because that was sure how he felt. Morgan's tongue and teeth on his ear short-circuited his brain, so he couldn't be sure.

They ground against each other, cock to cock, separated from each other by only a few layers of fabric. As he had the second time they'd fucked, Morgan took an aggressive lead, and Nick wondered with the tiny part of his mind still capable of thought if he'd be giving it up. He sure hoped Morgan had condoms.

Nick broke off. "Now?"

"Now," Morgan agreed, and he pushed Nick ahead of him as they ran for the locker room.

BRAD SUNDSTROM parked his car in the lot in front of the boathouse. It was an older Lexus that had belonged to his mother. It was also a wreck, at least on the inside: a rat's nest of fast-food wrappers and dirty workout clothes he kept meaning to wash but never managed to remember to bring inside, let alone get anywhere near the washing machine. He didn't care. Like virtually everything else in his life, his older brother had gotten it first. In Brad's whole life, he'd never had one thing that was his, just his. Until crew. He was big, but too awkward for basketball and too prone to injuries to handle the pounding of football. But with crew, all the big, awkward parts came together into a powerful whole that moved boats, made the numbers on an erg's monitor drop like rocks, and finally won him some attention from his old man.

Then Morgan Estrada had waltzed into the boathouse. At first, he was barely on Brad's radar. Then he beat Seth Settlemeyer, who promptly quit the team in shame. Or maybe he just preferred to concentrate on beer. Brad didn't really care. Settlemeyer had bored him. But then he noticed Estrada's erg scores. They were getting faster, and they were approaching his.

Suddenly Brad had to work on his game like he'd never had to. It wasn't enough to pull an oar through the water. He actually had to have some technique behind it; he had to pull on that erg handle for all he was worth, and his dad had made it pretty clear that was all he was worth. Even though he wasn't much of a thinker, it still kind of hurt, just as it had the first time Morgan beat him on an erg test, an indoor-rowing contest.

Brad hadn't told his dad about it, but somehow he'd found out anyway, probably by looking up the scores on the Internet. The race organizers posted the scores, so it couldn't have taken much effort, but Mr. Sundstrom didn't usually take much effort where Brad was concerned to begin with.

Well, that certainly didn't take long, Bradley. Brad could still hear the tired tone of inevitability (he'd once heard the phrase, and it fit, so he remembered it) in his dad's voice.

Even before he knew it, Brad had sworn he'd get that top score and his father's respect back both. Sometimes he wondered why he bothered, and why it bothered him that his only value to his father was in relation to someone else.

But bother Brad it did, so down to the boathouse he slogged whenever he had a spare moment. Since he was a PE major, he had a number of those, and he spent them at the boathouse on the erg or on the weight equipment. Longer endurance pieces, shorter pieces to develop power, and weights to increase brute strength. He was going to recapture that top spot if it was the last thing he did.

That the boathouse was open wasn't unusual. He could see the open door from the lot. That just meant that one of the other guys was there, or that Coach Bedford was working on something, or both. In fact, that might've been Estrada's car in the lot next to Coach Bedford's old beater.

Brad paused in the doorway just as Coach Bedford hurried by, Morgan Estrada in hot pursuit. They ran into the locker room.

Brad stood there, mouth agape. Coach Bedford. Morgan Estrada. It didn't take a genius to figure out what they'd been doing. Or what they were about to do. Suddenly all the little hints clicked into place. He nodded slowly. Now he understood.

Brad returned to his car. He sat there for what felt like a long time, thinking. *Who knew Coach Bedford liked cock?*

Brad's thoughts turned in on themselves, running in circles. He couldn't have cared less that Coach was apparently gay. Coaches and athletes weren't supposed to be involved with each other, and Brad was pretty sure that whatever was going on in the locker room counted. There had to be some way to turn this to his advantage, some way to spike Morgan's wheel.

Brad started his car and drove back to his apartment.

MOTION sensors turned the locker-room lights on as soon as they entered, and Nick turned to face Morgan, the lockers at his back, aroused by and a little afraid of the beast stalking him. "Do you have supplies?"

"Supplies?" Morgan said, one eyebrow raised.

"You know, condoms and stuff," Nick said. The pressure against his briefs was intolerable. He unbuttoned his pants and slid his hand in, grasping his cock. He couldn't help it. He groaned and closed his eyes.

"No!" Morgan said roughly. In seconds, Morgan was on him. He grabbed Nick's hand, pulling it off. "Mine!"

With that, Morgan grabbed Nick's other hand and shoved him back against the lockers. Nick moaned.

"You like that, huh?" Morgan said. He kissed Nick roughly, nipping his lips, his neck.

"Yeah… uh-huh," Nick moaned. He would never have guessed that inside Morgan's calm exterior lurked this masterful and assertive man, but he liked it and was surprised by the liking. He'd never thought of himself as all that submissive, but he wanted to submit to Morgan. Or maybe love just made the sex hotter.

Morgan's mouth rampaged across Nick's face, kissing and biting him until Nick's head swam. But something finally intruded into Nick's faltering mind: he wasn't doing anything for Morgan.

Wrenching his hands free of his lover's grip, Nick pulled Morgan's T-shirt up. He ran his hands over Morgan's chest, lightly at first, just enough to tease him and to let him know there was more to come. Nick's thumbs found Morgan's nipples as he leaned in to kiss him.

Nick's hands roamed around to Morgan's back as he leaned down to nip and suck at one of Morgan's nips. He pulled off just as Morgan's breath started to grow ragged.

Nick had other ideas. He wouldn't be fucking Morgan from the sound of things, but that didn't mean he couldn't doorbell-ditch at Morgan's back door. Nick's fingers teased Morgan's entrance and danced away just as he started to moan.

Then Nick attacked Morgan's nipples again, sucking, nipping, and licking at one to ease the sting before starting over again on the other one. All the while, his fingers circled Morgan's entrance, stoking his pleasure but never quite seeking entrance.

"Damn," Morgan breathed. "You're driving me insane."

Nick smiled and dropped to his knees. He pressed his face into the hard planes of Morgan's lower abs, kissing and licking.

He ran his hands along Morgan's waist until he found the drawstrings of his shorts. After fumbling for a few infuriating seconds, he settled for jerking the shorts down. "Gotta love Spandex," he breathed.

"Damn," Nick said when he looked down at Morgan's cock, hard as steel and pushing out from under a jockstrap. Precum already pooled at the slit. With one finger, he rubbed the clear fluid around, slicking the head of Morgan's prick.

He paused for a moment, just breathing. The scent of sweat and man and Morgan rising from the pubes behind the jockstrap went straight to Nick's lizard brain and groin, short-circuiting thought. He crushed his face to the jockstrap, inhaling his lover's scent and moaning.

Nick mouthed Morgan through the jockstrap, sucking and chewing and pulling the taste and scent through the fabric even as his fingers sought out Morgan's ass again. He dropped a hand to his own cock, stroking it.

Morgan reached down and pulled the jockstrap down, freeing his cock. Nick stopped fingering him and grabbed his penis, plunging his mouth down over it.

Nick couldn't get enough, greedily sucking and slurping Morgan deeper into his mouth. Pheromones or manstink or the man he loved, Nick didn't care. He lost himself in breathing it in, taking Morgan in as far as he could to get closer to the source.

"Nick…," Morgan panted. "So good."

Nick grinned around Morgan but kept on working his cock with his tongue.

"That's right, suck the cock that's going to fuck you blind."

Nick looked up and saw the hottest sight ever: his lover rising above him. Now he understood what "all his naked glory" meant. Canting his head ever so slightly, he looked up to see Morgan's abs, covered with soft, dark hair. Without stopping the action, he ran his hands up Morgan's sides, thrilling to the feeling of the man beneath them. Above and just out of reach, he saw Morgan's nipples, still red from his earlier attention. The sight of the man lost in pleasure above him made him almost as hard as the thought that it was he, Nick, who made him feel that way.

Then Morgan pulled Nick up and spun him around, pushing him up against the lockers with just enough roughness to be totally hot, for Nick to feel slutty in a good way. With a lascivious grin, Morgan pulled Nick's pants down the rest of the way.

"I do love the sight of a man with his pants around his ankles," Morgan said.

"I'm finding out all kinds of interesting things about you," Nick said.

"Like?"

"That you're an example of why you've got to watch the quiet ones. I'd never have guessed that you had this in you," Nick said, looking over his shoulder.

"What else?" Morgan asked, stroking himself.

"That I love you. That it's true: it finds you when you don't expect it," Nick said, burying his disappointment that he hadn't heard it back.

"Anything else?"

"That I really want you to shut up and fuck me."

"I think that can be arranged, at least the second one," Morgan said. He reached down to caress Nick's ass. "But the first? Not gonna happen. You've got an awesome body, Nick Bedford, and you're going to hear about it."

"You like to talk dirty, don't you?" Nick said.

Morgan knelt down. "You like it too. Admit it."

"With you? Almost anything."

Morgan kissed one ass cheek. "I'll have to remember that." Then he kissed the other. "And I've got something else you may like, something involving my tongue."

"Oh? Ohhhh," Nick moaned as Morgan kissed his way lower. Morgan gently pulled Nick's cheeks apart to reveal his ass, still kissing his way lower.

Nick closed his eyes. It had been a long time since anyone had rimmed him. It took Morgan a few minutes to get the hang of it, and Nick shivered, his cock hardening further as Morgan's stubbled cheeks abraded his tender skin. Nick knew he'd have beard-burn around his hole, but that just made it hotter, somehow.

Morgan licked around Nick's entrance, but leisurely, like a cat taking his time with grooming. He was in no hurry, and the anticipation of where that tongue would lap next only heightened Nick's expectant pleasure.

"That's right, give yourself to me," Morgan said.

Nick groaned, slumping against the lockers. He didn't need to stroke himself. Morgan's ministrations alone made him needy and wanting. Wet, hot pleasure slowly tormented the nerves around his entrance, each one ratcheting him closer to ecstasy. Nick's hole was twitching before Morgan had even circled it once, and—oh! Nick sucked in his breath as Morgan stabbed in and out of his hole, nailing him with his tongue like he was about to with his cock.

Nick had forgotten what it felt like and how it turned his knees to jelly. If Morgan did that too long, he'd have to fuck him over one of the benches, because there'd be no way he'd stay standing. Assuming he didn't come from the rimming alone.

Morgan reached around to stroke Nick lightly, just enough to make Nick shiver. Nick didn't know which to focus on, the front or the back. He just hung there, poised between the rival pleasures as they fought to see which would overwhelm him. "Please," Nick begged, "now."

There was a brief pause while Morgan fumbled behind him, and then fingers cool with something slick probed at his hole.

"Jeez, you're tight," Morgan breathed. "Are you sure this is okay? I don't want to hurt you."

"You can't hurt me," Nick said, arching his back to give Morgan easier access to his ass. When Morgan hesitated, Nick pushed himself back onto those slick fingers. "C'mon, do it."

Morgan didn't need any more encouragement. Two fingers quickly replaced one finger and were shortly followed by three, each one bearing a load of lube, each one loosening his tight hole with a tenderness at odds with Morgan's dominant demeanor.

"You keep condoms and lube in your gym bag?" Nick said, slowly fucking himself on those slick fingers.

"I do since we started going out. Besides, are you gonna argue with the results?" Morgan said, spiking a finger into Nick's gland. Nick gasped and jumped.

"Are you ready?" Morgan asked.

"Please," Nick whispered.

Nick felt Morgan's fingers against his entrance, followed by something bigger pushing into him. It hurt a little at first, a dull, hot burning that threatened to swamp the pleasure until Morgan grabbed his cock, slowly stroking it. "I'm going slow. Just breathe. Relax."

Morgan paused to give Nick time to adjust, the head of his own cock just inside the tight ring of muscle.

"It's okay," Nick said, impaling himself. "Damn, you're big. It's been a long time since…."

"Since anyone fucked you up against a wall?"

"No one's ever fucked me against a wall. Only you," Nick breathed as Morgan slowly pushed himself all the way in. "Only you."

"Only you," Morgan echoed, pulling out. He let go of Nick's cock to hold his shoulders.

Morgan kept a slow and steady rhythm with no hint of urgency or any acknowledgement that they were fucking in a public place. Even so, Morgan's thrusts pushed Nick against the lockers. He didn't notice the cold, hard metal against his face, only the sensation of Morgan sliding in and out, incredible fullness followed by a void, only to be filled again. He closed his eyes, the better to feel his lover behind and in him.

Morgan picked up the speed and grabbed Nick around his torso, pulling him back and holding him tight, trying to say with his body the words he hadn't been able to speak earlier. The change in position altered Morgan's angle of attack, and where he'd glanced across Nick's prostate with each stroke, he now nailed it dead on. As Morgan's cock pistoned in and out of Nick's ass, Nick could only hang in his arms, his head thrown back to rest against Morgan's shoulder.

"Close," Nick whispered. He'd never been this close without someone stroking his cock, but Morgan hit him just right and in so many ways.

"Right there with you," Morgan grunted out. He grabbed Nick's cock, pumping it in time with his thrusts.

With no warning, Nick went from close to there, his orgasm exploding up and out, a tsunami of heat and warmth and release of a tension he hadn't know had built up, and Nick pumped cum out, hitting the lockers.

"Nick," Morgan gasped, and with one more shuddering thrust, he came, still holding his lover tightly.

Nick could've rested against Morgan forever, but Morgan spoke up. "Nick, my knees…."

Nick blinked and raised his head from Morgan's shoulder. "Not working real well right now?"

"Not so much, no," Morgan laughed softly, still a bit winded.

"That was hot, but there's just one problem," Nick said, standing up on his own, pulling off Morgan in the process.

"No cuddling," Morgan said.

"That, and the mess," Nick said, gesturing towards the ejaculate streaking the lockers.

"Think anyone would notice if we let it dry there?" Morgan said.

Nick glanced at the nametag on the locker door. "I think your bow seat might."

"I don't guess you'd let me get away with saying that was his problem?" Morgan said, wrinkling his nose.

"Next time we do it in the showers, if only for ease of clean-up," Nick said.

Morgan smiled. "Next time?"

"Yeah," Nick said with a half smile. The physical act had been amazing, but he still felt sad, just a little. Morgan hadn't said he loved him back.

Chapter
THIRTEEN

LATER that afternoon, Nick sat in the coaches' office at the back of the boathouse, finalizing the workout plans for the last weeks before the PCRCs before he left for his own class. He was in a sunny mood, still riding the high from sex with Morgan earlier in the day, despite the one-sided declaration of love. Could something that hot be called "making love" even if one of them wasn't sure? He didn't know, but he'd be thinking about what they'd done every time he sat down for the next day or so. It wasn't that his ass was sore, but he was aware of it in a way he wasn't usually.

Looking at his notes and the calendar, Nick decided it was time to go back to two-a-day practices before the final taper just before the regatta. In fact, next Monday. He made a note to himself to tailor each practice to drills to sharpen either technique or endurance. It took the sting off the double days. He could do drill work with the crew on technical matters, which didn't take all that much physical effort, while still devoting a daily practice to ramping up their aerobic conditioning. Just to mix things up, he decided to alternate which they did on a giving morning or afternoon, so technique on morning and conditioning in the afternoon, followed by conditioning the next morning and drill work in the afternoon.

Nick kept track of it all on a large dry-erase board that took up one wall of the office. He stood before it, pen in one hand and notes in the other, when the phone rang. Grumbling, he dropped pen and notes on his desk to answer the phone. "CalPac Crew, Nick Bedford."

"Hi, Nick, George Hillier here. How're you doing?"

"Mr. Hillier! Just fine, sir," Nick said, his mind kicking into overdrive, trying to figure out why the athletic director, to whom he'd spoken exactly twice since he'd been hired, would be calling him out of the blue. "How're you, sir?"

"Just fine," Hillier said, "but we've got a bit of a problem."

We, Nick thought. "What's wrong?"

"Nothing's wrong per se, but my office has received an anonymous complaint about you, so I'm letting you know. Unofficially, of course."

Nick had always thought the phrase "blood runs cold" was just a rhetorical flourish, but that was what it felt like to hear those words. He tried to speak but only managed to squeak. "I'm sorry, sir, you said a complaint?"

"My secretary just found a note in my inbox complaining that you had a physical relationship with one of your athletes. I took a look at it myself. It's not signed or anything. All it says is that Coach Bedford and one of his athletes are... well, you can imagine what word was used," Hillier said.

"Oh my God," Nick whispered.

"Don't get all worked up, now. You know what collegiate athletics in this conference is like. Someone's always got his panties in a twist about something, so this probably isn't all that serious. Besides, I don't put too much faith in anonymous reports. It could just be a disgruntled athlete. Come to think of it, it might not even be from someone in the CalPac family."

Nick's mind had checked out. "What?" he said stupidly.

"Seriously, it could easily be from a competitor, you know," Hillier said. "You boys have a big race coming up soon, don't you? It could easily be some rival trying to throw sand into the competition's gears. I've seen this sort of thing before."

"That's... diabolical, sir," Nick said.

"That's one word for it. Listen, you know what you're doing. Just be careful. I mean, why would this even be an issue? You coach men's crew," Hillier said. Then, mock seriously, he continued, "It's not an issue is it? You're not… what was that line from *Brokeback Mountain*? You're not 'stemming the rose' with one of your rowers, are you?" the athletic director chortled.

"No, sir, what a thought," Nick said. He tried to laugh.

"Anyway, just a heads up. Gotta run. Good luck with that race thingy," Hillier said before he hung up.

Nick fell back into his chair. *You know what you're doing* echoed in his ears. He clearly did not. He'd let his hormones get in the way of his job. He'd tried to walk a tightrope, balancing work and romance, and had fallen off.

In the space of mere moments, Nick's world, which had seemed so fair, had tilted on its axis. He almost made it to the bathroom before he vomited.

IT WAS late that evening, hours after the Friday Massacre, as Nick mordantly called it. It'd been hours since the call from the athletic director, but he didn't know how many, as there was no clock under his pillow.

He'd barely made it home from the boathouse before he'd thrown up again. *When did I turn into a puker?* he'd wondered as he wiped his mouth on the bathmat, the closest textile at hand.

He'd gone right to bed after that, and that had been hours ago. He called in sick to the class he was scheduled to teach at State and skipped his own class. Based on the intermittent bleating of his mobile phone, a number of calls and text messages had come in while he was hiding, many from Morgan.

He didn't care.

Nick wondered why he even should care. He'd cared for Morgan, loved him still, even, despite his rising anger, and what had it gotten him? He'd violated every rule for Morgan, and what he'd gotten in return was, "I'm not sure if I can say the same." That was nothing. No, worse than nothing. Instead, all he'd heard was, "You know what you're doing" from the athletic director. He had no idea what he was doing, that much was clear. Fucking one of his athletes. Jeez. He couldn't even claim temporary insanity. He'd known what he was doing on that score, at least. He'd scrupled against it but did it anyway, in the end. But those boundaries he'd so willingly violated existed for a reason. He was furious, and it'd be all too easy to take it out on Morgan, but Nick knew he had only himself to blame. He'd violated his every code and didn't even have a lover to show for it, not really. He had an "I'm not sure if I can say the same" instead. *And excuse me, that's not a relationship. Make up your mind how you feel and then call me*, he thought angrily. *And then don't do that, either.*

That was it. He was done, and when word of this leaked out—and it would—he'd really be done. He'd see this season out as coach and then quit. He had enough savings to live on while he got into a PT program, and he could always work as a personal trainer to pay bills. He'd miss coaching, but you didn't shit—or fuck—where you eat.

Nick looked at the clock. Twelve thirty a.m. There was no way he'd be in any shape to run practice in six hours. He rolled over and looked at the ceiling, considering.

Decision made, he picked up his cell phone and fired off a quick text to Stuart with a nasty erg workout. For the first time since he'd gotten his first part-time job in high school, he called in sick when he was perfectly healthy. The PCRCs might be in three weeks, but he was in no condition to face Morgan.

Then he burrowed back under his pillow and blankets and tried to forget that he and Morgan had slept there together just weeks before.

NICK had just fallen asleep when the squawking of his landline phone pulled him up, or so it felt to him. He groaned. Who the hell was calling him?

He checked caller ID. Drew.

Nick rubbed his face. That was right, he'd called Drew last night. "Yeah?"

"What's up? You sounded dreadful on voicemail. *Sound* dreadful."

"Only a perfect storm of suck. I told Morgan I love… loved him," Nick said.

"That's great! Isn't it? It's not, is it? Why isn't it?" Drew said, rocketing through a range of emotions in record time.

"He 'likes me a lot', that's what's wrong with it. Fucking brat," Nick spat, furious all over again. Then he felt horrible for saying that and mad at himself for feeling guilty. *God, I'm a mess.*

"Wow, I'm sorry. I know how much you care… cared? What're we feeling here?" Drew asked.

"I don't know," Nick groaned. He pulled the phone back under the covers. He felt safer there. "I still love him, I guess, but suffering Christ, I was afraid this would happen."

"You were afraid you'd fall in love with a guy and he wouldn't love you back? That's the oldest story in the book," Drew said. "So what's got you so upset, other than that it's happened to you?"

"They found out, Drew. Exactly what I was always afraid would happen happened," Nick said.

"Slow down," Drew said. "You've lost me. Who found out what?"

"The school. Somehow the athletic department knows I'm dating one of my athletes," Nick said.

"Shit," Drew breathed.

"Exactly. Actually, CalPac doesn't believe I'm fucking one of my athletes, but they've been told."

"That's clear as mud. Start at the beginning," Drew ordered.

After Nick explained everything, from Morgan's arrival at the boathouse and his "I like you a lot" on Friday morning to the call from the athletic director, Drew exhaled noisily. "Okay, it's not as bad as it could be. From what you've described, the school doesn't know for sure, since it's just an anonymous report and your boss thinks it's a joke or even sabotage. Wait… why aren't you at practice? It's Saturday morning. You shouldn't even be home now."

"I called in sick."

"I guess it was unavoidable, but you know you can't avoid him forever, either," Drew pointed out. "You should at least talk to him."

"Only as much as I have to for coaching. There's three weeks until the PCRCs, and then we're done, and I'll never have to see him again," Nick said spitefully. He sighed. "This is all exactly what I was afraid would happen. All of it. I hate dating."

"But you like being in a relationship, and the only way to do that is to date," Drew said. "As Dan Savage keeps pointing out, every relationship you'll be in will fail… until one doesn't. You haven't done anything rash, like dumped him, have you?"

"I've done what was necessary," Nick said.

"That's what I was afraid of," Drew sighed.

When Nick was done spilling his guts to his best friend, he turned the phone off and ejected it from under his blankets. He and Morgan were supposed to get together that night, but that would happen right after hell froze over. A terse text message ended that, and then Nick was alone with his guilt, anger, and self-loathing.

"GOD damn it, Estrada, you're deep. Again," Nick bellowed through the megaphone. He shook his head, glaring as Morgan corrected the depth of his oar on the next stroke. "That's better. Barely."

They rowed in silence, since Nick was calling the shots from the launch. They were into the second to last week of practices, and suddenly no one did anything right anymore. More often than not, the coach's launch was mere feet from the end of the oars, with Coach Bedford red-faced and screaming correction after correction.

"Sundstrom, it's a river, and you're an oarsman. Drop the oar blade in, pull the fucking blade through the water in a straight line, extract the blade from the water. Repeat. You're treating it like a swizzle stick, in, then out, then in, round and round. You could do it last week. What the fuck happened?"

"Brad, try pulling through with just a bit of extra pressure from the middle finger of the hand on the end of the oar handle," Stuart said quietly through the shell's sound system.

"If I wanted you to coach these pussies, you'd be sitting in the launch," Coach Bedford snapped at Stuart.

"Jawohl, mein Führer," Stuart muttered. To Brad and the rest of the crew, he added, "I call this 'middle finger' drill."

In five-seat, Morgan tried to keep calm and row, but he kept tensing up, his shoulders knotting up, and whenever they did, there was his coach to catch him and bellow. For the first time ever, Morgan found himself hating crew and the man who represented it, Nick Bedford.

"Quit trying to plug your ears with your deltoids, Estrada," came Coach Bedford's voice. "Relax and you'll row better."

Morgan thought he heard something along the lines of, "You couldn't row any worse than you are right now," but he couldn't be sure. He just prayed practice ended soon as his coach moved on to another target.

At the end of practice, when Coach Bedford zoomed ahead of them to reach the dock, Stuart, carefully controlling the sound so it was no louder than necessary, said, "Team meeting tonight at my and Morgan's place, eight p.m."

"WHAT'S the deal?" Brad demanded as he walked in ten minutes after everyone else had arrived. He flopped down on the sofa next to Stuart.

"I think it's pretty obvious what this is about," Stuart said. "Coach Bedford."

"No, I mean, where's the pizza and beer?" Brad said.

"We thought you were bringing them," said Ricky Craft, their stroke seat.

Garth Stroud sighed. "Now that His Majesty has seen fit to grace us with his presence, can we please get started? I've got a Latin paper due in two days, and it's not going to write itself."

Brad stuck his tongue out at Garth and said, "I'm not the queen, Morgan is."

"Ha, ha," Morgan said flatly. Since his relationship with Nick had inexplicably blown up in his face, his sense of humor was AWOL. That Brad knew for sure he was gay—and was being an ass about it—was the icing on the shit cake.

Stuart elbowed Brad sharply. "Awww, I'm sorry," Brad said. "I'm just trying to lighten things up a little. Practice has sucked lately. Seriously, dude, what'd you do to Coach Bedford?" Brad continued. Morgan met his eyes but saw only a question there, and even concern, as if Brad had somehow grown a conscience or turned considerate. "He hates you."

"It sure looks that way," added Kristof Wood, who rowed at two-seat.

Ryan McDonald, who sat behind Morgan at four-seat, said, "We can't do anything right anymore, as a crew or as individuals, but he's got it in for you, buddy. Brad's right, as shocking as that is to say."

"Hey, what's that supposed to mean?" Brad snapped.

"Only that a big dumb ox like you surprises the rest of us when he gets something right," Morgan said.

"Other than being first in the chow line," murmured the three-seat, Mike Conrad, who'd been quiet up 'til that point. "Somehow he's always first where food's concerned."

"Hey, I'm a growing boy," Brad protested.

"Yes, but generally that phrase refers to the vertical dimension, not your gut," Stuart said. "Now shut your pie hole if you don't have anything useful to add."

"I don't think anyone really has anything to say," said Garth. "We just know there's a problem. I just wish I knew what to do about it."

"I hesitate to bring this up, but it's something we've got to consider," Robert said. "If this keeps up, we should notify the alumni oversight committee."

"That's rather extreme. It's just been a week. We need to see where this goes. I mean, maybe it's just tension before the PCRCs," Morgan said, wondering why he was defending Nick all of a sudden when he'd spent the previous three or four days in a blaze of pain and confusion.

Robert held up his hands. "I just said we should think about it. I'm graduating, but if something's changed with Coach Bedford, then those who're rowing next year need a coach, not a power-tripping martinet."

"Let's shelve that for now," Stuart said, but Morgan could tell he was troubled by the thought. Stuart met Morgan's eyes. "Anyone got anything else to add?"

Morgan looked away. He'd never made a big deal about his orientation because he'd never had to. He just assumed everyone knew he was gay, but he didn't feel comfortable telling everyone he was involved with their coach, if involved he still was. He went back and forth on that score, aching for the old Nick and then remembering what an asshole his coach had become. He just couldn't help but lament that it wasn't supposed to be like this.

He felt Brad's eyes burning into him. There was something in Brad's eyes, something serious where there was usually just pussy and beer. There was something Brad wasn't telling them, Morgan sensed, but a deep and sensitive Brad was almost as confusing as what had come over Nick, and he just couldn't deal with anything else.

"I'll be back," Morgan said, getting up. "I need some air."

Morgan knew there was one person he could call, but should he?

THE next day, after another demoralizing practice, Morgan picked up his phone. He knew he'd never get any work done on his term paper until he straightened this mess out. He wasn't usually the kind to worry about calling people. He just picked up the phone and called, but this was different. He and Drew hadn't exactly parted on the best of terms, but Drew knew Nick better than anyone.

Praying the number was still in his phone's log, Morgan flipped through until he found it. Taking a deep breath, he hit "call back" and waited.

"Drew St. Charles."

"Hi, Drew, it's Morgan Estrada."

"Hello, Morgan. This is certainly a surprise."

"I know," Morgan sighed. "But… can we talk?"

"What's wrong?" Drew said, suddenly suspicious.

Morgan could hear the sound of construction in the background. "Where're you?"

"At work, I suppose. I flip houses on the side," Drew said. "One of the many things we could've discussed and didn't on our date."

"Don't remind me," Morgan groaned, suddenly sorry he'd called.

"I know, it was pretty bad, wasn't it? Was this a social call, or did you need something, because I'm kind of busy," Drew said, his gentle tone robbing the words of their sting.

"It's about Nick," Morgan said softly.

"Then I can be done here, at least for a while. Can you meet me in about an hour? I really need to get cleaned up before I see anyone who counts," Drew said.

Buoyed by thought he still counted with someone, Morgan agreed to meet Drew at a coffee shop and hung up.

An hour later, Morgan sat across a table from Drew at an anonymous coffee shop in a suburban strip mall.

"What a charming location," Morgan murmured over his cappuccino.

"Would you prefer that every fairy in the enchanted forest knows your business?" Drew said. "Because if we'd met at one the 'gayborhood' places, that'd be what happened."

"Golly, Drew, how'd you get to be so smart?" Morgan said, making his eyes wide and voice vapid.

"Stop that. Was this a social call? It sounded like you had something on your mind," Drew said, resisting the urge to kick this kid under the table.

Morgan took a deep breath, then let it out. "Have you noticed anything different about Nick?"

Drew was instantly wary. "Why do you ask?"

"Because he's turned into an absolute monster in the coach's launch, that's why," Morgan snapped, all his frustration and anger pouring out. "Now he's got it in for me. Suddenly I can't do anything right, and he's nasty about it too."

"That doesn't sound like Nick," Drew said, frowning. "What else is going on? You two all right?"

Morgan threw his hands in the air and leaned back in his chair. "I thought we were. He told me he loves me, and we had awesome sex in the locker room"—at Drew's raised eyebrow, he said, "Like you've never done that?"

"No, I haven't, but do continue," Drew said.

"Anyway, he tells me he loves me, and then goes one-eighty on me. He's been an epic asshole at practice ever since. He blew off our last date, and by text message, no less, and now won't take my calls or anything," Morgan said miserably. "That's the worst part. He's just blown me off after telling me he loves me… loved me? Drew, I don't know what to do."

"Let me ask you something," Drew said. "Do you love him back?"

Morgan nodded slowly. "It took me a while to realize it, but by the time I realized it, he'd already flipped on me. Love and hate aren't polar opposites. They're next-door neighbors. I want to kill him these days, but I also know that with one word from him, I'd be at his feet, begging him to love me back."

"Then you should've told him."

"You knew," Morgan said. "About all of it. You knew, and you let me go on and on."

"I wanted to hear your side," Drew said, his face unreadable.

Morgan wanted to scream. He wanted to sob on Drew's shoulder. He wanted his boyfriend back. "What do I do, Drew? You're his best friend. Tell me what I should do to make this right."

"I really don't know," Drew admitted. "I've never seen him this hurt, but there's something else you need to know. Somehow, the athletic department knows about you two. He's scared shitless about keeping his job. I know he's talked to you about those issues too, about coaches and their athletes."

Morgan felt like someone had punched him in the gut. "How?" he whispered.

Drew shrugged. "I don't know. I don't think Nick does, either. Maybe 'how' doesn't matter, but the athletic director called him on it. I really don't know what to tell you to fix this. Right now, I'd say just get through the PCRCs and then sort this out this summer. This is the thing about romantic disasters and being young; everything seems like it's an emergency but probably isn't. If you and Nick are meant to be together, you will be. If you're not, then don't let this ruin the last few weeks of the semester for you. But also remember this: you're worth being treated with respect just for who you are. If you're not getting what you're due, call him on it." Drew stood up. "I've got to run, but good luck sorting this out."

"Thanks, Drew," Morgan said, standing too. On impulse, Morgan hugged him. "You're a good friend."

To someone, I hope, Drew thought.

DREW watched Morgan drive off and then pulled his own phone out and dialed Nick's numbers, land and mobile. Based on the time, he should've answered, but after four tries, all he got was voicemail.

So Drew drove to Nick's apartment, and sure enough, there was Nick's car. *Play it that way if you want to*, Drew thought.

He knocked on the door to Nick's apartment, and when there was no answer, he let himself in with his key.

"What—" Nick said, coming out of his bedroom. "What're you doing here?"

Drew sat down on the sofa and kicked his feet up. "You ignore my calls, I break into your apartment."

"I'm not really in the mood for company," Nick said sullenly.

"Yes, I've heard. Really, darling Nicky, this isn't like you," Drew chided.

"I don't want to talk about it," Nick said, glaring.

"You blow me off, fine," Drew said, "but don't you dare blow that kid off."

"Blowing that kid is what got me into this mess," Nick muttered.

"He's still a little young in some ways, and it may've taken time for him to figure it out, but he loves you, and if you're going to panic and end this just because of that call, then at least grow a set and do it cleanly," Drew said.

"I'm doing the best I can," Nick protested.

Drew stood up. He'd made his point. "But is it good enough?"

Chapter
FOURTEEN

MAYBE Drew's words hit home, because at the next practice, when Nick watched his crew's mediocre performance at the end of the piece, instead of screaming through the megaphone until it deafened them all with feedback squeals, he just said, "C'mon, guys, this is not how we row. We're all better than that. Do it again."

"Oh hell, no," someone said from the boat. It sounded like Morgan. Sound carried on the water, and his rowers never quite figured that out.

"Technique is what you have left after your energy's gone," Nick said. "Technique is going to carry you across the finish line first, not those leg muscles, and right now, it's not there."

Nick pretended not to hear "fuck you" drift over the water as Stuart directed the rowers to turn the boat and do the piece over again. It was a hard piece. He knew why they didn't want to do it again, but he had a perspective they lacked. That was why crews had a coach in a motorboat running beside them. That, and safety.

The crew did the piece again. Their performance had definitely fallen off lately, but whose fault was that? This time, Nick could see them trying. "That was much better. Take it in."

Then the engine on his launch died, and he spent a good five minutes field stripping the evil little rebuilt two-stroke engine that, thanks to California's air-quality laws, could only be replaced with something cleaner-burning and hence more expensive, more expensive than the CalPac Crew budget allowed. When it came down to choosing between shells and oars for the crew or a used motor for the coach, the oversight committee favored the crews, and Nick agreed. But that didn't mean he didn't curse them to the seventh generation while he poked and prodded at the motor.

When Nick puttered back into the dock, he found that the crew had put away the shell and the rest of the equipment. Well, other than his launch, but no one had been doing much with that lately.

Nick lugged the giant safety-kit bag into the boathouse and found himself face to face with a mutiny.

"We need to talk," Morgan said. His voice was steady, but his eyes were red and suspiciously wet-looking.

Nick looked at Morgan and then at the eight men arrayed behind him. "Perhaps, but I'm not sure this is the time or the place."

"No, this is the time and place, Coach. Right here, right now. Isn't 'communication' one of your Five Cs? Well, we're going to *communicate*," Stuart said. Then, more gently, "Go ahead, Morgan."

"Oh?" Nick said.

Morgan took a deep breath. "You've been working us hard lately. There's a big race coming up, I get that. But all of a sudden no one can do anything right, and me least of all."

"I don't know what you're talking about," Nick said, crossing his arms over his chest.

"You yell, you swear, you insult me… us," Morgan said. "What the fuck?"

Nick kept a tight leash on his temper, despite the almost overpowering urge to scream at these insolent pups. "The PCRCs—"

"It's more than that, Coach. It's like you've got it in for Morgan. Suddenly he can't do anything right. He's a great rower," Brad said. Admitting it hurt, but it was true.

"We used to be a team—coach and crew," Stuart said. "But now? You're out to get us, Morgan most of all. We just want to know why."

Nick had never heard of a crew taking on their coach. He wanted
to scream and throw things, but he made himself consider their words.
After several deep breaths and counting to ten, and then again, he
realized that they had a point. He had been pushing them hard, and he
was furious—hurt and angry and vengeful—at Morgan. He could've
been taking it out on Morgan. He thought about the last week and a
half, and he knew he'd been doing just that.

Nick looked each of them in the eye in turn. "Maybe I do push
you—all of you—but only because I know what you're capable of. I've
let my own nerves, my own expectations, get in the way, but only
because I share this with you, at least on land, on the ergs. I can't be out
there racing with you, so I have to make sure I've given you my best
before I let you go. I can't row in the boat with you, but everything
else—I've tried. I've tried, damn it, to give you everything I've got,
and if I've sensed I wasn't getting it back from you, then yeah, I've
yelled, I've cursed, I've done what I thought I had to do to make you
the fastest crew I could, and not only that, to make you the best crew I
could, and there's a difference." His eyes settled on Morgan. "We've
got one more double day, and then the taper starts. Maybe you nine can
decide whether or not you're going to give this race your all. Let me
know what you decide."

Nick pushed past them and fetched his keys from his office.
Without looking back, he walked to his car, leaving his words and his
crew behind him.

As Nick drove home, however, he admitted he hadn't been
entirely honest with them. He thought about the Five Cs, and
communication, coach, and his commitment had definitely been less
than they could've been, less than they should've been. There was an
essential part of himself he had not communicated to his crew, and
because of that, he had erected a barrier between coach and crew. As a
result, when something major had happened, he hadn't been able to
communicate it to his athletes, and with the one of them who mattered
most of all.

But Nick knew it was more than that. He'd allowed his
commitment to many things to flag. He hadn't been doing the best he
could, and what he'd been doing wasn't good enough. He'd allowed his

personal feelings to affect how he coached, and that was just shitty. That it was one of the things he'd feared when the entire question of dating one of his rowers came up. Not only was it highly unprofessional, it violated his own personal code. He owed those athletes better than they'd received, and that it was before a major regatta only compounded the fuck-up. Starting tomorrow, he'd give them his all back.

Nick felt like he'd failed as a man too, but it was all tied together. Seeing Morgan red-eyed and miserable in the boathouse told him all he needed to know. He still loved Morgan. He was hurt that Morgan hadn't said "I love you" back, but that didn't mean the man—the younger, less experienced man—didn't love him, it just meant he didn't know his feelings. Since when was that a capital offense? That Morgan was so miserable cut Nick like a knife. It also gave Nick hope. Maybe Morgan still cared.

Sitting at a traffic light, Nick resolved to talk to Morgan right after the regatta. He'd done enough to the man without adding further emotional turbulence to the final days and weeks of the rowing season and school year. He wanted Morgan back, and he was prepared to beg. But Nick had to prepare himself for something else too. If Morgan refused him, Nick could only blame himself.

If Morgan would have him back, Nick would quit. The crew wouldn't want an out coach, and if Nick had to choose the job he loved or the man he loved, he'd choose his boyfriend. If he were still Nick's boyfriend. No, he resolved to come clean and quit, whether or not Morgan took him back. This was what the lie had gotten him: nothing. He'd done everything he could to protect the lie, rather than live life on the up-and-up with his head held high. He wouldn't have a job, he might not have a boyfriend, but at least he could reclaim his self-respect. After the PCRCs, he'd explain everything to the crew and then beg Morgan to forgive him.

Good job, Nick, he thought. *You've really screwed the pooch this time.*

"FAR cry from the last time we were here, isn't it?" Drew said. The early May day was sunny and bright without a cloud in the sky. Not even the slight headwind was enough to ruin the racing.

"Yeah," Nick replied. He hadn't said much to Drew that morning, and what he said was with a soft voice. "Last time, I had a boyfriend."

Drew flinched. "Sorry, that was thoughtless."

"No worries. You didn't get yourself in a snit and then panic like a frightened bunny-rabbit. I'm capable of ruining my relationships all by myself," Nick said. He smiled sadly. "I'm a big boy."

Drew glanced down. "Big enough, as I recall."

"You're bad," Nick laughed.

"Bad enough, but I got you to laugh, didn't I?" Drew said.

Nick had to smile. He was lucky to have a friend like Drew, even if he was there to mack on one of his rowers.

The CalPac races were early in the day's racing, and the air was a bit cool, but Nick and Drew still wore shorts and hoodies. The rowers were all covered in various layers of technical-fiber warm-ups.

The racing shells were already off the trailer in slings, and Stuart had already set the crews to re-rigging them. Now the CalPac rowers warmed up and stretched in advance of launching and warming up on the water.

While the week of the taper during which Nick kept up the intensity but not the volume of their training had improved the atmosphere of the boathouse, he still felt the distance between him and his athletes. That pained him. As a coach, Nick had long prided himself on the close relationship he cultivated between himself and his rowers, but all it had taken to end that was a week of spectacularly bad coaching and moodiness on his part.

Or maybe it was all in Nick's mind, and his rowers were only waiting for him to extend the olive branch. After all, as he once pointed out to Morgan, the relationship between coach and athlete was asymmetric, so he bore the burden of making things right.

Nick knew what he was going to do, but he'd done enough to upset the apple cart before the biggest—and last—race of some of these men's collegiate rowing careers. He planned to keep his peace until after the races were done and, he hoped, won. Over the course of the last week, he'd checked the results from previous years for the other schools in their event and then compared them to the schools' recent performances. The competition was fierce. CalPac faced some of the country's rowing powerhouses.

"Okay, this is it. This is the race we've prepared for all year. Everything up 'til now has been practice. The other races were important," Nick told them, "but only insofar as they gauged your progress. I won't lie to you. You're up against Cal and the University of Washington, and that's some tough competition. That said, I've run the numbers. You have a chance. You're in this race—"

"Yeah, someone's gotta come in last," Brad snorted.

Nick looked at him. "If you really believe that, why're you here?"

"Aw, I'm just kidding, Coach. Everyone's been so serious lately," Brad apologized.

Nick nodded in acknowledgment. "As I was saying, you're in this race. You're not here for comic relief. Every race is different, and every year is different for each crew. Based on what I've seen, this is a good year for the CalPac Crew, and it could even be a great year.

"I'm not going to tell you much else. You're the varsity squad. You know how to row. Stay relaxed during the warm-up and carry that into the race, and you'll do fine," Nick said, his voice growing thick with emotion. "We've had a good season, and I thank you for that. Since it's time to launch, I'll hand you off to Stuart, but guys? I'm proud of you."

"Thanks, Coach," Stuart said. "All right, hands on!"

Nick got out of the way and let Stuart do the job he was so very good at. They all were, each in his own way. CalPac's crew might've been a small program, and he didn't have a large talent pool to draw from like bigger schools did, let alone the recruitment budget of the rowing titans at the University of Washington, but Nick knew he'd been damned lucky with the men who'd walked through his boathouse door. Never mind having any replacements or bringing someone up from the junior varsity squad, he'd never needed to cut anyone.

The junior varsity. Morgan had risen up from the JV in a hurry, his natural talent and drive standing out even when he was a freshman.

"Hey, you okay?" Drew said. "That was a nice little speech, by the way."

"Thanks. I decided to save the emotional tear-jerker speech for afterwards," Nick said.

"I always knew you were secretly a girl," Drew said.

"Pretty big words for someone looking to be Brad's bitch, a man who's straight, by the way," Nick said.

"Fortunately, I'm too much of a gentleman to respond to such vulgar aspersions," Drew sniffed.

Nick laughed. "Thanks for the distraction."

"Any time, my friend, any time. Now let's go watch some races. There's one in particular I want to see," Drew said.

"Me too, oddly enough. I brought my camcorder too."

"I'll pay you twenty bucks if you zoom in on Brad for the entire race," Drew promised.

"I'm not sure which is more insulting, that I'd do something like that or that I'd do it for so little," Nick said. "Let's go."

They managed to find a place on the viewing platform with the other coaches, and Nick wasn't the only coach filming his crew. They all smiled and made nice with each other, but they were rivals, and they knew it.

"You're surprisingly calm," Drew observed.

"If fidgeting would help, I'd do it," Nick said, shrugging, "but it's just a waste of energy."

"So much for needling you," Drew sighed. "I'm as nervous as a long-tailed cat in a room full of rocking chairs."

"You? Why?" Nick laughed.

"This means a lot to you, so it means a lot to me."

"I'm reminded again that it really was a shame we never worked out," Nick said softly. "You've always been a good friend."

"And who helps me every summer with flipping houses?" Drew replied. "And won't accept nearly the money he's worth?"

"Hey, learn a skill, take a break from school, and help my best friend out while I support myself, it's a win-win," Nick said. "But all this gooey introspection? This can't be good for us."

"Then let's stop. I believe I've succeeded in diverting you until the crews are heading for the starting line," Drew said.

And then all of Nick's nervousness roared back.

Much like the last race at Lake Natoma, the PCRCs started from a platform floating in the river, which was dammed to create the lake. The coxswains guided their shells into alignment, a cumbersome process for sixty-foot-long boats powered only by eight oars.

Nick couldn't hear Stuart, but he certainly looked masterful as he issued orders, and the eight men under his command responded instantly. Nick bit his lip. Based on that, his crew certainly looked relaxed as they sat at the ready.

The CalPac Crew was in the second lane, and sure enough, Cal Berkeley was on one side and the hulking oarsmen of UW on the other. But Nick's rowers didn't look to one side or the other. Their attention was on Stuart, right where it should've been, and even Brad kept his eyes straight ahead.

"We have alignment," came the announcer's voice.

"Three… two… one. Go!"

And the crews were off.

The CalPac Crew put the tension of the recent past behind them, Nick could see that much through the viewfinder of his camcorder. While fierce and determined, they still rowed with an easy grace he didn't often see on them or on any other crew. Stuart issued his commands and encouragement in a steady voice, and that voice was the extent of his rowers' world. When done well, rowing was a thing of beauty, and that day, Nick's crew took his breath away.

"Wow," Drew said. "They're firing on all eight cylinders today. Just… damn."

But the other varsity crews rowed just as well, and past the five hundred meter mark, CalPac was bow-to-bow with UW, with Cal less than a stroke behind.

"C'mon, boys," Nick breathed while Drew vibrated in place next to him.

At the six hundred meters, Cal pulled ahead, followed instantly by UW.

"What's Stuart doing?" Drew demanded.

"I don't know, but he's there, and I'm here. We have to trust him," Nick said, thinking that if Stuart didn't call up the final sprint *now*, then Nick would run out there and beat him to a pulp.

Then Stuart did what Nick prayed and called his rowers up just past the six hundred mark. "Thank God," Nick said. "It's early," he explained to Drew, "but he's got no choice if he wants a chance at the win."

Slowly, inexorably, the CalPac Crew pulled ahead. No longer did it look effortless. Nick's rowers pulled harder than they'd ever pulled, and the exertion showed. Now, he could hear them, hear the *thunk!* of the oars turning in the oarlocks, hear the fast, loud commands pouring in a torrent from Stuart's mouth, even hear the grunting of the rowers as they pushed themselves to the breaking point. For Stuart. For Nick. For themselves.

UW and Cal weren't going down without a fight, and as soon as CalPac moved ahead, the other coxswains were forced to call up their final sprints.

Even going into the final moments of the race, no crew was the clear winner, but at the last minute, Stuart screamed, "Now, damn you, now!" and the CalPac oarsmen went even deeper into the pain cave. There was no grace, no beauty, only raw strength applied through a haze of torment and tunneling vision.

It sufficed. Barely. But even those few feet were enough.

UW crossed the line a fraction of a second behind, and Cal right after that.

"Did they?" Drew gasped.

"I think so," Nick breathed. "I… yes, they did. They did!"

Nick hugged Drew, and together they jumped up and down, ignoring the looks of the other coaches. Nick didn't care. His crew had just pulled off a stunning upset. He accepted the congratulations of other coaches as he and Drew made their way down to the water.

Nick handed Drew his wallet and the keys to the rental truck. Then he pulled off his CalPac Crew hoodie. "They'll be throwing me in."

"Why?"

"Tradition. When you win a race, the coxswain for sure goes in, and the coach, if they can catch him. Besides, they've earned it," Nick said.

"More than, I'd say," Drew replied.

The CalPac boat was almost to shore by the time Nick and Drew got down there. Of the nine men in the boat, only two did anything other than sit, their shoulders slumped, heads bowed with exhaustion: Stuart, who, while somewhat hoarse, had expended only mental energy in the race just won, and Brad, who looked around with an increasingly worried expression until he caught sight of his coach and Drew. Only then did he let go and relax. He exhaled noisily and fell backwards practically into Morgan's lap.

"Would you get up, you dumb beast?" Morgan said, still weary.

Nick and Drew waded out to collect oars even as Stuart climbed out, then steadied the shell as he gave the orders for the rowers to do the same.

Brad looked at Drew, who was waiting for his oar, and smiled. Then he caught himself and blushed and looked away. Drew just had a goofy smile on his face.

Nick caught it all but shelved it. He had enough on his plate right now. "Guys… I don't know quite what to say. I'm pleased and so very proud. Let's get the boat up, and then we can take care of the rest."

Stuart nodded. "Right, guys. Oars up, then hands on."

Buoyed by their victory, the CalPac oarsmen carried their oars from the beach to the trailer and then brought the boat up to the assigned CalPac staging area and left it in slings in short order. The best junior varsity men would be taking it out during their race as a treat, which freed them from de-rigging duties, at least temporarily.

Then Nick fetched the team's medals from the judging stand while the rowers stretched or ate. Then the CalPac Crew, including coach and coxswain, posed while Drew snapped pictures. It was a golden moment that they all wanted to remember.

"There are certain traditions that're usually observed by a victorious crew, so we'll take care of those, and then I have some things to say," Nick said, somber despite the crew's victory.

While Nick spoke, Stuart removed his sunglasses and shirt, setting them on a nearby picnic table. Then the eight much larger men he commanded picked him up and, with three swings and a loud cheer, tossed him into Lake Natoma.

Then, grinning, they turned to Nick. He didn't fight, and they tossed him in too, right next to Stuart, who waited and splashed him before wading out.

Nick could only smile and shake his head as he waded out of the lake, water streaming down his chest. He looked up to see Morgan's eyes on him, and he gave a shy, one-sided smile. Morgan smiled back, and Nick's heart soared. Maybe there was still hope.

Nick dried off and called everyone around. It was a bittersweet moment. His crew had just finished its best race ever, possibly the best race in the history of the CalPac Crew. And it was his last.

"First of all, I want to congratulate you. You were magnificent, and that race was amazing. Whatever you tapped into during the end of your sprint made the difference. For those of you who're graduating—Brad, Robert—I'm so glad that your final race for California Pacific

College was this one. For the rest of you, I hope you'll continue on and row this fall. I also hope this is a race you can build on to carry the varsity boat on to greater things this fall and next spring. Regardless, this race is one for the record books, at least our record books."

Nick stopped then. This was the hard part. He swallowed the lump in his throat and felt his eyes sting with unshed tears. "All of that said, this was my last season as your coach." He held his hands up for silence. "Recent weeks have made it very clear to me that I can't juggle the demands of my personal life and my duties as your varsity coach. So I'm stepping down."

This time, Nick let them interrupt. He'd just dropped a bombshell on them, but the only reaction he was interested in was Morgan's. Morgan looked shocked at first but quickly recovered, or at least covered it up. Then he looked wary, wondering if there were another shoe to drop and, if so, where it would land.

"This was bound to come out sooner or later, but it's best that you hear it from me. I'm under investigation by the athletic department and I'm sure, in good time, by the NCAA."

"What!"

"Why?"

Nick sighed. This was the hardest part. "Because I'm dating one of my athletes." That quieted them down. They all looked at Morgan, who nodded his confirmation, his lips pressed into a thin, tight line. "Yes, I'm gay, and it's become very clear to me that I have to choose between my personal life and my job. The reasons why are private, but I know I've said and done some things lately that I regret very much, both as a coach and as a boyfriend. I certainly haven't been the kind of coach I want to be, let alone the kind of significant other.

"All of you, but one of you in particular, deserve better than what I've given you. I'll stay, on an interim basis, while a new coach is hired, but this was my last season as coach of the varsity men's team of the California Pacific Crew, and probably my last season coaching."

Nick was silent for a moment, then wiped his eyes. There. He'd said it, and now it was time to go. He walked slowly away. He couldn't tell if he was slinking away with his tail between his legs or not.

"Could you not have warned me?" Drew hissed as he hurried to catch up.

"Just think how much more natural your reaction was this way," Nick said, faking a smile.

"Oh, Nick, what am I going to do with you?" Drew sighed.

"Probably what you always have," Nick replied.

"I keep hoping we can do better than that."

"Guess not."

Chapter
FIFTEEN

"ALL right, who's the fucker who ratted out our coach to the athletic department?" Brad demanded in the wake of Nick's announcement. His eyes flashed and anger rolled off him in waves, but he knew the answer.

"Go after him! You're the only one he'll listen to," Stuart said to Morgan.

Morgan stared at him, torn by his own emotions. It sounded like a peace overture from Nick, and that made his heart sing, but there'd been more than enough hurt to go around, and he was angry himself now.

Morgan caught up to Nick and Drew very quickly. "Drew, would you excuse us, please? There's something Nick and I need to talk about."

"You think?" Drew said. Shaking his head, he walked away.

"Well, I guess they know which one of you I was dating," Nick said, trying to make it sound light and failing.

"Hilarious, Nick. What the hell is this all about?" Morgan snapped before Drew was more than a few feet away.

"I can't do both," Nick said, sighing.

"Just like that? You don't even talk to me first," Morgan said, voice rising. "Did it ever occur to you I might have something to say about all this?"

Nick's jaw dropped. "But... I stepped down so I'd be free to make it work with you!"

"And you're doing *such* an amazing job of it, Nick Bedford!"

"I don't think you really appreciate both what this is costing me and the risks I took," Nick spat. "Whatever happens between us, I could still end up barred from coaching."

"But you're quitting anyway!" Morgan said.

Nick threw his hands in the air and turned to walk away. Morgan had a decision to make and a split second to do it. He reached out and grabbed at Nick. "Nick... wait. Don't walk away from me," he said, lowering his voice. "I'm younger than you are, but I'm not a moron. Look, I'm sorry I hurt you that day on the dock. You have no idea. It took a bash upside the head, but... I love you too," Morgan said in a small voice. "Can... can I have another chance?"

Nick sniffled, then nodded his head. "Only if you give me one too."

Then Nick struggled to keep his balance as Morgan launched himself into Nick's arms.

"I was an ass," Nick said. "I got scared when the athletic director called me, and I panicked. Then I took it out on you and everyone else. That's part of why I have to quit. It's part of why coaches can't date their athletes."

Morgan whistled. "That investigation... that's pretty scary stuff. But Nick? You're doing it again. You're making decisions that affect both of us without consulting me. Talk to me. *Communicate* with me. Isn't that one of the things you said makes the CalPac Crew great?"

Nick blushed. "Yeah. How'd you get so smart?"

"I've had a great coach," Morgan said, catching Nick's mouth with his.

"Does this mean you forgive me?" Nick said a moment later. He rested his forehead against Morgan's.

"Yes, if you'll forgive me too. I'm still sorry I hurt you... that I didn't know my own feelings well enough to say I love you back, because I did, and I do. I love you very much. It just took the thought of losing you to make me realize it." Morgan paused, considering. "Well, that and hating your guts for a week or so and realizing I wouldn't be so pissed if I didn't love you. You're the one I want to spend my future with."

Nick tipped his chin up and kissed Morgan again.

Behind them, a rower in the colors of one of the crews CalPac had just beat yelled, "Get a hotel room, you fucking fags!"

"Shut the fuck up, you fucking son of a bitch!" Brad screamed, bounding out of nowhere like an avenging angel. He got right up in that other man's face and bellowed at the top of his lungs. "You say one more goddamn thing, I'll rip your goddamn lungs out and beat you to death with 'em!"

Nick and Morgan stopped kissing, but Nick held on to Morgan's hand. "C'mon, let's get that boat de-rigged before we have to bail him out of prison. The JV should be done with it by now, anyway."

"WHO'S the fucker who ratted out our coach to the athletic department?" Somehow, despite catching them in the boathouse that day and turning in that anonymous note, Brad was as stunned as anyone when Coach Bedford made his announcement and then walked away.

Then he heard Stuart say, "Go after him! You're the only one he'll listen to."

Brad was up and in motion before he realized Stuart wasn't talking to him. He shook his head, wondering how long it'd take before he stopped jumping when short people told him to.

But since he was up and moving, anyway....

He crept stealthily down the path that Morgan and Coach Bedford had gone down. He spied them in the distance but circled around because Coach's friend Drew was blocking the path.

Drew. Why did he keep thinking about that guy, anyway? He'd been around for a while, but suddenly, Brad saw him everywhere. When Drew tried to help carry up those oars at the WIRAs, he made a

total mess of it, but that just made Brad smile. It was so sweet of him to
try.

Brad shook his head. Since when did he think guys were sweet?
Or that guy, at least. Drew was a total flamer, but Brad couldn't get him
out of his mind, and he definitely didn't want to think about why he'd
been so happy when he saw Drew standing next to Coach Bedford
when the crew had hit the beach after their win.

Brad came around the other side and saw Morgan and their coach
hug, then kiss. He guessed he'd missed the arguing, since it looked like
it was time for the making-up part.

He watched the two men embrace, then kiss. It was quite a kiss
too. He wasn't the smartest guy, he knew that. But the look of peace
and contentment that came over those two when they were in each
other's arms even he could see.

"Damn," Brad breathed. He'd never felt that with any of the
women he'd banged. Never. How could that be wrong?

"Get a fucking hotel room, you fucking fags!"

Brad was moving again before he knew it, right up in the faces of
that asshole insulting his coach. "Shut the fuck up, you fucking son of a
bitch! You say one more goddamn thing, I'll rip your goddamn lungs
out and beat you to death with 'em!"

Brad was big, even for a rower, and he made his point very well.
"Ha!" he yelled as the asswipe ran like a schoolgirl.

This was his fault, Brad thought as he stalked back to the CalPac
trailer, still flying on adrenaline and something that might've been
sentiment. He'd fix it. He'd tell the athletic department he'd made it up
because he was mad about boatings or something. Then he'd deal with
the alumni oversight committee. He had an idea about that—his dad
had been pestering him for some idea for a graduation gift. Brad had
been leaning towards a new car, but inspiration had struck. He'd ask his
dad to buy the crew a new racing shell. Then the oversight committee
would kiss his ass.

Brad nodded in satisfaction. Yep, some pretty fancy figuring for a
dullard, and it just might work.

Chapter
SIXTEEN

Six weeks later

"THAT wasn't too traumatic, was it?" Morgan said when he and Nick returned to Nick's place.

"I think your oldest brother was a little skeeved that your boyfriend is the same age he is," Nick replied.

Morgan shrugged. "He'll get over it. Besides, my parents liked you when they met you last week, and I'm sure they'll put in a good word."

"I've never been that nervous in my life," Nick laughed.

"I wasn't worried."

Nick shook his head. "I was worried enough for both of us. At least there was none of that 'what're your intentions towards our brother' nonsense. More like the other way around. You're a far bigger perv than I am."

"Not yet," Morgan said, wiggling his eyebrows at Nick.

"Oooh, is that a threat or a promise?" Nick said. "I think your brother was worried that I'd derail your education somehow."

Morgan shrugged. "Tony's always been too focused for his own good, but I'd say you put that to rest. Your description of your graduate work alone shut him down pretty fast. Between teaching, grading, taking classes of your own—"

"And oh yeah, research," Nick said.

"And research," Morgan continued, "I think you reassured him that you won't distract me from my schoolwork."

Nick snorted. "Maybe the other way around. His eyes had glazed over before I even started in on the planning that coaching involved."

"And there it is," Morgan said. "The dead elephant in the corner. Have you made any decisions about what you want to do?"

"Not really," Nick sighed. "The athletic department's dropped its investigation, so as far as California Pacific's concerned, there's no reason I can't continue. The alumni committee's another matter entirely, however, and until it weighs in, I don't really know whether or not I have a job beyond next year. But so far, they haven't advertised for a men's varsity coach position, so that's something."

"It is, indeed," Morgan said, heading to the kitchen to make tea. "I'll graduate next year, and you're supposed to, assuming you can keep juggling that schedule."

Nick made a face. "Yeah, assuming that. What I can't figure out is why the athletic department dropped its investigation, just like that," he said, snapping his fingers. "One day it's a phone call about a note with dire allegations, and the next it's a friendly email from the athletic director telling me all's well and have a nice summer."

"They never spoke to anyone on the team, either," Morgan said. At Nick's questioning look, he shrugged. "I asked around."

"Whatever the reason, it ought to shut the NCAA investigation down, but even if it doesn't, I'll be okay for a while, and as you said, we'll both be done in a year," Nick said. "If I graduate and leave coaching, then a ban won't matter."

Morgan thought for a moment. "You know what strikes me as odd about all that? Brad. He seems pretty smug these days."

"Brad's always smug. He has been as long as I've known him," Nick said.

"Yeah, but more than usual," Morgan said.

Nick set mugs out on the coffee table in the living room as Morgan brought the teakettle in from the kitchen. "You don't think he had something to do with it, do you?"

"I really don't know. His dad's loaded," Morgan said, pouring the tea, "and the athletic department's nothing but a bunch of whores."

"And there are rumors of a new racing shell." Nick shook his head. "Did I tell you the latest? I've gotten three emails from Brad since graduation, and in each one, he manages to ask about Drew."

Morgan choked on his tea. "Jeez, can you warn me before you say things like that?"

"I'll grant you that it's an unlikely combination," Nick said, handing Morgan a napkin to wipe up spilled tea, "but why the shock?"

"I really don't want to think of Brad as gay, thank you very much. I used to change clothes in front of him, you know," Morgan said.

"Maybe he's just gay for Drew," Nick said. "What he doesn't know is that Drew's been hounding me about him for months, but I am so not getting into the middle of this. I'll pass on email addresses or something, but no more."

"You mean you won't be hosting a bride-finding ball for them?" Morgan said. "What if I want to? I need a project this summer…."

"You… please tell me you're kidding."

Morgan shrugged, a secret smile on his lips. "Maybe, maybe not. Maybe I'll just make them dance for a while. Who knows, perhaps there'll be two matches to come out of your days with the CalPac Crew."

Nick looked at his boyfriend. Morgan still took his breath away. Just the thought that this man, this wonderful, intelligent, playful man thought he, Nick Bedford, was worth the time of day…. "I got what I most longed for out of that job. Those two are their own problem." He stood up and held out his hand. "But I also don't want to talk about that right now."

Morgan rose and took Nick's hand. Nick pulled it to his lips and kissed it, meeting Morgan's eyes.

"Why, Nick Bedford, are you trying to romance me?" Morgan said, actually blushing.

"I'll never stop, Morgan Estrada," Nick said, leading Morgan by the hand to the bedroom.

Nick closed the door behind them and led Morgan to the bed, gently pushing him down. Nick lay on his side next to him, one hand on Morgan's chest. He wove his fingers through Morgan's and brought Morgan's hand up for another kiss before releasing it.

Morgan met his eyes and found them overflowing with a welter of emotion. Passion, certainly, the sure knowledge of how this evening would end, but also gratitude and love, a love that was only just pushing into bloom, a love that promised to grow and flower for the rest of their lives, deepening over the years into a shared lifetime's love and affection.

Morgan blushed hard and looked away, or tried to. But Nick reached out and turned Morgan's head back. "Not so fast. I have plans for those lips," Nick breathed, kissing Morgan's mouth. "And those eyes." Feathery kissed whispered across Morgan's eyelids as they fluttered closed for a moment.

Nick unbuttoned Morgan's shirt. "And that heart," he said, kissing his way down Morgan's neck to his chest.

"And all the rest of you," Nick said. He kissed his way down, following the treasure trail to just about the waistband of Morgan's pants. He rested his head on Morgan's hard belly, savoring the scratch of the hair against his cheek even as his hand dipped down beneath pants and underwear.

"Even that?" Morgan rasped, his breath growing ragged as Nick palmed his hardening cock.

"Especially that," Nick said, grinning. He sat up and unbuttoned Morgan's jeans as Morgan lifted his hips. He slid Morgan's pants and underwear down, grinning when he saw what greeted him. "Nice," he breathed.

Morgan reached down to touch Nick. "You're too far away. You're wearing too much."

"I can fix all that," Nick said. He sat up and pulled off his shirt.

Morgan lifted himself up on his elbows to watch, still unable to believe that this man was his. "You are so beautiful. How'd I get so lucky?"

"I'm the lucky one," Nick said, "and you're the beautiful one."

Nick climbed back on the bed. "Now, where was I? Oh yes," he breathed, "I remember."

Nick bent down over Morgan's cock. He breathed on its taut skin, up and down the shaft, his hot, wet breath teasing as he stopped over the head, dark with blood and leaking precum. He flicked his tongue over the slit, tasting Morgan. Then again, making Morgan gasp as a shudder ran through him.

"Nick...."

"You like that, do you?" Nick said, grinning. He ran his hands over Morgan's abs before bringing them down across his pelvis and circling around his cock and sac, now drawn tight against his body. "I think you do."

Even as Nick stopped teasing Morgan's cock and took it in his mouth, he moved his hands farther down, circling his sac and rubbing his taint.

Morgan lifted his legs, moaning as Nick's long fingers continued their exploration. "I know what you want tonight," Nick said around Morgan's shaft, "and it's your lucky night."

"Soon?" Morgan whined.

"When it's time," Nick said.

He brushed his fingers past Morgan's hole even as he resumed servicing his cock. Morgan could only make needy little gasps as Nick slowly traced one finger around his puckered opening, feeling it twitch in anticipation.

Morgan's breath came in short gasps. "Is it time?"

"Not yet," Nick said, abandoning Morgan's shaft for his mouth. He put one finger right on the opening, slowly working his finger around the first few millimeters of the entrance. "Is this what you want?"

"Uh-huh," Morgan gulped.

"Or this?" Nick said, pushing one finger deeper inside and working it around.

"Niiick...."

Nick smiled down at his lover. He reached over Morgan to the nightstand to pull out condoms and lube. But Morgan leaned up and latched onto on nipple, licking and nipping. Nick could only prop himself up, gasping as Morgan hit the button that short-circuited his brain. "Morgan...," he panted. "You're not getting fucked this way."

"S'okay, worth it," Morgan said, using his tongue and teeth to torment Nick in just the right way.

Nick, struggling to keep his eyes from rolling back, managed to flip open the cap on the lube and slick up his fingers. Morgan obligingly canted his pelvis up, and Nick pushed two fingers into his hole.

"Yeahhhh," Morgan breathed as Nick loosened him.

Two fingers became three, and Nick brushed the tips over Morgan's gland. "Please," Morgan said.

Nick positioned himself in front of Morgan and then rolled a condom over his own cock, catching the leaking precum inside the tip. He greased Morgan and then himself, then positioned his cock against Morgan's hole.

Then Nick paused, looking down at the beautiful man beneath him and then into his eyes. He could only smile, a shy, sweet smile that told Morgan exactly how he felt. Morgan had never felt more loved than at that moment. "I love only you," Morgan said, looking into Nick's eyes as Nick slowly pushed his way in.

"Only you," Nick breathed, looking down into Morgan's eyes.

CHRISTOPHER KOEHLER has had what his mother refers to as an incestuous relationship with books since he learned to read, but it wasn't until his grad school years that he realized writing was how he wanted to spend his life. Long something of a hothouse flower, he's been lucky to be surrounded by people who encouraged that tendency and the writing both, especially his long-suffering husband of nineteen years and counting.

He loves many genres of fiction and nonfiction, but he's especially fond of romances, because it's in them that human emotions and relations, at least most of the ones fit to be discussed publicly, are laid bare.

While writing is his passion and his life, when he's not doing that, he's a househusband, at-home dad, and oarsman with a slightly disturbing interest in manners and the other ways people behave badly.

Visit him at http://christopherkoehler.net/blog or follow him on Twitter @christopherink.

Romance from DREAMSPINNER PRESS

LaVergne, TN USA
23 February 2011
217670LV00003B/4/P